BLADE

of

SECRETS

TRICIA LEVENSELLER

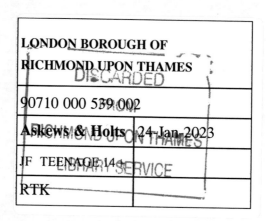
Pushkin Press
71–75 Shelton Street
London WC2H 9JQ

Copyright © 2021 by Tricia Levenseller

First published by Feiwel and Friends, an imprint of Macmillan Publishing Group, LLC. All rights reserved

First published by Pushkin Press in 2022

9 8 7 6 5 4 3 2

ISBN 13: 978-1-78269-364-2

Offset by Tetragon, London
Printed and bound by CPI Group (UK) Ltd, Croydon, CRO 4YY

www.pushkinpress.com

This one's for you, Dad.
Don't let it go to your head.

KEY

☀ *Capital*
✦ *City*
• *Village*

Galvinor

PRINCE RAVIS'S
Territory

PRINCESS
LISADY'S
Territory

✦ *Briska*

• *Amanor*

PRINCE SKIRO'S
Territory

Lirasu

N
W   E
S

CHAPTER ONE

I prefer metal to people, which is why the forge is my safe space.

The heat is relentless in here, even with all the windows open for ventilation. Sweat beads on my forehead and drips down my back, but I wouldn't give up being a smithy for anything.

I love the way a hammer feels in my hand; I love the sounds of metal chiming against metal, the slight give of heated steel, the smell of a raging fire, and the satisfaction of a finished weapon.

I pride myself on making each of my weapons unique. My customers know that when they commission a Zivan blade, it will be one of a kind.

I drop my hammer and inspect my current project.

The flange has the right shape. It's the sixth and final of the identical pieces that will be attached to the mace's head. After quenching the blade, I take it to the grindstone to sharpen every curve of the outer edge. I've already made grooves into the mace using a hammer and chisel. Now all that's left is to weld all the pieces together. Using separate tongs, I place everything into the kiln and wait.

There's plenty to do in the meantime. Tools need cleaning. Scraps of metal need disposing of. I work the bellows to keep the kiln over 2,500 degrees.

Shouts interrupt the peace of my workspace.

My sister, Temra, runs the shop at the front of the forge when she's not assisting me with larger weapons. From there, customers can purchase more simple items, such as horseshoes, buckles, and the like. My magicked horseshoes ensure the horses run faster, and my buckles never break or lose their shine. It's a simple magic—nothing like what's involved in bladesmithing.

"Ziva is not seeing customers now!" Temra yells from the other side of the door.

That's right. No one steps into the forge. The forge is sacred. It is *my* space.

Judging the steel to be ready, I pull the mace head and first flange from the oven, lining up the blade with the first groove.

"She *will* see me!" a voice screams in response. "She needs to answer for her defective work."

That word prickles. *Defective?* That's unnecessarily rude. If I were a person who handled confrontation well, I might go out there and give the customer a piece of my mind.

But I needn't have worried; my sister *is* that person.

"Defective? How dare you? Get yourself to a healer and stop blaming us for your idiocy!"

I wince. That was maybe a bit too far. Temra never has been much good at controlling her temper. Sometimes, she can be downright terrifying.

I do my best to block out the argument and focus on my work. This is the part where the magic will set. The metal is heated, primed. I thought long and hard about how I would make this weapon special. A mace is used for bashing and smashing, something that requires brute strength to wield. But what if I could increase the power behind it? What if every time the weapon absorbed a blow from an opponent, I could transfer that energy into the next swing?

I close my eyes, thinking on what I want the magic to do, but I jolt upright as, to my utter horror, the doors of the forge slam open.

I feel the extra presence in the room as though it were a weight pressing down on my shoulders. For a moment, I forget entirely what I'm working on, as I'm unable to think about anything but the discomfort coursing through my veins.

I hate feeling as though I don't fit right in my own skin. As though the anxiety takes up too much space, pushing me aside.

As footsteps draw closer, I try to compose myself. I remember the mace and focus on it like my life depends on it. Maybe the intruder will take the hint and leave.

No such luck.

Whoever he is, he stomps to the other side of my anvil, where he's now in my line of sight, and shoves an arm under my nose.

"Look at this!"

I take in the large gash across the man's lower arm. Meanwhile, a ball of nerves roils in my stomach to have a stranger so close.

"Get out of here, Garik. Ziva is working!" Temra says futilely as she joins us.

"This is what your blade did to me. My *sword* arm! I demand a refund!"

My face heats, and I can't think for a moment, can do nothing but stare at the man bleeding over my workspace. Garik is perhaps in his early thirties. Lanky rather than well built, with a hooked nose and too-big eyes. It's no surprise that I don't recognize him. Temra handles most of the commissions that come through the shop so I can focus on the actual forging.

Garik looks at me like I'm stupid. "Your weapon is defective. It cut me!"

"You cut yourself!" Temra shouts back. "You will not come in here and try to blame the weapon for your carelessness."

"Carelessness! I am a master swordsman. The fault certainly doesn't lie with me."

"Really? How else does a man cut his sword arm with his weapon? What were you doing? Practicing twirls? Throwing the weapon up in the air and trying to catch it? Was there a large audience to see you stumble?"

Garik sputters for a good minute as he tries to find his words, hinting that Temra's guess is exactly what happened.

"Perhaps you should try acrobatics if you're going to use your sword in such a manner instead of how it was intended," Temra bites out.

"You stay out of this, you little heathen! I'm taking this up with the smithy. Or is she incapable of speaking for herself?"

That has me dropping my tools and giving the foul man my full attention. It's one thing for him to come in here and attack me, but to call my sister names?

"Garik," I say with confidence I don't feel. "You will leave now before we bring the city guards into the matter. You are no longer welcome in the forge or the shop or anywhere near our land."

"My arm—" he tries.

"Is not nearly as hurt as your pride, else you would be at a healer's and not here."

His face grows red as blood drips onto the ground.

I can't look at him any longer. It's too much. My eyes find the laces at his shirt instead and focus there. Maybe that was stupid. Did what I say even make sense? If I say something more, would I only be rambling?

I decide to add, "I would be happy to take a look at the weapon to ensure its effectiveness. Perhaps in front of all your friends? Though, by the excellent gash in your arm, it appears to be working just fine."

That does it. He storms out the way he came, but not before taking a swipe at the worktable along the way and sending my tools cascading toward the ground.

Then he's gone.

"Horrible man," Temra says, and she goes to put the worktable to rights.

But I can't really hear her. I'm looking at my tools, then back at the spot where Garik once stood. The entire ordeal is replaying in my mind over and over again, completely out of my control. He was here. In my forge. I had to speak. Had to question myself. Had to feel like I was going to boil from the inside. Logically, I know neither my sister nor I were in any real danger, that such confrontations don't mean the end of the world is nigh, but that doesn't mean my body is convinced.

I can't breathe. Or maybe I'm breathing too fast.

"Ziva? Oh dear. Everything is okay."

Everything is not okay. Temra tries to approach me, but I step backward, nearly falling over as I do so. My hands are shaking, and my body temperature goes from uncomfortably hot to unbearably so.

"Ziva, he's gone. You're safe. Look around the room. It's just us. Here, hold your hammer." She thrusts the instrument into my hand. "Now listen to my breathing and match it." She exaggerates the sounds of her own breath, slowly dragging it in and out.

I fall to my knees in front of my anvil, my head level with the unfinished mace, my hammer held loosely in my hand.

You are no longer welcome.

I can't believe the things I said. I insulted him. He's going to tell other potential customers about the ordeal. Everyone will know that I said something stupid. They'll all want to take their business elsewhere. I'll be ruined. Humiliated.

Everyone will know there's something wrong with me.

"Breathe. You're safe. Breathe," Temra says, cutting through my tangled thoughts.

"What if the sword was defective, and I just—"

Temra says, "The sword was perfect. Don't think like that. Come on, Ziva. You're amazing. Just breathe."

Time falls away as I try to crawl out from under the weight of my own panic.

I've no sense of how long it takes before the attack recedes, before my mind can understand that there's anything else besides impending doom. But it passes, easing out of me like a fruit being juiced.

I've always been a naturally anxious person, but being around people makes it so much worse. And sometimes these attacks happen—when it's a particularly nasty encounter or if I'm simply feeling overwhelmed.

I'm tired and overstimulated, but I still welcome the hug my sister wraps me in. She lets me decide when to pull away.

"Thank you," I say as I set my hammer back on one of the many worktables in the forge.

"I'm sorry, Ziva. I really did try to keep him from entering."

"Trust me, I heard. But I hope you know that if anyone is acting dangerous, I insist you show them in. I don't ever want you in harm's way."

She scoffs. "How can a man who injures himself with his own weapon be dangerous?"

We share a laugh, and I turn back to the unfinished mace, trying to decide whether to continue working or to rest for a bit.

Only . . . the weapon has already been magicked.

There's no physical change that I can see, but I sense it. A slight pulsing of heat.

I pick up the mace by the metal handle and bring the head toward my face for inspection, careful of the single flange that is still cooling.

"Something happened," I say.

"Did Garik ruin the weapon?"

"No, it's already imbued with magic."

"What did you do?"

"Nothing. I was welding the first flange on, and then Garik came in. I set it on the anvil, and then . . ."

"Then?" Temra prompts.

"And then I couldn't breathe."

I head outdoors, Temra following. Our city is located in the middle of a conifer forest. It rains every other day of the week, and the sun is constantly battling the clouds for dominance in the sky. Today the sun shines brightly, warming my skin through the light breeze.

Our parents kept chickens and a goat in the backyard when I was little. I remember helping Mother collect the eggs each morning. But neither Temra nor I care for such responsibilities, so the land mostly serves as an area for me to demonstrate my weapons.

When I judge myself to be a safe distance from the house, I grasp the mace tightly before taking a swing in the direction of the old cedar tree.

Nothing magical happens.

Though rare, there have been a few times when I've unwittingly magicked a weapon and had to figure out how it worked.

It's rather frustrating.

I try bringing the shaft down against the dirt-packed ground, but that does nothing either. On a whim, I breathe onto the mace, since my face had been so close to it during my attack.

Still nothing.

"Let me try," Temra says.

"Absolutely not. You might hurt yourself."

"I've handled your weapons before."

"But oftentimes my weapons have long-range effects. Until I'm sure what it does, I won't let you—"

Temra falls to her knees, her hands going to her throat as she makes a gasping noise. I'd started twirling the weapon over my head, and I immediately stop and rush over to her.

"What happened?" I ask. "Did you swallow something?"

A burst of air fills her lungs, and she stares wonderingly at the weapon. "I didn't swallow anything. It's the mace. Do that again."

"What?"

"Spin it over your head in a circle."

I give one full rotation of the weapon, and this time Temra is ready. "I can't breathe when you do that."

I stare at the mace in shock before handing it over to her. "Now you can try."

She does, and I feel the effects instantly. The mace is sucking the air away from me, toward itself. I step farther and farther away. Once I reach about ten feet, I can breathe again.

Temra stops the motion. "Incredible!"

"I'm glad my sheer panic is good for something."

Temra looks on me sadly. "It's all right, Ziva. Whenever it happens, I'll be here for you."

As the older sister, *I* should be there for her. But more often than not, she is the one saving me. Temra should have been the one to receive our mother's gift for magic. She is so much stronger and braver than I will ever be, but I don't think she realizes how much my gift took away my own childhood.

I'm glad that, at sixteen, Temra is able to concentrate on more trivial tasks, like flirting with boys and focusing on her schooling. But me? I've been providing for us since I was twelve. I often wonder if spending so much of my formative years locked in a forge somehow made me fearful of everything else. At eighteen, I hate to leave the house and be around people.

Or maybe it's simply an effect of the magic itself. I've no one to ask for answers about magic. Mother was killed when I was five, long before my gift manifested.

"The local tournament is only months away," Temra says. "I'm sure we'll have many more customers passing through the city between then and now. Everyone is going to want a Zivan blade."

She's trying to make me feel better. I appreciate the effort, but I'm still reeling from the effects of my attack.

"It's a phase," Temra says, reading my thoughts. "It will pass eventually."

"I'm sure you're right."

But I don't believe it for a moment.

CHAPTER TWO

It's Tuesday, which means we go out for dinner.

I hate going out.

There's a small relief when I see that our usual table is free. I make a beeline for it, taking the far chair. It's my favorite spot because my back is against the wall. No one can get behind me, and I can see the whole room.

I don't like feeling as if people are staring at me, and it's a sensation I can't shake off when my back is exposed to a large space.

Temra and I make a show of raising the menus, but we both already know what we want.

The waitress greets us both by name before taking our orders. "I'll have the cauliflower soup and fresh bread," Temra says. "She'll have the lamb and steamed vegetables."

I nod with a forced smile on my face toward the waitress. It's an arrangement Temra and I have. We're both terrible cooks. Everything seems to be burned or soggy when we try. Still, I'd rather eat poor food and be safe at home than out and about where strangers can watch me eat. Temra, on the other hand, loves eating out, so we have a deal. We can eat out for half the week; the other half we take turns cooking at home. And Temra always orders for me so I don't have to talk to anyone but her.

I place my hands atop the table in front of me and twist my fingers together, a habit I've had since childhood. A light buzzing sensation has taken root just under my skin. In an attempt to distract myself from my discomfort, I say, "The governor came by to collect his weapon this afternoon while you were at school."

"He came in person?"

"Yes."

"He must be really excited about the mace. How did he like it?"

I try to hide a cringe, but I must not manage it, because Temra says, "He didn't like it?"

"No, no. He liked it just fine."

"Then what's the problem?"

"He . . . invited us over."

A bright smile fills my sister's beautiful face. She makes it so difficult to be appropriately upset at times.

"That's wonderful. Ziva! Don't you know what this means? We must make a good impression."

"I tried to say no," I explain. "The man wouldn't let me."

"Oh, it'll be fun! A party is just what we need."

"It's not a party. I was assured it would be a quaint dinner affair."

"That's fine. The governor's son will still be there."

Her mischievous smile can mean only one thing. "Attractive, is he?" I ask.

She sighs in response.

I wish the food would get here more quickly so I'd have something to do with my hands. My fingers have turned red from all the fiddling; I hide them beneath the table.

I can tell Temra wants to discuss the governor's son in greater detail, but I just can't be bothered. I've never really felt attracted to anyone before. I'm not sure if it's the anxiety keeping me from getting close to people or something else. Whatever the case, it just hasn't happened for me yet.

It's not that I don't want to connect with people. I desperately do, but even more than that, I want to feel safe. No one but Temra has ever felt safe.

I do a quick sweep of the restaurant. Only four other tables are filled. Two couples are seated at separate tables: a pair of middle-aged women holding hands, and a bickering man and woman trying to keep their voices low. The woman storms out of the establishment. The man throws down some coins before following.

How awkward.

Then there's a lone woman sitting in a chair by the window, sipping a glass of wine.

And the fourth—

Is staring right at me.

I lower my eyes instinctively, my face heating to be caught staring. Except, he was looking at me first, wasn't he?

Temra is talking about something, but I barely hear it as I risk glancing out of the corner of my eye back at the man.

He's still watching me.

"Temra," I whisper. "Someone is staring at us."

"How many times do I have to tell you? No one is staring at you."

"No, I mean it this time. Look, the fellow behind you."

She turns in an obvious way to meet the eyes of the man near the door. He doesn't have any food yet, and he's certainly not looking at the menu held open in front of him.

Temra gives a quick half wave at the man before turning back around. "He's handsome, if you can forget what he's wearing. Maybe I should go talk to him?"

"Don't you dare leave me," I mutter between my teeth.

"I'd just invite him to join us."

"No!"

"I'm teasing! I'll wait until after dinner before—"

At first, I think the waitress has arrived with our food, but then I realize the far table is empty and the man has sauntered over. I turn my attention to the wood grain again as Temra twists delightedly toward the stranger.

"Hi there," she says in a voice she only uses with men.

"Hello," he says. "Forgive my interruption, but is there any chance you'd let me join you?"

Temra looks to me, but I can't say anything. I still can't look up properly. So she answers, "Please," and indicates the free chair.

The hairs on my arms stand up at the close proximity of the stranger. I feel as though my insides are being kneaded like dough. I want to be anywhere else.

"I'm Temra," my sister says.

"I'm Petrik," the stranger says.

"Petrik," Temra repeats, trying out the name. "I haven't seen you around before."

"I'm not from here. I came from Skiro's Territory."

"What do you do in Skiro?"

How does she do that? She just effortlessly knows what to say and how to say it. I manage to talk to my customers in the shop sometimes. Weapons I know well, and I don't have too much trouble discussing them. But anything else?

I'm helpless.

A pit of longing rests in my gut. A wish to be more like my sister. So at ease with the world, so comfortable in her own skin.

"I'm a scholar from the Great Library," Petrik continues in his deep tone. "I specialize in ancient magics."

My eyes flit upward of their own accord, my interest piqued.

"Magic?" I question.

The man grins, and I find the courage to look at him properly. He's somewhere around my age. He wears his hair shorn close to the scalp, a thin strip of black fuzz. He has full lips, a wide nose, and his skin is a deep brown with matching eyes.

His clothing is unusual. Most opt for tunics and leggings and sturdy boots, but this man wears a deep sapphire robe that covers his hands and ankles. In fact, all I can see of him are the pointed tips of his boots and his head. It would appear the robe has a hood, but he wears it down, so I can see his face.

"Yes, from the seeresses in the northern continent to the animal speakers in the western isles—I've read into all of it. I'm compiling my own book. A quick guide of sorts to every known magical ability in the history of the world."

Temra's eyes narrow, and she looks pointedly at me. She raises her brow, as though trying to communicate something silently to me. After a moment, she gives up and looks heavenward. "And this study has brought you to Ziva," she says.

"Precisely," Petrik says. "I was hoping Ziva might allow me to ask her some questions and inspect some of her work."

At first, I feel delighted. A man my age wants to talk to me about my work? Is this the opportunity I've been waiting for? A promise to stay in safe conversational waters while getting to know someone new?

But then I remember he said this was for a book.

Other people will read it. Petrik will quote me. Describe me and my processes. I'll be scrutinized. What if I say something wrong? What if he thinks my magic is boring and he rejects me and leaves? What if everyone who reads the book thinks I'm a hoax and I lose all my customers?

Even if I know most of that is unlikely to happen, I can't shake the fear. Agreeing to talk with him doesn't feel safe at all.

"No, thank you," I say, and turn my attention to my hands in my lap.

The waitress comes then, delivering our food. She looks to Petrik. "Have you decided on anything?"

"Not yet," he returns.

She leaves, silence and steam the only things filling the air in her wake.

"So, Petrik," Temra says, flipping her hair over her shoulder. The rich mahogany locks catch the light with the motion. "Tell me about Skiro. I've never been there before."

I can tell he's staring at me. I can feel it. Temra makes her best attempt to direct the scholar's attention back to her, but Petrik all but ignores her.

"I must have spoken too hastily, Ziva. I apologize. It's been a long journey, and I didn't mean to ambush you at dinner. I hadn't expected you to walk into the very restaurant where I was eating. I meant to seek you out. Set a proper appointment and explain the whole arrangement. I would of course compensate you for your time. Perhaps I could come by your forge sometime so we could discuss the matter further?"

"No, thank you," I repeat.

"May I ask why?"

"The forge is Ziva's safe space," Temra explains. "She doesn't like anyone intruding. She's a very private person. I'm sure you understand. Maybe I could talk to you to help with your book. I assist Ziva in the forge frequently. I'm familiar with her process and have extensive knowledge of all the weapons she's made. Maybe the two of us could get together sometime. We could meet up for dinner again."

Yes, I like that idea much better. Just leave me out of the entire thing, and Temra can flirt with the supposedly handsome boy.

"Are you certain I can't do anything to convince you otherwise?" Petrik asks, his attention never wavering from me.

I need to be direct. Confident. If there's any hint of uncertainty from me, he'll likely keep hounding me. So I raise my gaze, look the scholar firmly in the eye. "I'm certain. I have no desire to be questioned or to have my life scrutinized."

Then I pick up my fork and knife and start cutting pieces out of the roast lamb. I try not to repeat what I said in my head. I don't want to fixate. I don't want to worry. I just want to enjoy my dinner.

Petrik rises without another word. Instead of retreating back to his table, he exits the restaurant altogether.

Good riddance.

"Can you believe him?" Temra says.

"I know," I say. "How many times do I have to say no for him to understand?"

"What? Oh, right. But also, he completely ignored me! Rude. He just used me in the beginning of the conversation to get to you."

That's a first. People usually mistakenly try to talk to me to get closer to my pretty sister.

"He's gone now," I say, and I finally take a bite of the mouth-watering food. It's delicious, as always.

Temra only dips her spoon in her soup, never actually bringing it to her lips, her mind clearly still on the strange encounter.

"Don't worry about it," I tell her. "Soon I'll have enough money for us to leave Ghadra and retire in the northern continent. He won't be able to track us down there." We've been talking about it for years, ever since I opened my own business. The northern continent is beautiful, and few people can afford to live there. No one will know who I am. No one will seek me out for weapons. I love what I do, but I'd prefer forging for no one but myself. When I finally have a comfortable amount for

Temra and me to be set for life, we'll leave behind this place and settle somewhere out in the country. Just the two of us. It's all I want. To feel safe all the time and never worry if someone is going to surprise me with a social visit when I haven't mentally prepared myself.

I do very well for myself as the only magical smithy in existence—at least I've never heard of another one.

People seek me out from all over the world for weapons. Some have been for nobles who want to boast their wealth and superiority. Others have been high-ranking officers of private armies. City and castle guards receive small salaries, so I've never had one of them grace my doors.

But the bulk of my customers?

They're mercenaries.

Sellswords.

Fighters for hire.

There's been a high demand for them in recent years.

Our former sovereign, King Arund, had a bit of difficulty with his younger brother, who constantly tried to usurp him and steal his throne. The story goes that the king eventually had to sentence his brother to death after a failed assassination attempt on his life. He loved his brother dearly and hated that the crown had come between them.

In an attempt to do away with future familial animosity, Arund decided he would divide the kingdom of Ghadra between his six beloved children.

New boundaries were drawn. Six territories arose, each named after the prince or princess who rules it. Ghadra became divided.

And opportunities arose for unsavory sorts.

It was only a decade ago that the split happened, and there were many who took advantage of it. Bandits have become more common than flies on the roads. They move from territory to territory, making it impossible for any one ruler to stop them. No one wants to allocate men or funds toward criminals when they're no longer in their territory. Then there's the problem of six new rulers trying to create their own courts, build their own economies, finance their individual rules.

The people have suffered greatly for the change.

And I've heard tales that not all six royal children are content with one little piece of the pie. Rumors abound about revolts and plans for takeover, but that's all they are at this point. Whispers on the wind.

Regardless, my business has become a necessity, and I make very good money doing it. Countless individuals have tried to hire me as their personal smithy. Given my abhorrence for people, I've always refused. Lately, these requests have become more frequent. Knowledge of my abilities has started to spread to the far reaches of Ghadra. Probably because I've been taking on more commissions lately, trying to reach our goal faster.

Temra and I are so very close to being able to leave. Just two more years, I think. If I want to be able to retire and afford the higher cost of living for myself and my sister for the rest of our days, we need a bit more.

"That's great, Ziva," Temra says, pulling my mind from images of her and me alone in paradise.

She still doesn't touch her food.

"Have you given any more thought as to what trade you'd like to commit yourself to?" I ask, hoping to distract her.

"Not really. I love to act in the local city performances, so maybe I could join a traveling troupe someday."

I don't see how she would stay with me in the north if she intends to go traversing about for her trade. She clearly hasn't thought that one through very much.

"Or . . . ," she hedges, "maybe I'll do something with weapons. I've basically been apprenticing under you my entire life."

Yes, I like that idea much better. "Of course! There's always a place for you in my forge."

"That's not what I meant. I can't be in your shadow my entire life, Ziva."

My shadow? How curious she would put it that way, since it's always been me who's tried to hide behind hers.

"You'll find something that will make you happy. I know it," I say.

"I'm already happy, but I know I'll figure out the future, too. What about you?"

"Me?"

"Are you happy?"

My instinctual response is yes, but I pause. I do live in constant fear of others. Sometimes it's overwhelmingly hard to leave the house.

"I'm happy," I decide in the end. "I have everything I need. You and my forge. I just wish the rest of the world would disappear."

"That'd be an awfully empty world."

"Exactly."

"Then what need would you have of me, if I'm not scaring away most of your customers?"

"I'd get lonely if it were just me," I joke.

"And what about me?"

"What about you?" I ask.

"What am I to do while you're in your forge making weapons for nonexistent people? I can't be an actress without an audience."

"You could get a hobby."

"I have hobbies!"

"I don't think flirting counts. Besides, there are no men in my world."

Temra shakes her head in astonishment. "One day, you're going to fall madly in love. You'll find someone who will make you want to leave the forge. You won't even see him coming."

"The day the world runs out of iron ore will be the day I leave my forge. But even then, I'm sure I could figure out something with copper."

Temra flicks droplets from her spoon into my face.

CHAPTER THREE

There is nothing more terrifying than a well-attended party.

"It will be a small affair," Governor Erinar had said. "Just my family and a few friends at dinner to celebrate Ghadra's most talented smithy. You must come. I won't take no for an answer."

And I, in my haste to get rid of the governor after finishing his mace, agreed.

I wish I'd had it in me to be rude to the man. Instead, I'm stuck at a party that has more than a hundred guests in attendance. Either Erinar is related to everyone in the city or someone really needs to explain to him that his idea of a "small affair" is terribly misguided.

Either way, I'm trapped. As the guest of honor, I can't escape without notice.

Even now I feel the eyes of those in attendance on me like lions tracking a herd of antelope. I clasp my hands together and fiddle with my fingers.

I will not panic.

I will not run.

I *probably* won't die.

Has being social killed anyone in the history of the world? Surely not, but that does not seem to matter to the lead weight in my heart or the buzzing insects in my stomach. My whole body ripples with discomfort at so many eyes on me, at so many people surrounding me.

My sister—bless her!—materializes before me.

"What are you wearing?" Temra asks, eyeing me up and down before I can demand why she's arrived so late.

"A dress," I say with disgust. I pick at the fabric, missing the lightweight material of my typical loose tunic and trousers. They're perfect for combating the heat in the forge, and right now I swear it's hotter in the governor's home than it's ever been in my workspace.

People make me sweat.

Temra blinks slowly, as if to compose herself. "Why didn't you put on something nicer? Where is that dress I bought you for last Sisters Remembrance Day?"

"It's in my closet." Buried somewhere deep, but there, nonetheless.

"It's so lovely. Really brings out the blue of your eyes."

I don't recall the color of the dress, but I smile as though I remember it or care just how lovely it is. My current ensemble is a light tan. Nondescript. Lacking any fancy embellishments. Perfect for hiding.

Or so I thought.

"Ziva, all the other girls in attendance are in bright colors. You're practically wearing your work clothes in dress form."

"Don't be ridiculous. My work clothes have stains," I say, proud of myself, but as I scan the room, I realize she's right. My bland dress no doubt makes me stick out like a lone weed in a flower garden.

It's honestly been so long since I've been to a social gathering, I'm completely unaware of the latest styles in clothing. I probably look like I'm trying to snub the governor at his party.

Not that this was supposed to be a party at all.

So, really, who's more in the wrong here: me or the governor?

I peer at my sister more closely. "Your hair is rumpled."

Her hands fly to her curly locks, attempting to flatten the strays.

"You were with a boy," I accuse.

Temra doesn't embarrass easily. There's no telltale reddening of her cheeks or sheepish eye lowering, but I know I've struck true all the same.

"The time got away from me, is all," she says.

I want to press her further, but it's awfully hard for me to be angry at her when I'm trying so hard to block out the stimulants around me.

I suspect the governor's husband has a fondness for blue, for the whole room is spattered with it. Azure hand-stitched rugs cover the floor, the dining area is speckled with sapphire flowers

I don't have a name for, even the wax of the candles spread over the decorative tables has a cerulean sheen to it.

Beautiful marble columns hold up the ceiling at even intervals. On the far wall, a painting of the Sister Goddesses hangs proudly so they can watch over us all.

And there's the happy couple, arm in arm, striding toward me, their faces upcast in delight.

I grip Temra's arm in a vise. "Hide me."

"Don't be ridiculous. You're going to thank our hosts and smile through this whole affair like you couldn't be more delighted."

"I can't."

"Then next time, don't agree to a party."

"It wasn't supposed to be—"

I cut off once the pair is in hearing range and plaster a smile over my mouth that hopefully doesn't look forced.

"Miss Tellion!" the governor says. "I'm so delighted to have you in our home!"

"We are most grateful for your generosity in hosting us!" Temra says. "I'm Temra Tellion, Ziva's sister, and she's simply been gushing about how honored she is to have forged a weapon for you."

"A pleasure to make your acquaintance. This is my husband, Reniver, and our son, Asel, is around here somewhere."

"There he is," Reniver says.

We follow his extended finger to where a man our age is surrounded by girls. He's tall and muscular, with a symmetrical face that's likely the reason he has so many admirers.

"He's a very sociable boy," the governor says, stepping in front of the scene to block my view of his son. "So popular."

"Just like his father," Temra says politely.

"Oh, well, thank you."

A silence falls. Perhaps the couple is wondering why I haven't said a word. Everyone wonders why I can't make polite conversation. It's just not one of my strengths.

But I try. "Governor, you mentioned the weapon was a gift for your husband when you commissioned it. How long have you trained for the mace, Reniver?"

There, that's a normal question, right?

"Oh, I'm no mace bearer," Reniver explains, "but the gift is everything I could have hoped for! We're going to take the guests by to see it as soon as supper is over. And after a toast in your honor, of course!"

"To see it?" I echo. Just where is the weapon?

"But of course you'd wish an early peek! So proud of your work! Asel?"

I jump as Reniver shouts the young man's name, but Asel obeys, excusing himself from the horde of women.

"Father?" he answers.

"Would you show Miss Tellion where we've proudly displayed her work?"

Asel turns his head toward Temra first, and a delighted grin smears above his chin as he takes in my beautiful sister. Her dark hair bounces in the most perfect curls when she walks. The sun has brightened her skin to a glorious tan over the summer, and she's a perfectly regular height at just under five and a half feet.

The governor, seeing his son's eyes light on my sister, says, "No, this is Ziva, the magically gifted blacksmith." He indicates me, and Asel's face loses its delight.

I'm a behemoth at just over six feet tall. Taller than most of the boys, and Asel is no exception. My dull brown hair is flat as a board, and I wear it up and out of my face always. I never bother with makeup like most of the girls my age (what's the point when I'd just sweat it off while I work?), and as a result, my freckles stand out in stark relief over my nose, forehead, chin, cheeks. Everywhere.

As I wait for Asel to finish his perusal, I'm not filled with shame. Only the fear that comes from being so closely examined. From being forced to interact with people. From worrying I'll say or do something stupid. From worrying that he'll be able to guess all my weaknesses just by looking at me.

Asel quickly composes his features. "A pleasure to meet you. Shall we?" He holds out his arm, and I think I'm supposed to take it. The color must drain from my face—touching strangers makes everything so much worse—because Temra takes my arm instead and says, "Lead on, Asel. We'll follow."

Bless my beautiful, wonderful sister.

But the governor says, "Actually, Miss Temra, would you accompany me to the kitchen? I simply must get your thoughts on the dinner menu for tonight."

Temra looks to me for permission. Not permission, really, but acknowledgment that I'll be all right on my own. I most certainly will not, but I can't say so in front of the most powerful man in the city.

I nod as I realize just what this is.

A setup.

The governor and his husband want me to take a fancy to

their son. Wouldn't it look splendid to have one of the few people in the world possessing magic as a member of the family?

I want to gag.

Asel, having taken the hint the first time, merely steps beside me without offering an arm this time, and leads me out of the receiving hall. We traverse up a set of stairs in silence, the noises from the party growing fainter as we leave everything behind and enter into some sort of study. I note a desk made from a purple wood and books lining most of the walls. On one end of the room, a fireplace stands, empty of logs or heat at the moment. But above the mantel, atop polished metal hooks, my mace has been placed.

Displayed.

"What is this?" I shriek before I can stop myself.

"Your work, I'm told," Asel answers.

"This mace steals the breath of surrounding enemies! It can kill without even touching an opponent, and yet it sits above the mantel as though it were a—a—*decoration*!"

As soon as the words are out, I remember myself and turn to Asel in a panic. He's going to report back to his fathers, and I'll be—

He starts laughing. Then, as though he finally finds me interesting, he turns his body toward me. "Did you think my father intended to take it into battle? Wage some war against my other father's opposers?"

I look down at the ground, a smile surfacing on my lips, because I cannot help it. "Maybe. Or just wear it threateningly, in case anyone thought to bear ill will toward the governor."

"I'm afraid this is only supposed to make a statement and

perhaps be a great conversation starter when other politicians are visiting."

"What statement?"

"He who bears this mace bears great wealth," Asel says in a deep, mocking tone.

I laugh again and find the courage to raise my eyes. "So you won't tattle on me?"

"Whatever for?"

"My outburst regarding the mace's resting place."

"Not at all. I do find it curious, though, that you would care where the weapon ends up. You were paid regardless, yes?"

"Yes, but . . ."

Asel takes a step forward, showing he's truly interested in the answer. "But?"

"I want to make the world a safer place. My weapons are supposed to do that."

"But not if they're attached to a wall."

"Exactly."

Asel purses his lips together in thought. "If I promise to use it if anyone should break in, will that make you happy?"

"Yes, it would," I joke back.

"Then I promise," he says, taking another step forward.

I realize a flurry of things at once. One, I've been hunching again, because Asel and I are at eye level. Two, he's much closer than I originally thought, close enough to touch. And three, what I'd been doing was maybe confused as flirting, when really all I was trying to do was survive a conversation.

He leans forward, his lips puckering.

I step back, rise to my full height. "What are you doing?"

"Making you feel better about the mace."

Oh no. What do I do? Run for it? Or say something? Which would be less embarrassing at this point?

"No, thank you," I say, and then I want to slap myself. What a stupid thing to say to someone trying to kiss you. But what else do you say? I haven't ever had someone try to kiss me before. I haven't prepared for this kind of confrontation.

"What?" he asks.

I cringe. I probably didn't make sense the first time. "I don't need you to make me feel better. I'm just fine."

"Kiss me anyway," he whispers in some sort of deep tone that I haven't heard from him yet. He leans forward once more.

Goddesses. Why is it happening again?

I can't say *No, thank you* again.

"I don't want to," I say instead. Is that any better? Why is it so hot in here? I feel like I can't breathe in this dress.

"No one will ever know," he says, following me across the room as I try to get away from him.

"I'll know."

At that, Asel freezes in place. His eyes shrink behind his eyelids as he scrutinizes me. As though he's looking for just what's wrong with me.

And I know there's something wrong with me, but him looking at me like that isn't helping my state of mind.

"What's wrong with you?" he asks, confirming my thoughts. "I made you laugh twice."

"You were counting?" I mean, *I* was counting, but that's because no one but Temra ever makes me laugh. And why should those two comments of his go together unless—

Oh.

I see now what all of Asel's words were meant to do. Not make me feel better at all about the mace but to lead to something that he thought would make his night more enjoyable.

He's a despicable lady hunter.

The panic recedes, replaced with fury.

"You think saying a few nice words to me earns you a kiss? That's not how it works."

He blinks once before standing straighter, trying to match my height, but he still falls inches short. "Most women would kill to get me alone."

"I very much doubt that. Most women are far too sensible to have such poor taste."

He scoffs in outrage, dares to step forward. I cross my arms over my chest, hopefully hiding my shaking hands, and letting my biceps bulge with the muscles there.

Thinking better of trying anything, Asel steps around me and all but rushes out of the room.

I'm left alone, the faraway chatter of a hundred people lightly filling my ears. I take a seat in one of the elaborate sofas facing the weapon.

Now that the threat is gone, my thoughts turn back to the conversation. Everything I said. Everything I did. Did I really flex in front of him?

My thoughts tumble out of control, fixating on each mortifying sequence of events, down to the horror of having to stand up for myself.

I'm distracted as another presence fills the room.

A woman enters in an almost lazy manner, a glass of wine

held in front of her. She looks once at me and then to the weapon on the wall.

"Are you her? Ziva, the blacksmith?"

I don't know if I can take being social for one second longer. I manage a nod, before sinking further into the chair.

"I saw the governor's distasteful little brat running from the room. Good for you," she says. "Whatever you did, I can promise he deserved it."

I manage to breathe out a sound similar to a laugh. "Who are you?"

"Warlord Kymora Avedin," she says, approaching the mantel to get a better look at the mace. "A pleasure to make your acquaintance."

A warlord? I've never met one of those before. But I've heard of her. She served under the late king before he split the kingdom into territories. Kymora is smaller than I would have thought someone with such a title would be, but at my height, most girls seems short to me. She wears her tan hair pulled back into a bun, with one lock twisted into a braid and pinned to the side of her head. A scar runs from the center of her right cheek to her ear, but it was well tended to, the line smooth and white, rather than puckered and pink. A broadsword hangs at her side, but by the slight bulges in her clothing, I gather it is not the only weapon on her person. I place her at about forty years of age, though it's hard to tell, as she's certainly taken great care with her physical health.

"Exquisite work," she says, reaching out to touch one of the flanges. "Such a shame it's being wasted on a wall. Utterly ridiculous for such a fine piece." She takes a sip of her drink.

I like her. She's so upfront, dismissing with any formalities. It puts me at ease immediately.

"Thank you. That's exactly what I was just saying."

"I'm in town to commission a piece from you," she says without any more preamble. "Something to wear at my side, not dangle in front of guests, I assure you. I'll be stopping by the forge later this week."

"I'd very much like to make something for you," I say, and I mean it.

"Excellent. I'll see you later, then. Think nothing more on this," she says, indicating the mace. "Maybe you'll get lucky and someone will rob the place."

I've a wide grin on my face as she leaves the room just as casually as she entered it.

I wonder how much longer I can hide up here.

I give it a few more minutes before forcing myself back down the stairs to the main room. I assure myself that I'm only imagining everyone's stares. No one is looking at me. No one knows about the embarrassing situation with Asel. No one cares that my dress is brown. Someone laughs nearby, and I have to tell myself it's not at my expense.

I can survive the rest of the night. I'll be cool and collected like Warlord Kymora. Exuding power and unaffected by anyone else's opinions. I can't wait for her to visit the shop. I start thinking of all the intricate metalwork I could do on the hilt of a broadsword.

Temra finds me, and I link my arm through hers before realizing the look of panic on her face.

"We need to go," she says. "Now."

That's usually what I say. "Are you all right? Did something happen?"

"Ziva, just trust me."

"Okay," I say, letting her lead me toward the exit—secretly delighted that I'm getting out of the party early.

Then bodies block our path.

Asel is at the front of them with his fathers, his arms crossed in front of his body in an imitation of the threatening posture I just displayed to him upstairs.

"Ziva," the governor says. "It's come to my attention that you've insulted my son after we've welcomed you into our home."

"Erinar," Reniver says, gently tapping his husband on the arm. "Perhaps this isn't the best place."

"I want this settled now. What do you have to say for yourself, blacksmith?"

"Um . . ." The whole receiving hall is watching. A hundred bodies stop their conversations to stare at the scene before them, and I seem to have forgotten every word I've ever learned.

"Did you or did you not strike my son?"

That brings me up short. "Why should I have reason to do that?"

"Asel says you were furious at the mace's placement on the mantel. You then became enraged and attacked him."

"I did what?"

"Governor," Temra says, "my sister doesn't have a violent bone in her body. I'm sure Asel is mistaken."

"I am not," Asel says.

"You appear perfectly fine," Temra points out. "I see no

marks. No tears in your clothing. Where exactly is my sister supposed to have struck you?"

He huffs proudly. "I don't need to explain myself."

"I think you do, son," Reniver says.

"How can you doubt him?" Erinar says.

"You know how he can be. I'm worried we don't have the full story."

"What kind of parents would we be if we don't believe our child? And if the blacksmith were innocent, perhaps she'd have more words to disclose."

My face heats, and I feel wetness at the corners of my eyes as fury and fear take hold within me. Words. Find my words.

"Asel—he—" Breathe. "He made unwanted advances toward me. I may not have said the kindest things in response, but I didn't lay a finger on him."

Reniver nods, as though he feared that's what happened.

"Is that true, Asel?" the governor asks.

"No, Father. I swear it happened as I said."

Both the governor and his husband look between Asel and me. I watch as they check my knuckles. Reniver nods to himself, as though unsurprised to find unbroken skin there. The governor seems to notice for the first time the large scene he's caused and the people all looking on.

"I'm going to have to ask you to leave," the governor says to his guests. "It appears my husband and I need to have an important chat with our son about honesty."

A vein stands out on Asel's face, and the young man looks positively mortified. I become embarrassed for him instead of myself.

Reniver begins making apologies and ushering guests out. The governor takes a step toward me. More quietly, he says, "I apologize for the night being ruined and for the actions of my son. You can expect a formal apology from him in the future."

"That's not necessary," I hurry to say. The last thing I need is to see Asel again, this time in my home.

But the governor doesn't hear my response. He's begun assisting his husband with apologizing to the other guests as they leave through the doors.

Asel stomps toward us. "This isn't over. You're going to regret this."

"Go run to your fathers. Sounds like you're about to get a scolding," Temra says smugly.

I grab her arm so we can depart.

Our horse, Reya, is waiting for us in the stables. I breathe in the smell of her cool hide, forcing my thoughts to the here and now. To safety. Temra bought our mare a few years ago so she could ride into the city more quickly for her lessons, though I've seen her saddle the horse a few times at night to sneak off to meet boys, which resulted in me revoking her horse-riding privileges from time to time.

Wordlessly we saddle Reya. Temra tells the eager stable hand to leave us be as she tightens the girth. Meanwhile I strap on her bridle.

We hoist ourselves up. I let Temra take the reins and position herself up front, while I climb on behind her, wrap my arms around her waist, and lean my forehead against the back of her neck.

We trot out into the night, then adjust to a walk when the governor's estate is far behind us.

Temra taps a finger against one of my hands. "Tell me what happened?" The question gives me room to refuse, but I want to tell her everything.

"He was so nice at first, and then he tried to . . ."

"To . . . ?" she prompts.

My thoughts take a dive. I was forced to attend a *party*. Asel tried to kiss me. He dared to lie to his father when I refused him. He caused that big scene. There were so many eyes on me. He threatened us before we left. What more does he intend to do?

Over and over again, I see his lips puckering, his affronted look of confusion when I didn't want to touch him. Because he expects *everyone* to want him. And then he pitches fits when he doesn't get what he wants.

Just like that, I'm angry again.

"The governor said it would be a small affair. Just a dinner, not a party. I wasn't able to properly prepare myself for that event." My voice rises to a near shriek. "And then he has the nerve to sic his son on me! Because, what? He thinks it'll make himself look better politically to be connected to me?"

"I think he just wanted you to meet his son. He couldn't have anticipated that Asel would—"

"And then Asel has *the nerve* to try to kiss me. Just because he made me laugh. He thinks that entitles him to a reward. Well, I have news for him. He's not as attractive as he thinks he is! In fact, his shallowness would rival a dog's piss puddle!"

The horse nearly comes to a stop as Temra's grip on the reins tightens. "He tried to kiss you? And what else?"

"What do you mean, *what else*? That's what he did. That's what happened. He tried to kiss me, and I told him no. Then he got angry and stormed off."

"You're telling me that boy made a big scene over a kiss! I thought he tried to assault you or something."

"He *did* try to assault me. He tried to assault me with his lips."

I'm staring at the back of her head. I wish I could see her expression. But when she starts shaking with laughter, I can imagine it perfectly.

"I love you, Ziva," she says once she gets her giggling under control.

"I love you, too."

CHAPTER FOUR

It takes me a whole day to convince myself that Asel's threat was empty.

Then Temra comes home from school in tears.

"What happened?" I ask.

"I don't want to talk about it." She heads for her room upstairs without another word.

Later, I'm able to pry more out of her. I forgot that Asel is one year above her in school. I didn't have a formal education. I only apprenticed as a smithy. The dynamics of an educational setting are completely foreign to me.

But somehow, Asel has turned all her classmates against her. Temra's friends have shunned her. Apparently everyone has taken Asel's side in the matter, despite the fact that Temra had nothing to do with the incident in the governor's home.

I may hate confrontation, but I'm not about to sit by while that brat makes a mess of Temra's school life.

"Where are you going?" Temra asks when she sees me trade my work boots for walking boots.

"To the governor's home."

"You can't!"

"I absolutely can."

"If you tattle to his parents, that'll only make things worse for me! Please, Ziva!"

She makes me promise I won't go, and though I tell her I won't go today, I make no such promises not to do so in the future.

But then things get worse.

I'm working alone in the forge when five men let themselves in. At first, my mind starts whirring from the thought of having to talk to so many people at a time, but when I take a second look, I realize these boys aren't here to talk.

They're friends of Asel's.

I instantly relax and raise my hammer in one hand and the fire-red tongs in the other. "You'd better think very carefully about your next move," I say.

I'm not intimidated by any of them. They're tiny things, really. Hardly taller than five and a half feet each. There's not one of them I'd lose to in an arm wrestling match. Together, however, they could overpower me.

But with a pair of tongs fresh out of the kiln? I don't expect them to attack me.

And they don't. Instead, they make their way around the forge, overturning tables and throwing tools across the room.

They can't actually break anything. Everything important is made of metal.

But the mess is devastating to watch.

Only when the last of my castings is on the floor do they turn around and head back the way they came, making the same mess in the shop.

I've no choice but to report the incident after they leave. Temra goes with me for support as I relay what happened to a city guard. As I describe each man who entered the forge, Temra supplies his name. She knows them all from school and needs very few descriptors from me before knowing exactly who the vandalizers are.

And then we return home to clean the mess.

Temra sweeps up broken glass from the displays, while I right all our items for sale in the shop. With heavy hearts, we discuss our options.

"I could quit school," my sister says. "Find work now. Then I wouldn't have to deal with those idiots, and we could get out of town that much quicker with the two of us working."

"Not an option I'm willing to consider."

"The only other option is leaving now. We can't live like this. Fearful of vandalizers or thieves or maybe even something worse. Who knows how things might escalate?"

"We really should involve the governor, not just the city guard."

"It won't help. Asel will only make our lives worse. The governor isn't about to imprison his only child and his friends, and I guarantee that incarceration is the only thing that'll stop—"

The bells at the top of the shop door ring as the hinges swing inward. We both turn in surprise, because we put out the Closed sign while we cleaned.

Two men in scarlet uniforms bearing falcons on their chests enter the shop. They give Temra and me disinterested looks before doing a sweep of the area. One of them goes into the forge. He leaves the door open behind him, and I watch as he opens a few of the larger cupboards—those big enough to hold a person, I realize.

"What do you think you're doing?" Temra demands before I can. I rack my memory for anyone I know with a falcon as their sigil.

When done, the guard who stayed in the shop knocks on the door twice, and another figure joins them.

The warlord.

I'd completely forgotten about my conversation with Kymora, and I'm embarrassed that she's arrived to see the place in such a state.

Temra looks the woman over, forgetting the rude guards. "My lord, welcome to the Zivan Smithy."

"Warlord," I correct her.

Her eyes widen, and she looks at the woman with blatant fascination. "Warlord. Please do forgive the mess. We had trouble with some vandals today."

Kymora doesn't comment on the state of the shop. She says, "Ziva, good to see you again."

"And you," I say.

Kymora walks around the shop, taking in what remains of all the displays. She pauses at a row of daggers behind a now broken glass case.

"Everything in the shop is imbued with magic, Warlord," Temra says, ever the perfect saleswoman. "Those daggers never dull."

Kymora strolls around the space, looking for all the world like she couldn't care less about the broken glass at her feet. She picks up objects seemingly at random before replacing them. Temra is quick to tell her what everything does. She does not insult her by relaying prices. A woman of the warlord's status would not be encumbered by something so trifling as money.

Kymora comes to a stop in front of a quiver of arrows. She draws one out to examine the point.

"Those were designed to hit flying targets," Temra says. "For hunters of geese and other fowl. They'll never miss the heart of the bird they're aimed at."

"It's all extraordinary," Kymora says at last. "I see why word of you has spread to the whole of Ghadra, Ziva. I've had occasion to run into some of the weapons you've forged, including a pair of daggers that shattered anything they came into contact with. I finally decided to make the trip myself to commission a weapon."

"Thank you, Warlord," I say, remembering the weapons in question. I made them last year for a mercenary who wanted something that wouldn't weigh her down on long journeys.

"Is there somewhere we might talk in private?" she asks.

Temra narrows her eyes at the woman, assuming—and probably rightly so—that she's the one who isn't supposed to overhear the conversation.

"We could step into the forge, but I'm afraid it's worse off than the shop, since we haven't even started setting it to rights."

"It'll do fine."

I precede her through the back doors; a harsh tingling pricks along my spine at having my back to her, but there's nothing else for it.

Kymora shuts the doors behind her, leaving her men with my sister. No—to guard the only entrance into the shop. Someone like her likely has hundreds of enemies if she needs to take such precautions.

It's unusually cool in the forge. The embers in the kiln have died, and evening is approaching. The windows are open, as is my habit to do so first thing each morning. Kymora promptly closes them so she won't risk being overheard. Candlelight illuminates her form.

"I have a proposition for you," she begins. "Something I think will greatly benefit us both. I want to commission a weapon, and if you make it up to my standards, I'd like to offer you a job at my estate in Orena's Territory. The position will pay handsomely, and you'll be making magicked weapons for my soldiers."

"You want me to come work for you?" I echo.

She's not the first to offer me such a position. I've had major noblemen send missives with similar offers, and I even received one from Prince Verak. As word of my abilities began to spread, more and more powerful people wanted to use me. I've turned down every offer, of course. I like my independence. Thankfully, no one is in a position to try to force me to do their bidding. Not with the young territories still trying to find their footing. Powerful people have much more important things to focus on at the moment. This is just another reason why Temra and I need to make our way to the northern continent as soon as possible. I'm becoming too well-known.

But Kymora's offer is the first I've wanted to accept. I like the warlord, and this position could be the answer to all our problems. It's in another territory. Far away from the governor's son's influence.

"Thank you. Your offer is very generous."

"This isn't a service I'm doing for you. You need to prove yourself first."

"Of course. Your weapon."

She nods. "I'm fond of the broadsword." She pats the weapon hanging off her waist. "I'd deeply enjoy a magicked one."

"Swords are one of my specialties." Temra and I always say this to customers, regardless of what kind of weapon they want. Truth be told, I'm good at everything involving iron. Part of the magic that courses through my veins.

"Excellent." Kymora takes a turn about the forge, eyeing my tools and castings on the floor. With her back to me, she says, "I want you to outdo yourself. I want you to treat my sword as though it is the weapon you've been practicing for your entire life. It is to be of immense power. Something that can defeat many opponents at a time. Something that could bring nations to their knees."

She turns. "Do that, and I will pay you triple your usual rate for the weapon in question, and the position at my estate is yours."

I allow myself only a moment to worry over her request. "It will be a challenge, but I like challenges."

"Good."

"There is one other thing."

Kymora inclines her head.

"My sister—"

"Oh, I thought that girl was your hired help. Very well. There will be accommodations for both you and your sister on my estate. Is there anyone else I need know about?"

"We have a horse," I joke.

She smiles then. "I look forward to seeing the finished weapon. I have business in Ravis's Territory. It should keep me for about three months. Is that sufficient time to make my broadsword?"

It'll be tight, but I'll just cancel any other commissions I have scheduled. "Yes."

"Good. I will return then." She heads back for the doors to the shop, seeing herself out.

I stare after her in bewilderment.

When she passes by the front desk, which Temra has taken position behind, Kymora unties a purse from her waist and sets it before her. "Half upfront—that's how it works, is it not?"

"It is," Temra confirms.

"As I told Ziva, I'm willing to pay triple the usual rate if she can do what I ask. Here is half of your usual fee. There will be much more when I return. Perhaps you can encourage her best work."

She starts for the door before turning once more, as though remembering something. "You needn't worry about the miscreants who did this." She twirls a finger around the shop. "I'll deal with them." Then she and her men leave without a backward glance.

Temra shivers. "Something about her makes me uneasy."

"The arrogance," I suggest.

"The power, I think. How many people do you suppose she's killed? Maybe that's it. All the death that surrounds her."

"I'd imagine it's somewhere in the hundreds."

"Thousands, I bet," Temra says.

We both stare in the direction of the door she exited.

"When she said she'd *deal with them*, you don't think she meant . . ." Temra lets the words drift off.

"She's not going to kill them." But as soon as the words are out, I reconsider them. *Would she kill them?*

"Is it terrible that I kind of hope she kills them?"

"Yes!"

"You're right. Too extreme. Maybe just maim them."

"Temra!"

"They're awful! I can't wait to find out what she does to them! She's incredible. Can you imagine the looks on those boys' faces when she appears at their homes?"

"I don't want to imagine being on the receiving end of her hostility."

"Then we'd better not disappoint her," Temra says. "What did she want from you? And how do you know her?"

"She introduced herself to me at the governor's party. She wants me to make her a broadsword, and then she's invited us to live with her." I share all the details of Kymora's offer.

"Wow," Temra says. "That's awfully convenient."

"You think we should turn the offer down?"

"No. I'm honestly just a little awestruck by the woman. How does one become a warlord?"

"Are you considering it as a profession?"

"Maybe," she says.

"Kymora was King Arund's general over his armies. When he split Ghadra between his children, there was no longer a standing army. She employs her own private army now." That's all I know about her.

"For what purpose?"

"I don't know. Because she can? To scare off any other kingdoms from thinking they can invade us now that we're divided? I, for one, feel safer knowing Kymora is watching over Ghadra's territories."

Temra taps her fingers along the desk. "Can you do what she asked? Make an all-powerful weapon that can take out many opponents at once?"

"There's only one way to find out."

Another pause. Then Temra asks, "What do you think she will do to us if you fail?"

"I'd rather not think about it. I need to be alone for a bit. Today has been particularly rough." I retreat back to the forge to get started on cleaning it.

"If it's all the same to you," Temra says to my back, "I think I'd prefer not to come in to work the day she returns. Not that I doubt your abilities or anything, but there's no sense in both of us dying."

"Very funny."

Kymora did not kill Asel's friends or maim them, but Temra says they won't look in her direction.

"It's not like before when they were shunning me," she says. "Now, it's as if they're afraid. Like something really bad will happen if they look at me. They keep their distance, even run away if I enter the same room."

"The warlord threatened them?" I guess.

"She must have. Oh, I wish I knew what she said!"

"If everyone is leaving you alone, then maybe we don't have to flee the city anymore."

Temra's eyes widen. "No! It's not the same as it was before. I've still lost friends, and Asel still complicates everything every chance he gets. We may not be dealing with his friends breaking in anymore, but we are not safe in this town. Especially if Asel aspires to go into politics one day. He can still make our lives miserable. Besides, I want to live on Kymora's estate. I need to learn from this woman!"

She's right, of course.

I don't like change. I don't like doing new things. But leaving is our best option. In fact, it's likely our only option.

And if I work for Kymora, I bet Temra and I could retire to the north even sooner!

With that thought lending my heart strength, I throw myself into my work, determined to construct my best weapon yet.

Lirasu, our city, is pressed up against the Southern Mountains, and I pay the miners for a steady stream of iron ore, which I then turn into steel using a crucible.

Swords are one of the simpler weapons to make. Any weapon is certainly a lot of work, but a sword's overall shape is straight and uniform, unlike a mace, for example, which requires many pieces coming together.

Shaping a sword requires endless hours of hammering. It starts out as a fire-heated glob of steel. It's pounded and reheated again and again until it flattens out into the right shape. The trick is in keeping the steel the right temperature and pounding with just the right amount of force—enough to shape but not break it. The smithy I apprenticed under told me it takes decades to master this, so either I'm a prodigy or the magic has a hand in helping my instincts.

When the sword finally has its shape, I set my mind to the magic.

It's tied to my senses. To the sound of my voice. The heat of my breath. The fervor in my eyes. The way I soothingly caress the metal or listen to what it has to say. It's not something I'm fully conscious of most of the time, but what I have learned is fire-heated steel is not to be shouted at or reprimanded. It is to be coerced with gentle whispers and encouragement.

So far, I have not failed to make it do what I want. And occasionally, it surprises me by doing something wonderful that I hadn't even anticipated.

I want you to treat my sword as though it is the weapon you've been practicing for your entire life. It is to be of immense power. Something that can defeat many opponents at a time. Something that could bring nations to their knees.

Suddenly feeling daunted by the task, I decide to procrastinate the magic and turn my attention instead to the hilt while I wait for inspiration to strike.

I chisel and shape and reheat. Reheat. Reheat.

I pour my strength into my work, knowing that I can't fail. My sister and I have too much depending on this.

Yet no ideas are forthcoming every time I turn my attention to the magic.

Something that could bring nations to their knees.

I stare at the useless length of sharpened steel before thrusting it deep into the kiln to heat the metal. The magic will only set on heated steel. When it's most malleable.

The warlord will return in two weeks' time. I've reheated the sword more times than I can count, trying to will magic into the blade.

Nothing is taking, because I have no idea what I want the sword to do.

I have made daggers that shatter anything with which they come into contact, a mace that steals the breath from those surrounding it, a longsword that knocks nearby attackers off their feet when struck against the ground, a halberd that calls forth the power of the wind, blinding any enemies.

Countless weapons with countless magical properties—and then, when the most important client of my career comes to me?

Nothing.

I'm useless.

I pull the sword out with a pair of tongs and set it on the anvil. A breeze from the windows stirs the wisps of hair that have come free from my ponytail, and I close my eyes at the brief relief.

The fire-bright tip of the broadsword grows darker as the metal cools, and I wonder how many more times I'll have to reheat it before inspiration strikes.

"Get out of the road!"

My eyes lift to the windows, where I see a man swerve around a horse-drawn cart. The shouting owner of the cart turns her voice down low to coo at the horses. Meanwhile the man turns to glare after her.

I don't recognize him from this angle, but that's not saying much. I hardly know anyone in the city, because I never leave my forge if I can help it.

The man lifts his head heavenward, as though to ask the Sister Goddesses just what the world has come to.

Then he turns, facing my forge, his eyes meeting something above the line of windows.

And I nearly drop my hammer.

Because the man, whoever he is, is—is *beautiful*.

There's no other word for him.

He's tall—a whole head over me. Golden-red locks hang down to his shoulders, the top half secured in a band at the back of his head. The shade is unlike anything I've ever seen. He wears an impressive longsword on his back. Not one of mine, but the sheer size of it is a testament to his strength.

Though his figure is intimidating, there's something about his face that belies that. His features are smooth, gentle almost. So inviting.

And very pleasing to the eye.

I don't know what's happening. I feel like something's been lodged in my throat. I can't stop staring at the stranger, and liquid heat seems to be moving through my veins.

I almost want to . . .

I want to touch him.

I'm startled by the unfamiliar thought almost as much as I am by the fact that I've inadvertently whispered the words aloud.

A flare of heat hits me from below. Confusion and wariness and some powerful unfamiliar feeling all battle for dominance within me. But the broadsword demands my attention.

It's . . . pulsing.

But in the time it takes me to draw my next breath, it stops, and the temperature spike disappears. I look back out the window to find the man moving on.

I just stand there, breathing. But I can see the red-haired man in my vision perfectly, and another wave of heat that has nothing to do with the sword rolls through me.

What is this?

The faintest sprinkling of magic pulls on me from below, and I force myself to wipe the stranger from my memory.

I consider the weapon carefully. It's as if I've started the magicking process but not finished it. What was it I'd said right before the weapon pulsed?

"I—I want to touch him," I repeat, my cheeks heating.

Nothing happens.

I raise my hammer and bring it down against the hot metal, but before the two can meet, the hammer bounces back up, despite not quite making contact. Intrigued, I try again.

It's resisting my blows.

Now why would it do that?

All right. What I'd done was say something about the man who wandered past my windows. Perhaps if I try that again?

"He's quite tall," I whisper. "With beautiful hair."

Nothing happens. No pulse of heat.

So it wasn't talking specifically about the man that did it.

"It's hot in here," I say, trying for another fact, but that obviously does nothing for the sword.

Think harder.

What I'd done was whisper a thought I had aloud. I told it to the blade.

No, not just any thought.

A private thought.

A *secret*.

"After Temra goes to bed, I sometimes sneak extra sweets from storage."

The blade glows white, and a flare of heat rises like before.

Thrilled, I tell the sword more. "I wish I could be more like my sister. She's so fearless and outgoing. I envy that." I plunge the sword back into the fire to make the steel more pliable. More prepared for my secrets.

"She doesn't remember Mother or Father. When she asks about them, I lie and say I don't remember, either, because it's too painful to talk about them."

Weights lift from my shoulders as I unburden myself on the sword, whispering all the secrets I can think of. Nothing particularly scandalous. I don't get out enough for that, but I tell it *the secrets of my mind*.

"I worry all the time that I haven't done a good enough job raising Temra. She deserves her mother, not me."

The secrets of my heart.

"I wish I weren't so alone. I love my sister, but sometimes I long for more. A partner. Someone to spend my life with. But I've never felt strongly about anyone. I've never even felt attracted to anyone."

At that word, the handsome stranger blazes in my memory. I realize all at once what I'd been feeling when I saw him.

Attraction.

Goddesses, is that what it feels like?

Why now? Why him?

But the sword isn't done with me yet. I can feel it. So I press on.

"I would rather die than talk to a stranger one-on-one. I can build the fiercest weapons the world has ever seen, but force me to talk about something other than weaponry with people I don't know, and I won't survive. But I long to have someone in my life. Someone to share my burdens with. Someone to love."

The secrets of my soul.

"I want my parents back so fiercely. If I ever find out who murdered them, I will kill them myself."

That one surprises me, even as I say it. Because it's true.

I abhor violence. I make my magical weapons to *discourage* violence. Only a fool would cross swords with a magical blade.

And yet, if I were to learn who took my parents from me, all those beliefs about violence would go right out the window.

Truth after truth spills from my lips, rushing out of me and into the sword. I don't know how long I stand there. Hours maybe? But my voice turns raspy, the flames die down, and my mind feels so serene. As if the sword has taken the burden of my secrets upon itself.

When I can think of no more to say, I thrust the blade into a bucket of water. The liquid instantly evaporates, and I have to jump back from the onslaught of steam or be burned by it. The bucket cracks in two, and the sword drops from my grip.

The glaring white glow is so intense for a moment, I have to shield my eyes. When that subsides, I can do no more than stare at the sword, watching it hum from the dirt floor.

I do not fear it exactly, but something about this weapon feels different than the others I've made. Perhaps because I put more of myself into it? It's heavier than it was when it only consisted of steel, the weight of my secrets adding to the bulk of it.

Cradling the weapon to my side, I leave the forge once the sword cools, taking it to our small backyard. It's usually filled with straw dummies and wooden planks for my customers to test their new blades. I haven't replaced the last batch yet, so I settle for the single tree that provides some shade.

When I come to a stop in front of the large cedar, I hold the broadsword in both hands, cock back the weapon, and swing toward the trunk.

Many things happen simultaneously. I lose my grip on the sword. A powerful force knocks me onto my back in the tall grass, and a cracking sound shatters my ears, followed by wind whistling through leaves, and a loud crash.

When I rise to my feet, I find the tree on the ground, severed all the way through right where I'd struck the trunk, *which had been at least four feet wide*. Thank goodness it missed the house! The surrounding grass lies flat, as though a fierce wind bent everything ninety degrees.

And the sword is humming from where it fell to the ground, as though it's alive and incapable of remaining silent.

But the most truly remarkable thing is that the sword cut the tree in half *before it even came into contact with the trunk*.

It has long-range abilities.

As I look at the destruction all around me, I can't help but feel a little giddy.

I think I've just made my most powerful weapon yet.

CHAPTER FIVE

What is going on with you?" Temra asks the next day. I told her all about the sword when she returned home from school. She, of course, demanded I let her have a go with it. I stepped far back as I explained the sword had two abilities that I knew of. It could cut through anything, and it cut things before even coming into contact with them.

Now I sit with the sword in my lap, carefully polishing the metal, holding the blade steady so there's no hint of a swing in the motion. Otherwise it might demolish the counter in front of me. "What are you talking about?"

"You're humming."

"I sometimes hum when I work."

"No, you don't. You never hum. And you've had a ridiculous grin on your face all day. Care to share the good news?"

I can feel the blush on my cheeks. "Obviously I'm excited about the sword." Though that wasn't what I'd been thinking about at all.

Temra stops sweeping and leans the broom against a display case. "Spill, Ziva."

I'm obviously not a very good liar. "I saw someone, if you really must know."

"Why should seeing someone put you in a good mood?"

"Temra, let it go. It was no big deal. This guy just walked by the forge, and—"

"A guy! Your cheeks are brighter than tomatoes."

"He was . . . attractive."

"You don't think anyone is attractive."

"I'm aware of that, Temra! Can we stop talking about it now?"

She slides into the chair next to me and tries to wrest the cloth from my grip, but I snatch it out of reach.

"No, you're going to give me details," she demands.

"There's nothing to tell. He was tall. Golden-red hair. Carries a sword."

"Did he wear a uniform?"

"No."

"Too bad. Men in uniforms are extra handsome. I wonder if he's a local or if he's just passing through? We should check all the inns on this side of the city. Just in case."

"Absolutely not!"

"But this is a huge thing for you!"

"Don't make a big deal out of this. I feel weird enough as it is."

"But you should talk to him. Maybe do other things with him." Her wicked grin is out in full force.

Is it possible to singe my own brows off? Because I think my face might be reaching extreme temperatures.

"I don't want to do any of that."

"But—"

"I'm not you. That's not how I work." I don't bother to try to explain how it's not worth the discomfort and anxiety. My panic is so overwhelming at times, I simply couldn't bear to be near him. And if he ever looked at me—

I can't even imagine how I would react.

"You pushing the matter is just going to make me run in the other direction," I finish.

Temra lets out a frustrated growl, but after what appears to be a mental argument with herself, she sighs. "Fine. Do what you will. But your handsome stranger might not be in town long. Just think about that. Now, I'm going to be late for class."

She leaves me alone with my thoughts, and I pick back up the tune I'd started. It's a love song, I think. Something Mother would sing to me when I was little. I don't remember any of the words. Just the tune.

The doors open, and I look up, expecting Temra. "Did you forget something or are you back to make fun o—"

I drop the sword, but it isn't followed by a clatter so much as a *shink!*

Instinctively, I look down—the broadsword landed point first, and it went right through the floor, stopping with the hilt protruding out of the ground.

My gaze flits madly between where the sword lies imbedded in the ground behind the front desk and the man who entered the shop.

My man.

No, not my *man.*

But *the* man.

The golden-red-haired stranger with a longsword on his back.

"Sorry, should I have knocked? This is a shop, right? Not a private residence?"

His voice is like the deep cadence of water running over rock.

How is even the sound of his voice attractive? One shouldn't be attracted to a voice, right? Maybe there is more wrong with me than I realized.

Or maybe there's just something wrong with him. He shouldn't exist. It isn't right to look that perfect. To *sound* that perfect.

I make the mistake of meeting his gaze. Never before have I looked away so quickly. I think my whole body has gone red, and I know he can see that. Which only makes me more embarrassed and awkward *and I want to be anywhere else.*

After a silence that progresses too long, he says, "I'm here to see the blacksmith. Is Ziva in? I was hoping to commission a longsword."

Why didn't I put the sign out that says the shop is closed? I do that when Temra leaves for school, but I was too busy . . .

Thinking about *him*. Humming ridiculous love songs!

"Maybe I could leave a message for her? Or come back later?"

"No!" I say at last.

And then I want to impale myself on the sword. Except that it's stuck in the ground.

"No to the message or to coming back later?"

"Both."

"Am I in the wrong place?" He does a sweep of the shop, taking in all the weapons on the walls.

"No."

"Is Ziva closed to commissions right now? Because I'm certain I can make it worth her while. I came a very long way just to see her."

My heart skips a beat at those words. He came a long way to see me?

Of course he did. You make magical weapons. He wants a weapon. A million customers have said this to me before, but this one . . . makes my heart do strange things.

I'm torn between trying to come up with something—*anything*—to say to this man and deciding whether or not to attempt to retrieve the sword. This likely results in me looking awkwardly hunched from what the stranger can see of me on the other side of the counter.

"Are you . . . all right?" he asks.

"Fine. I'm fine."

He grins, showing the tips of his teeth, and to my utter horror, he comes closer, leans himself against the counter, and asks, "What's your name?"

And I swear by the sacred names of the Sister Goddesses that I don't know the answer to that question. I cannot remember it or anything else when he looks at me like that.

So I look back down at the sword wedged into the ground. Kymora will be here in less than two weeks' time . . .

"Come back in three weeks and the smithy will see you," I say. By then, Temra and I will be long gone, and I won't have to endure this again.

"What about you? Will you be in?"

For the love, will he just leave?

"I really should get back to work."

"Of course." He steps back from the counter, and I can finally breathe again. "Do tell Ziva I look forward to doing business with her."

That's the third time he's said my name. I don't know why I kept track—only that I loved hearing the word on his lips.

What is wrong with me?

The stranger says something else on his way out the door, but I don't catch it.

I'm too busy finally getting the sword out of the ground.

After my mortifying encounter with the handsome man, I throw myself into my work, making all the little details on the sword pristine. I've shaped the hilt after Kymora's sigil. While the guard forms the wings of a great falcon, the grip serves as the body and tail. The fuller is pristine and even, the edges sharp, the point deadly.

I'm proud of it.

But is it good enough for a warlord?

It will serve her well in battle. Enemies will have a tricky time getting close enough to kill her, but I don't know that it's powerful enough to *bring nations to their knees*.

Still, it will have to do.

Temra comes rushing in to the forge. She closes the doors behind her carefully.

"The warlord is on her way."

"What?"

"I just saw her and her men coming up the road. They'll be here in seconds!"

"She's early!"

"I know!"

We both scramble for the storefront. I lay the weapon on the desk and shut the doors leading back to the forge. Meanwhile, Temra shoves her schoolwork behind the counter, hiding the mess.

I fidget uncomfortably during the ten seconds it takes Kymora to arrive at our doors.

As before, her guards enter first, surveying the area for threats. I try not to flinch when one of them enters the forge. I've left a mess in there. At least it can't possibly be worse than the state they saw it in last time.

When Kymora enters, her face is unreadable, and I wonder for a moment if she's come here assuming I didn't do what she wanted. She eyes the sword on the counter.

"Warlord, it is so good to see you! We weren't expecting you for another week," Temra says.

"I finished my business early, and I thought I would check in to see Ziva's progress."

Temra turns to me, letting me decide how to proceed.

"This is the weapon here. If you'll just follow me," I say, not bothering to look to Kymora to see if she'll agree. It's much easier not meeting her eyes at all.

I bypass her guards and step out into the yard. Everyone follows silently. Thankfully, Temra and I have restocked the place for a demonstration.

"Stand back, please," I say. The warlord crosses her arms over her chest, her face still an unreadable mask.

I raise the broadsword into the air, letting my arms adjust to the weight of it.

"Ziva has created for you a weapon with long-range abilities, Warlord," Temra says. "The weight might be more than you're accustomed to, but—"

"Is the smithy unable to talk for herself? Why isn't she showing me what it can do?"

I flinch at the words. Of course I *can* talk; I just prefer not to. But if I'm to work for Kymora, I need to be better at talking to her. I remind myself that I like this woman, and she has offered me and Temra a fresh start. I can do this.

I don't turn around as I say, "This blade can cut through anything, and it has long-range abilities. It's also quite heavy." Weighted with my secrets.

Holding the sword in both hands, I swipe across the dummy's middle. The weapon isn't even within four feet of its target, but straw flies everywhere, and the top half of the mannequin goes sailing off to the side. Without pausing, I move over to one of the wooden planks and swipe down. The board cracks, and the two ends soar up into the air, while the sword plunges into the earth. I have to keep a sure grip on it to avoid losing it to the soil.

When done, I glance over to Kymora, whose straight face has risen into one of wonder.

"My turn," she says, holding out a hand.

I grab the sword by the blade and extend it out to her. She takes it and proceeds to demolish what remains in the yard.

She takes out all three still-standing dummies with one swipe. She shatters every plank in the vicinity. Then, she strides over to the run-down, empty coop and takes it apart slash by slash. When there's nothing left to destroy, she puts herself through some stances, swinging the sword in arcs and lunges.

I instantly take back my earlier thought. I worried this weapon wouldn't be fit for a warlord, but that was before I saw the weapon in the hands of a seasoned warrior.

Legions of men would fall to this sword. Kymora took out three dummies with one swipe. How many foes could she fell before they were even upon her? The broadsword's reach could outdistance even a spear's considerable length.

When the warlord has worked up a fine sweat, she brings the sword close to her face to examine it. Carefully, she holds the sword away from her and brings one finger closer and closer to the blade until a fine line of blood magically appears on her finger. She doesn't so much as blink from the cut.

"Extraordinary," Kymora says. She thrusts the blade toward me, which is now marred with a line of her blood, despite not having come into direct contact with it. "Clean it," she orders.

I nod and take the weapon from her.

My fingers touch the grip and—

This is more than I could have hoped for.

My gaze snaps up to the warlord's.

This weapon will make me unbeatable in combat.

Though I hear Kymora's voice, her lips aren't moving.

I will crush Ghadra's pathetic rulers and reunite the regions under one rule once more: my own. The people will be enslaved to my will. The royal family will all bow before me. Right before I remove their heads.

I can't move. I'm barely breathing.

"Well?" Kymora says aloud. "Get that blood off my weapon!"

I rush into the shop, my mind whirring as I try to find a cloth.

The smithy is coming home with me. Once she makes weapons for every soldier in my army, we will be unstoppable.

The horrifying voice in my head doesn't abate until I wipe the streak of red from the steel.

What just happened? I heard Kymora, but she wasn't talking. Were those her real thoughts?

Her secrets.

The realization hits me in an instant.

"I'm very impressed with your work, bladesmith," the warlord says from behind me. She must have followed me inside.

It takes every ounce of willpower I possess to turn around and face Kymora.

"How does it work? The long-range abilities?" she wants to know.

"I—I—" *For your own safety and Temra's you have to pretend all is fine. Get it together, Ziva.* I pause and start again. Focus. "It's in the swing and the intent. You wanted to test its sharpness, so you cut yourself. When you're ready to sheathe it, the sword will temper down. You'll want to sheathe the blade slowly and make sure there isn't a trace of a swing in the motion. I've noticed that wearing gloves helps. Something about bare skin makes the weapon a bit more volatile. I haven't been able to determine exactly how far of a reach the sword possesses. Sometimes it won't cut things until they're within a foot of it. Other times, it will reach obstacles that are yards away. Again, I think it has to do with intent."

"Incredible." Kymora removes a purse from her side and sets the heavy pouch on the nearest worktable. "For your efforts. Now go and pack your things."

I look up from the heavy bag of coins. "What?"

"You passed with flying colors, Ziva. The position is yours. Let's get you far away from the governor's brat and his influence, hmm? We leave first thing in the morning."

So I can make weapons for her private army. Which she intends to use to conquer all of Ghadra.

I'm speechless for so long the warlord's face grows impatient. "Well, say something."

"I'm so honored you love the weapon, but it won't be ready by tomorrow morning."

Her eyes narrow. "It's done already."

"I'm afraid not," I say. "You arrived a week early. I need to give it a special, final polish in order for the magic to set in permanently. Then there's the matter of the scabbard."

"I have a scabbard."

"I wish to magic one to prevent any accidental cuttings of your own person. Please, Warlord, you did arrive early. Let me finish my work."

"And how long will that take?"

"Three days," I say. I would have liked to say weeks, but I know she won't go for that.

Kymora stares at me. Though her face is clear, her suspicion is evident. "You have until tomorrow morning. I will return then for my sword and you."

Unable to manage anything else, I nod. Kymora grabs her money before leaving.

CHAPTER SIX

I wait until Kymora and her men are long out of sight before turning to Temra.

"What's wrong?" she asks. "Why did you lie to the warlord? I've never once seen you polish something for the magic to *set in*."

I raise the sword once more. With slow deliberateness, I bring my free hand closer to the blade, until a light sting erupts on my middle finger. A small line of blood wells.

"Hold this," I say to Temra.

Though baffled, she obeys and takes the sword.

Only a moment passes before her eyes widen and she startles backward.

"What did you hear?" I ask.

"You weren't talking, but I heard you. You said you wished

you were brave like me. Ziva, that's ridiculous. You have your own kind of bravery. Why—" She cuts off as something else comes to her. "You were really underselling how much that handsome stranger affected you. Goddesses." Another pause. "You steal sweets out of the larder after I go to bed!"

Before anything else can happen, I snatch the sword away. "I was afraid of this."

"As well you should be," Temra says. "We're going to have a long talk about the taffies."

"No, Temra. It's the warlord! When she cut herself and handed me the blade, I heard her secrets. Remember when I told you how I made the weapon? By whispering my secrets to it? This sword not only has long-range abilities, it reveals the secrets of those it cuts. Kymora—she intends to enslave all of Ghadra and rule over everyone. She's going to take me with her tomorrow whether I wish it or not to make weapons for all her soldiers. Everyone is in danger."

Neither of us speaks as the weight of the words settle.

I wait for Temra to say something. Perhaps to ask if I'm overreacting. If there's any chance I misunderstood. Or if maybe we've got the sword's abilities wrong.

She says, "What do we do?"

I was so prepared for some kind of argument that I forget immediate action is required.

I have to save us.

There's really only two choices. I go with Kymora and build weapons for her army. Or . . . we run. We leave everything behind. My forge. My family's home. Temra's school. Everything we've ever known. Everything that's ever felt safe.

We give it all up to try to save Ghadra.

I'm ashamed that it takes me a moment to make the right decision.

"Pack a bag," I say. "Necessities only. Fit as much food as you possibly can. We have to leave."

"Where will we go?"

I pace back and forth and fiddle with my fingers. "We need a plan and quickly." Who would take us in? Is there anyone who would hide us? Certainly not in Lirasu. Not anymore.

I pause in place. "Do you remember that old painting we found in the back of Father's closet when we were going through our parents' things?"

Temra nods. "You want to track down Father's family?"

I remember the day we found that painting. On the front was a couple I didn't recognize standing before a beautiful waterfall, but on the back was written: *Sotherans. Thersa Falls.*

I thought to simply throw out the picture. After all, it was stashed at the back of the closet, but then I realized the similarities between the two in the painting and my father.

They're his parents. My grandparents. I knew my father took my mother's surname, but at the age of five, I'd never thought to ask what his original family name was.

It was all there on the painting. My father's family are the Sotherans, and they live in Thersa. We had no reason or care to seek them out before. But now—

Now I cling to that information like a lifeline.

There's no point in stressing over how we'll be received or if we'll be received or if we'll be believed when we claim to be relations. Our main concern is escape.

"We have to find them," I answer.

"But they don't know us. They've never met us. Did Father ever even talk about them?"

"Not that I remember. But they're family. They're our only hope."

"Okay," Temra says after a moment. She riffles through a bunch of tools atop one of the worktables and stalks over to me. "That's good. We have a destination. But we need to take precautions."

"Precautions?"

I hear a *snip*, and then my head feels significantly lighter. My hand flies to my ponytail, only to find it practically gone.

"Temra!"

She shoves the scissors at me. "Now you do me." She turns around, brandishing her curly locks.

"No!"

"Time is precious right now. We need to alter our appearances as much as possible. Now start snipping."

Maybe it's silly, but only now do I start to cry. I didn't cry when Asel wronged us. I didn't cry when I knew we'd have to leave the city or when I realized I'd have to betray the most dangerous individual in the world.

But as I cut through my sister's beautiful hair, I start sniffling.

Temra has no tears to shed. When she turns back around, she's as strong as ever.

"Kymora can never have the sword," she says.

I nod. It takes a few minutes to light the kiln, but once it's raging with heat, I carefully toss the sword inside. Let it melt and destroy the magic with it. Temra doesn't move as I do this. She stares off into the distance, lost in her own thoughts.

Though it kills me to say the next words, I push through: "Kymora didn't get a good look at you. She probably won't even remember you. You could stay. Not here, of course, but in the city. I can manage—"

"Oh, don't you dare," Temra says. "We're sisters, Ziva. We're in this together. I'm not leaving you. Not now. Not ever. Besides, Kymora saw me. She knows I'm your sister. If she couldn't find you, how long do you think it would take before she came looking for me to draw you out? I'm safest with you."

I shut my eyes, feel tears threatening again. "I'm so sorry, Temra. I never meant to put you in danger."

"We can discuss it on the road. You better make room in your pack for taffies."

And she disappears in the direction of her room.

I don't know how the Sister Goddesses blessed me with the most perfect sister, but they did. It's beyond selfish, but I am relieved and eternally grateful to have her with me for this dreadful turn in my life.

My hands shake as I pack.

I'm not going to panic. I'm not going to panic. There is no time for panic.

I keep my mind on the tasks I need to accomplish. That'll keep it off the danger.

Gather food. Clothes. Money. Pack the horse.

I have quite a bit of money lying around the house, but most of my coins are stored at the Lirasu Bank for safekeeping. Dare I go to collect more?

There's no time. The warlord could be watching the house for all I know. We can't risk venturing into the middle of the city.

In the forge, I grab what few weapons I possess. A staff. A shortsword. A spear. I wrap them all in a bundle and attach them to Reya. Temra and I take some of the daggers from the shop and hide them into our clothing wherever we can. We take extra shoes for the horse.

"Oh no," I whisper under my breath.

Temra raises a brow.

"What are we going to do for safety on the road? We'll be traveling at night. Two girls alone."

"That might be to our advantage," Temra says. "We'll likely travel unnoticed if we don't use the road."

"But we'll be slower if we don't take the road. We need to put as much distance between us and the warlord as we can."

Temra is quiet for a moment. She looks as though she wishes to say something. Then, "I think we should hire protection. I know of a mercenary staying at a tavern located on the edge of the city."

Though my whole body tenses at the thought of adding a stranger to our small party—in trusting a stranger with our safety—I nod. "It's our only option."

When Reya is all loaded up, Temra and I don our cloaks, and I take a long look at my home and sanctuary.

I expect to feel a sad longing, but all I can seem to think about is that sword and its magic. Magic that I can still feel . . .

I turn to Temra. "I need to check something."

I plunge back into the house as quickly as possible, making a beeline for the forge and the kiln in the center. As I peer into the dying embers of the oven, my stomach sinks to my toes.

It can't be.

Using a pair of tongs, I grasp at what I hope to be indistinguishable remains of the weapon.

But the sword is intact. Unmelted. Perfect as though I'd just finished it.

I'm not about to try breaking it apart with my tools; the sword would only resist my blows as it did after I imbued it with my secrets.

It can't be destroyed.

My head swims with panic. How did this happen? How could I have done this?

It's too late to dwell on your mistakes.

I quench the blade, dry it off, and carefully slide it into the black leather scabbard I completely lied about not having finished.

When Temra sees me approaching the horse once more, she asks, "Is that—"

I nod. "I did as the warlord asked. I outdid myself. It can't be destroyed, Temra. We have to take it with us. We have to keep it safe."

I wait for the outburst that is sure to come. Temra's anger at me for ripping her from everything she's ever known. For my foolishness in forging this weapon of destruction.

But it doesn't come. Temra quietly takes the weapon from my hands and adds it to the others already strapped to Reya's side. Somehow, Temra's silence is even worse. I don't know how she's feeling or what she's thinking. But I think we both need to process what's happening right now.

Just as soon as we're out of danger.

I start for the road, but Temra puts a hand on my shoulder.

"Don't go that way."

"But that's the road."

"And if Kymora is watching us, that's where she'll have men stationed. Besides, I know how to get out of here unseen."

Temra leads Reya to the backyard. A hidden trail I've never noticed before materializes in the tall grasses at the edge of the property, and Temra begins to follow it.

As I look over my shoulder, I note the trail is out of sight of my bedroom window.

"You've been sneaking out!" I accuse.

"Now really isn't the time, Ziva."

"How long have you been using this trail? Did you make it yourself?"

"Years and yes."

"Yea—" I can't even finish the word. "What have you been doing?"

"Do you want to raise your voice a little louder? I don't think the warlord can hear you."

I clamp my mouth shut, but I'm raging within. What if something happened to her? Where has she been going? And who has she been going with? I feel myself getting hysterical.

I focus on my feet and watch them as I walk. One step. Two steps. Three.

Just keep moving. Every step puts us farther away from danger. That's all that matters right now. Temra is safe. Focus on the now.

The trail eventually opens onto the city streets. It's just beginning to get dark, and the people are lighting the two lanterns that hang on either side of their doors. One for each Sister Goddess. For protection.

Though I haven't bothered to light ours in years, I also haven't taken them down. Lighting the lanterns certainly never did anything for my parents.

A stray cat peers at us from the compost bins outside the establishment Temra leads us to, which must be the tavern she mentioned. It doesn't look like a place of great import, with the sticky-looking and fogged-over windows, but the mirth bursting through the glass would suggest those inside are having a grand time.

"Just how do you know about this place or that there's a mercenary for hire inside?" I ask her.

Temra smiles. "His name is Kellyn Derinor. All the girls at school have been talking about him."

"Why?"

"You'll know when you see him."

"And this place?"

Temra shrugs. "It's a good place to meet men."

"You've been frequenting this establishment!" I nearly shout. "Have you been drinking?"

"I'm sixteen, Ziva. Of course I've been drinking and having fun—while being perfectly safe." She tries to stride inside the building.

"Oh, we are not done discussing this or your sneaking out."

"Maybe we could save it for when we're not trying to outrun a warlord?" she asks.

I narrow my eyes at her back as she pushes into the building. Handing Reya off to a waiting stable boy, I bark orders at him not to unsaddle her. We won't be that long, and I don't want him touching any of the precious cargo on her back.

I grab the sword and buckle it to my side before following after my sister.

Temra couldn't have beaten me by more than thirty seconds into the tavern, yet she's already seated at a table, surrounded by admirers. Three men and two women are laughing around her, and I watch as one of the men buys her a drink.

How does she do that? Temra has her own magic. A kind that draws people to her and makes it effortless for her to be around them. Jealousy blossoms within my chest, although it's mostly covered up by the fear of being surrounded by so many people.

Noises and smells are everywhere. Laughter, wailing, chewing, mead, sweat, leather.

Awkwardly, I walk over to my sister. The broadsword weighs me down heavily on my left side, and I have to adjust my stance accordingly. When I finally reach Temra, I hover at her shoulder. That brings the gazes of the others at the table straight to me.

I stare at the back of Temra's head, willing her to do something. Anything.

She reaches up, grabs my arm, and yanks me onto the chair so that half my rump is balanced in the air. And then, as though Temra's acceptance was all they needed, whatever conversation I'd interrupted resumes.

"As I was saying, Kellyn is a fine swordsman, despite being so young. There's talk that his father was a weapons trainer in the late king's castle, but that could just be a rumor." The man speaking pauses to take a hefty drink from his cup.

"But honestly, that's the least of his fine qualities," one of the girls says. She and the other woman at the table turn toward a corner of the room.

I nearly choke on my own spit.

Golden-red hair. Tanned skin. Longsword at his back.

It's the stranger who helped me create the sword. I wanted to touch him, and the blade ate up the secret, giving it power.

Secret Eater.

The name comes to me all of a sudden. Normally, I leave the naming of weapons up to my customers, but this one is now my burden to bear.

My thoughts circle back to the mercenary Temra wants to take with us on our journey. Kellyn. He already has a connection to the sword. Either it's a sign from the Sisters that he's our best option on our journey or that I should keep him far from the weapon.

"We can't use him," I say after leaning in toward Temra.

"Do you see any other options?"

But he's going to remember me, and it's going to be awkward and—

For Temra, I have to do this.

"Then what are we waiting for? Let's go talk to him."

Temra gives me an irritated glance. I think she's upset over how I chastised her for sneaking out. As if *I'm* the one in the wrong here. "You can't just walk up to someone like that, Ziva. We need to wait for the right moment."

I watch as Kellyn raises a cup to his lips and throws his head back. Half the contents spill down either side of his face.

"He's drunk!" I exclaim.

"Of course he is. This is a tavern."

"And this is a terrible idea."

We watch as one of the men seated next to the mercenary

says something, the sound lost in the cacophony of other voices. But whatever he said Kellyn doesn't like, because he tosses his tankard right at the man's face.

"Oh dear," Temra says.

The man opposite Kellyn draws his blade and tries to skewer the mercenary to his chair. Kellyn dodges just in time, finding his feet.

While the other man advances, coming around the table, Kellyn picks up the chair he just vacated and crashes it onto the man's head.

That gets the attention of the rest of the tavern. People turn in their seats to get a better look. Cheers go up as drunken men and women encourage the fighters.

Kellyn doesn't touch his weapon as the other man starts slashing at him like mad. He dodges and punches. Then, in a swift move, he disarms the other man, grabs him by the back of his shirt, and rams his head into the table, rendering him unconscious.

As the crowd cheers, Kellyn reaches over to his enemy's mug, raises it into the air in a salute to the room, and downs it in one go.

"Now," Temra says.

"Now what?"

"Now is the time to talk to him."

"I don't want to go anywhere near him!"

"What choice do we have?"

None. We have none.

Resigning myself to my fate, I follow Temra toward the big brute. She's careful to put herself directly in his line of sight.

"It's Kellyn, isn't it?" she asks, putting on a bright smile. She uses the tone I recognize as her "flirty voice."

"It is," he says, hailing down a serving girl for another glass of mead.

"I'm Temra," she says, sitting in the chair right beside him.

I panic for a moment. Should I stay back as Temra's shadow? No, I can't let her do this alone. Steeling my courage, I take the seat vacated by Kellyn's opponent, the one right across from him.

Kellyn's eyes fix on me, and I try desperately not to squirm in my seat.

"Don't I know you?"

"I don't think so."

"I swear I've seen you somewhere before."

My chin-length hair combined with Kellyn's drunkenness is the only thing sparing me from utter mortification right now.

"This is Ziva," my sister says.

"The magically gifted smithy!" Kellyn exclaims. "I came to this city to seek you out." He laughs as though that were funny before taking a drink. "Can I order you both a round?"

I have to turn my head to the side to hide my disgust. He thinks we're propositioning him!

"We're sisters," I hastily bite out.

"Even better," he says.

Temra laughs like he just told a joke. "I'm afraid you have us all wrong. We're interested in your fighting talents. Are you for hire?"

Kellyn takes a hefty swig from the new draft placed before him. "What's the job?"

"We're looking for safe passage to Thersa. We can pay a hundred ockles a day."

"If she makes me a magicked longsword, I'll take you anywhere you'd like to go in Ghadra."

"That's wonderful!" Temra says. "How soon can you be ready to go?"

Kellyn burps loudly into his cup, which only heightens the sound.

I find myself struggling to remember why I ever thought this man was attractive.

But then he turns those beautiful brown eyes on me. His lips raise into an openmouthed smile that makes my stomach do a flip. "As soon as I sober up!" He downs the rest of his cup's contents, sloshing more over himself.

I look to Temra in a panic. "Is there someone else we could hire?" I ask, hoping the universe will magically provide a solution.

"No. Well, he was an option." Kellyn nods at the passed-out man on the floor. "But since you just got a good look at his fighting skills, I doubt you'd want to hire him. But none of that! We have an arrangement, and I will be ready to leave posthaste!"

Kellyn stands with his empty mug, takes one step toward the stairs, which likely lead up to his room, then tips forward. He catches himself on a wooden beam holding up the ceiling, before lowering himself to the ground.

"Actually, I think I'll have a little lie-down first."

And then he's out.

Temra raises from her chair, leans down, and slaps him across the face.

He doesn't budge.

"What now?" I ask.

"Go get the horse, and I'll meet you outside."

"What are you doing?"

"Just trust me, okay?"

Gathering my cloak about me more tightly, I stride outside and pay the stable boy to bring Reya around. I reattach Secret Eater to the weapon's bundle.

Then we wait. I'm unsure what for, and every passing second makes me more and more anxious. What if something happened to Temra? What if she's been caught by the warlord's men? What if—

The doors open, and Temra comes outside, followed by four big men, carrying something.

No, someone.

Kellyn.

Temra directs them to lay him atop the horse and pays each of the men a coin.

I turn to her in horror. "This is your plan!"

She smiles. "What choice do we have?"

"We can't just *take* him!"

"Not like this. Help me strap him down."

"Temra!"

"Ziva, you got us into this mess. I'm getting us out. Now, are you going to help me or not?"

There it is. The anger I've been looking for. The outburst.

"Just what exactly are you two doing?"

I hadn't realized that one of the men didn't return inside with the others. I do a double take when I recognize him and his blue robes.

It's that scholar from the restaurant. What was his name?

"Petrik," I say.

"Hello again!"

"None of your business," Temra says in answer to his question.

"Can I be of further assistance?" he asks, undaunted by her tone.

"We're fine." Temra finds some rope from the stables and starts attaching Kellyn to the saddle. Wordlessly, I assist.

Petrik disappears back into the tavern at a run, but I don't spare him another glance.

It's only when Kellyn's secure and we're headed out of town that I say, "I'm sorry. For everything. For—"

"No. I used your own insecurities against you. I'm sorry. I needed you to go along with the plan. We're taking Kellyn. And you have nothing to be worried about between us. I love you. This isn't your fault. But we have to go, and we have to take him. Now let's be off."

She can be quite bossy.

Sometimes I forget who's the older sister.

CHAPTER
SEVEN

The irony of the situation is not lost on me. We carry an all-powerful weapon, yet we're running for our lives.

The broadsword might as well be useless to us. What are we supposed to do? Use it against Kymora before she's committed any crimes?

And with my sister and me traveling together, we can't even wield it in our defense. The sword has too long of a reach. It would be far too easy for me to slice Temra by mistake while I was trying to protect her. Such a weapon takes practice to master.

Not to mention the fact that *I don't want to kill anyone.*

And Secret Eater is not the kind of weapon that injures only. It's a killer. Plain and simple.

Of course, all my weapons have the potential to kill. I knew this as I was making them. But how could I have foreseen that someone would want to use one for world dominance? Kymora is well-respected. She and the late king parted on good terms. There's no way I could have predicted this would happen when I agreed to make her weapon.

These thoughts buzz in my mind as we lead Reya down the road at a trot, Temra and I jogging beside her. It's a good thing we're both in good physical condition, else I don't know how we'd manage to escape. We try to be as silent as possible, but the road consists of dirt and rock, and Reya's shoes clap against the stones.

Fir trees line the road, and I imagine large eyes staring at us, just waiting to pounce.

As if I needed that on top of worrying about whether or not we're sufficiently outdistancing Kymora.

Oh, and her personal *army*.

"Wait up!" a voice calls out, and I nearly jump out of my skin. A single figure strides down the road. Both moons are out tonight, and they shine on the swishing dark robes.

Reya throws back her head at the unexpected newcomer, and Temra is all forced smiles.

"Petrik," she says. "What are you doing here? And why do you look like you're ready to go on a long journey?"

He hoists the backpack higher up on his shoulders. "I happened upon two girls fleeing in the dead of night. I can't, in good conscience, let you go off alone. Let me escort you, whatever your destination."

Temra flicks what is left of her hair over a shoulder, not that the new length comes even close to reaching it. "And maybe Ziva will want to talk about her magical abilities along the way?" She says it like an accusation.

"That would indeed be a happy bonus."

"You're unbelievable!" I say to him.

"I just want to help, and I won't be a burden. I have my own food and travel supplies. Also, I bribed the tavern owner to let me into the mercenary's room so I could gather his belongings, since I noted you two were busy with other things."

Temra and I share a look. We hadn't even thought to grab Kellyn's possessions before taking him.

Temra looks the scholar up and down. "Are you hiding a weapon in there somewhere?"

"No," he says, puzzled.

"Do you know how to *use* a weapon?" she asks.

"No."

"Are you skilled in hand-to-hand combat?"

"Um, no."

"Then how exactly are you going to help us?"

"We can help *each other*! Another body on the road never hurts to deter bandits, and you could help me with my book."

"Absolutely not!" I say.

But Temra says, "Excuse us for a moment, Petrik."

With Reya's lead in one hand and my shoulder in the other, my sister steers us off a ways.

"What?" I whisper.

"I think we should bring him along."

"Why would we do that? We're about to be hunted!"

"Because he's a leading expert on magic, remember? And we need to get rid of a *magic* sword! This is perfect. You can pick his brain on the road."

Oh . . .

"How am I supposed to pick his brain without revealing just how powerful our cargo is?"

"You're smart; you'll figure something out."

I hate that she's right. I don't want another stranger with us.

"We'll be putting him in danger," I say. "We can't do that. What if he's caught with us?"

"If I could just interject." Petrik raises his voice to be heard. "There are other ways I can be of use! I may not look it, but I'm strong. I carried all these books across two regions just to find you. I can help with any chores. I know how to build fires and cook. I can—"

"You can cook?" Temra and I ask simultaneously.

"Yes, one of my many duties at the Great Library was being in a cooking rotation with other novices."

Temra and I share a glance.

Temra hands me Reya's lead. "I've got this." She returns to Petrik. "You may come with us, but we have some conditions."

"Name them," he says.

"You don't ask questions about where we're going or what we're doing. And you need to know that dangerous people are after us. It might not be safe for you if we're caught."

Petrik's hands drop from his shoulder straps as he deliberates. "How dangerous?"

"Very."

He only thinks about it a moment longer. "Well, then, I guess I just can't stick around too long."

"Really?" I blurt. "You really still want to come?"

"If I'm being totally honest, it sounds very exciting!"

He's mad, is what I want to say to Temra, but I can't tell her that now without Petrik overhearing.

"Then we can't delay any longer," Temra says. "You have to keep up."

And we resume running.

Even when the sun rises, we don't dare make camp. We're all tired, especially Reya, who's carrying all the supplies as well as the mercenary's bulk. We stop at a nearby stream to let her drink and graze a little but not for long. Temra picks the long grasses along the journey and feeds them to her as we walk.

Eventually, we pass by another set of travelers, a husband and wife sitting at the front of a covered cart, likely carrying goods for trade up to our city. The wife bears a very impressive crossbow for the dangers of the road. She eyes the drunken Kellyn with curiosity.

"Had too much to drink, this one," Temra tells them.

They nod in understanding before carrying on.

"I think we should get off the road," Temra says when they're out of earshot. "Ky—Our pursuers won't know which way we've gone. There are three roads leading out of the city, but if they question new arrivals to town, they'll be able to point out having seen us. How hard will it be to remember a pair of sisters?"

"Just a moment," Petrik says.

He runs back down toward the couple. They halt their cart and share a few words with Petrik. He hands something to them, and then they continue on.

"What was that?" Temra asks. "Now they're going to remember us for sure!"

"I thought I'd ask if they'd like some bread," he says.

"Bread?" I ask in disbelief.

"Yes, I informed them that my *wife* and her *cousin* made too much for our journey, and we'd love to share."

"Oh," I say, and Temra and I both look toward the ground awkwardly. Petrik was making himself more memorable. Hiding Temra and me. Even though he has no clue what's going on.

"Give me some credit. I'm not an idiot." Petrik steps forward, making a path through the trees and ferns at the side of the road so we can continue traveling more discreetly. We keep the road barely out of eyesight, checking occasionally to ensure we're still on track.

When we finally stop for an early lunch, everyone turns toward the mercenary. He's still out cold. Aside from the rise and fall of his shoulders, you'd think he was dead.

"We've got to cut him down," Temra says. "Reya needs a break for as long as we can give her."

We start with the saddlebags and weapons. Only when we can't avoid it any longer do we cut the ropes holding the large man in place.

Petrik helps us to lift the mercenary off the horse's back, but we only manage to get him halfway to the ground before he topples in our lopsided grip and falls the rest of the way.

The jolt from striking the hard soil wakes him right up.

"What—" Kellyn sputters. He tries to stand and reach for his longsword, which isn't on his back anymore. We attached it to Reya with the rest of the weapons so as to keep it from sliding out of its sheath from the angle Kellyn was perched on the saddle.

The motion, which was off-balance to begin with in his state, results in him crashing to the ground once again.

He is not happy. Sick from too much mead, cramped from the way he slept on a horse all night, the bright sun—none of this is likely to put him in a good mood.

Kellyn rises again, this time more slowly. He shades his eyes and takes in the three of us.

"Who are you?"

I look to Temra in a panic. He doesn't remember us.

"Your employers," Temra says, not missing a beat. "So far, we're not pleased with your performance."

Kellyn squints, as though that will help him see better. "I took a job?"

Temra glances at Petrik only briefly before saying, "Safe passage to Thersa for three." She can't very well not tell our escort where we're going. And it would be impossible to tell Kellyn without telling Petrik. So I guess everyone is in on our final destination.

The mercenary moves his free hand to his temple, as if willing his brain to remember last night. Kellyn asks, "How much did I agree to?"

"Not an amount. A Zivan blade. Ziva will make you a magicked longsword when we reach Thersa safely."

His alarmingly alert eyes shift to me, and I focus on my boots.

"I know you. You were in the smithy shop. *You're* Ziva?"

My eyes snap up. "What is that supposed to mean?" Does he find something wrong or distasteful about me? And why do I care?

"You didn't say anything last time," he says.

"I was busy."

"You two know each other?" Temra asks.

"I came by the shop to commission a blade," Kellyn says. "She told me to come back in three weeks. Wait, that's not until next week. Did you already know you would be leaving then? Were you blowing me off?"

My fingers are practically tangled in knots, and I can't find anything safe to look at. I'm sure to find judgy eyes from all three of my companions.

"The important thing," Temra says, drawing the mercenary's attention, "is that you're getting your weapon. Let's not worry over what happened before."

I can feel his eyes return to me as he asks, "Why do I feel as though I slept on a log?" He cricks his neck.

"You slept on the horse," Petrik says unhelpfully.

"You passed out on us," I add. "We didn't have many options."

"How far away from Lirasu are we?" Kellyn wants to know.

I fear he means to back out and leave us on our own, but we can't lie to him. He'd figure it out eventually when we reach our destination.

"An evening's hard ride," Temra says.

"Left in a hurry, did we?"

"Yes, we need to reach Thersa with haste."

"And we'll add in a bonus once we get there," I say. Goddesses, but I hate that we have to rely on so many strangers. Still, a little monetary incentive can't hurt if Kellyn's on the fence about this.

There's a nerve-racking silence as we wait to see what the mercenary will do.

"I'm a man of my word," he says at last. "If I agreed to take you to Thersa, then that's what I'll do."

He treads off a ways.

"Where are you going?" Petrik asks him.

"To take a piss. Is that all right with my employers?"

No one says anything, and Kellyn disappears into the thickness of the trees.

I sidle up next to Temra. "For a moment, I thought he'd abandon us."

"Remember, his kind will do anything for the right price. Quick thinking about the bonus." She nudges her shoulder against mine.

"We make a pretty good team," I say.

"Yes, we do," Petrik says, and we both just stare at him. "What? I was feeling left out."

"It's time to put your cooking skills to the test," Temra says. "Why don't you get started while we make a fire? Then we'll decide whether or not you're worth the trouble."

Petrik has sausages sizzling over a frying pan, eggs scrambled from a nearby pheasant nest I spotted, and mint tea boiling in no time. His cooking skills weren't exaggerated.

Kellyn bites into some fire-heated toast, before asking, "What exactly is the connection between you all? You're sisters, right? Your faces have the same shape. But who's this guy to you?"

Petrik introduces himself. "I'm working on a book, exploring the known magics of the world. Miss Ziva is kind enough to answer questions about her specialty on the road."

"And you're wearing a dress because . . . ?"

Petrik glares at the man. "These are *robes*. I was trained at the Great Library of Skiro. And I'll have you know I am a leading expert on ancient magics."

"And just how many people are in your field?"

The faintest red hue appears on Petrik's brown cheeks. "I don't recall the exact number."

"You sure? Because I'd bet you could count them on one hand."

I intervene. "You're being awfully rude."

I regret the words instantly, because Kellyn turns those big brown eyes on me, making my heart do a traitorous flip. "Being nice costs extra." He offers me a small grin. "I'm kidding. The man talks a big game; I just wanted to know how much of an expert we were dealing with. Sounds to me like someone just has a big head."

"Says the man who named his sword Lady Killer," Petrik grumbles.

Kellyn gives the scholar a startled look.

"You mumbled it several times in your sleep. Didn't take long for me to realize you meant your weapon. Ridiculous name."

"Now, there's no need to go insulting another man's sword. Lady Killer will be far more useful to us on the road than your *books*."

"I'm going to stop you both right there," Temra says. "Ziva and I acknowledge that you're both big important men. Now eat your food."

Petrik doesn't take his eyes off the mercenary. "Maybe if the brute could read, he wouldn't be so dismissive of—"

"I can read just fine," Kellyn says. "*And* I can swing a sword. One might say I have double your talents."

"When you're not passed out drunk," I mumble.

Kellyn shifts his gaze from the scholar to me. Before he can say another word, I rise and dust off my palms. "Ten more minutes before we depart, and you two better play nice."

Petrik heads for the stream to wash the dishes, his nose up in the air. Temra loads up Reya. Kellyn stretches out his cramped muscles.

And I leave. I put distance between myself and all the other people.

Because there's nothing I want more than ten minutes of alone time.

CHAPTER EIGHT

I spend ten blissful minutes feeling safe. Ten minutes where I don't have to worry that I'll say something stupid to embarrass myself. Where I don't have to deal with the sharp pains in my chest that come from being around Kellyn Derinor.

It's not enough.

I want a day to myself. A day to recharge and relax without having to worry about any of the people around me. Not to mention the fate of Ghadra should this sword fall into the wrong hands.

But I don't get what I want. What my body so desperately needs.

"Remind me again why you said we couldn't travel on the road?" Kellyn asks the next day.

"We didn't," Temra answers.

"Right. Well, consider this me asking. Why aren't we traveling on the road?"

"You're not being paid to know things. You're being paid to swing your sword," I say.

"All right, bladesmith," he says, raising his hands in defense. "I see your identity isn't the only thing you like to keep secret."

"Not my fault you didn't automatically assume I was the smithy when you walked into the shop."

"I thought the most talented bladesmith in all of Ghadra would be an *older* woman. Someone who had time to build a reputation and hone her skills."

"Still not my fault."

"You didn't have to lead me astray so blatantly! And blowing me off? What was that—revenge?"

I shrug, because talking to him has my body temperature rising to uncomfortable levels. I don't think I can manage another word. The only thing that's allowed me to talk this long is not being cornered in a room with him, and I'm keeping my eyes on the ground beneath my feet.

"Okay," Kellyn says at my silence. "It was my fault, and I deserved to be blown off. I'll agree with you there. You keep your secrets and leave the sword swinging to me." He resumes his position at the head of our party.

"Do you think we can keep trusting him?" I ask Temra quietly.

"The warlord can't have gotten to him before us. I think as long as he doesn't interact with anyone on the road, we should be fine."

We both go still as pounding hooves sound to our left. Peering through the trees, Temra and I watch as a rider in a red tunic goes by at a breakneck pace.

He's wearing Kymora's sigil.

We freeze to the spot, not daring to breathe even once the rider is out of sight.

"What are we looking at?"

We both jump into the air as Kellyn puts his head right between us, peering through the foliage.

"Nothing," I say.

"Who are you running from?" he asks.

"No one."

"Is it a love match?"

"*What?*" Temra asks before I can.

"Between one of you and the scholar. Are you running away because your parents want you to marry someone old and sickly?"

"No!" I shriek.

"Right. Look at the state of his robes. He doesn't look like he could afford a wife."

"Hey!" Petrik protests.

But Kellyn talks right over him. "Is he really a monk, then? Are you off to join him in a life of celibacy to escape the old and sickly man?"

"By the Twins, no!" Temra says.

"There is no old and sickly man!" I say. "What is the matter with you?"

"I am not celibate!" Petrik shouts.

We all turn to him, and I suspect his cheeks are warming.

"Not that I'm with anyone—right now, I mean—I just—" He cuts himself off and turns away.

The mercenary lets out a chuckle at Petrik's expense. "If you don't tell me what's really going on, then all I can do is guess. And by the way, if I end up having to fight some brute that one of you is betrothed to, that's going to cost you extra. I'm here for protection against bandits. Not lovers."

"Now he's a brute?" I ask. "What happened to him being old and sickly?" Then I mentally rebuke myself for engaging with him.

Kellyn turns to me and grins. Actually grins. Like he couldn't be more thrilled that I'm playing along with him.

"Never mind. I take it back. Don't answer that," I say. The longer he looks at me, the more uncomfortable I feel. Not because I feel threatened by him, but because I don't like being looked at by anyone. Being on display has always been Temra's thing. She's the one who likes to star in city plays, to take center stage during a dance, or be in the middle of a group of boys.

I want to be hidden.

I want to feel safe.

When we break for the night some evenings later, everyone goes to gather firewood, not straying far from camp. I, however, put as much distance as I can between myself and everyone else without being unsafe.

I put my back to a tree trunk, sit on the pine-needle-covered floor, and breathe out more easily. It isn't quite twilight, but the night bugs are already out in full force, buzzing and niggling around my ears. I raise my hands to block the sounds and close my eyes, pretending I'm home, sitting before the hearth or in my bed or in my forge. Somewhere the rest of the world isn't.

That's when I hear footsteps. They're light, as though trying to be quiet, and that naturally sends my mind spinning with all the possibilities. My eyes fly open as my heart pounds in fear of bandits or Kymora's men.

It doesn't slow down when I see it's the mercenary, carrying a load of firewood he's gathered.

"Why do you wander off on your own so much?" he asks. "Are you looking for trouble?" He smiles with the question. As though he knows just how attractive he is and he wants me to acknowledge it, too.

I swallow, torn between running and lashing out with words. I do not know this man. I do not trust him. And I don't want to be alone with him.

Yet, lashing out wins.

"You've been with us barely a week. It's hardly enough to start making assumptions about me."

"No? Haven't you already made some about me? All bad ones, I'd wager."

I despise one-on-one conversations with people I don't know. I always fidget, worrying I'll say the wrong thing, embarrass myself tremendously. I barely have time to think over my words before spitting them out.

"You have done nothing to impress me so far."

"We haven't run into danger yet," Kellyn says. Does he realize that the way he's carrying that stack of wood puts his biceps on perfect display?

Of course he knows. He must know.

"So your fighting skills are the only impressive thing about you," I say.

His gaze narrows on me, and he drops the stack of wood. Kellyn rises to his full six and a half feet, brushing off bits of bark and dirt from his shirt. He takes a few steps forward.

"Take a look at me and tell me it's the only impressive thing about me," he says. His grin is gone, and the look he gives me is a challenge.

My anxiety peaks at his proximity, but underneath it, I think I sense something else, too. I don't have a name for it, and all I want is for the mercenary to leave me alone.

"I am not impressed by superficial surface looks that are completely out of your control."

As if sensing how tense I am, Kellyn retrieves the wood and takes a few steps back. "What does impress you, then?"

I'm pushed off-balance by the question. Because the answer is that nothing impresses me. I have never been impressed by someone. Not enough to overpower the fear of being around them in the first place.

"Don't tell me," he says with a wink. "I'll figure it out on my own."

My jaw drops in outrage, but he's gone before I can say anything else.

To make matters worse, Temra sneaks out between two trees, nearly giving me a heart attack.

"Temra! Are you trying to kill me? How long were you standing there?"

"Not nearly long enough, it would seem."

I huff and lower my head into my crossed arms. "This is my alone time. Why is everyone trying to disturb it?"

Temra has only one long, thin branch in her hands. She drops it to the ground before sitting beside me. "We have very important things to discuss."

She's probably right. There are so many unknowns. The warlord. Our relatives. The two boys who could turn on us at any moment if they learn the truth.

"That boy is flirting with you," she says.

"Sorry?"

"You heard me."

"Yes, but you said we had *important* things to discuss!"

"This is important."

"Temra." I turn her name into a groan.

"It's him, isn't it? He's the one you saw when you magicked the broadsword?"

I give her a wide-eyed glance.

"You said he was tall with golden-red hair," she explains. "Our mercenary is an attractive man with those qualities."

"Yes, it's him." There's no point in lying. She'd see the truth anyway.

"And now you're stuck together on the road! This is wonderful!"

"And how do you figure that? I thought he was attractive *before* I met him. He's rude. Disgusting." I don't know if I can ever get the image of him drunk and belching out of my head. "Arrogant to a fault. And for all we know, he doesn't actually have any skill with that sword."

"Really, so I didn't see you ogling his arms just ten minutes ago? Eyeing him like he was a piece of meat?"

I turn away from her. Hoping she won't see my cheeks redden. "I don't think he's a piece of meat."

"Of course not. But that doesn't mean he's not pretty. I don't think I've ever seen you ogle anyone. This is fantastic."

"What?" I nearly shout. Being on the road must be getting to her. She's clearly gone delusional. "How is this fantastic? He's horrible, and I wasn't ogling. I just like his arms, is all."

"He's quite tall. Tall enough for you."

"Now a man has to be tall enough for me?"

"No, I'm just saying he's the perfect height."

"For what?" I hedge, dreading the answer.

She raises her eyebrows twice in quick succession.

"I'm not interested in that," I say.

"Fine. Don't jump straight to the kissing. Let's start with something simple. Talking."

"That's not simple."

"I saw you talking to him just now!"

I find a twig on the ground with my fingers and start breaking it in half over and over again. "I was angry. It's easier when I'm angry. It overpowers the fear."

"You really shouldn't judge him based on the first two days on the road with him. He was coming off a nasty night of drinking. That would make anyone unpleasant."

"I don't care."

"So you've made your decision, then? You don't like him."

"Of course."

"Well, that's even better."

I've given up trying to make sense of anything she has to say regarding boys.

"No, listen to me. He'll be practice for you! And because you don't like him and don't care what he thinks about you, it'll make it easier for you!"

"What are you talking about?"

"Flirting, Ziva. Flirting."

"We are on the run for our lives!"

"All the more reason to make the time count. You're so lucky you have me."

"Yes?" I respond like it's a question.

"It's not that hard. Repeat after me. Kellyn, tell me about yourself."

"What?"

"Go on. Say it. Kellyn, tell me about yourself."

"No, this is ridiculous." I stand and try to move past her, but she stays me with an outstretched hand.

"It's not. What's ridiculous is that you've never properly flirted with a man. Now say it."

"No."

"Say it, or I'll tell Kellyn I saw you ogling him."

I glare at her. "You wouldn't."

"Wouldn't I? The days are sure to grow long and boring. I could really use the—"

"Kellyn," I say through gritted teeth. "Tell me about yourself."

"Good," she says enthusiastically. Like I'm some small child who's accomplished a feat far greater than my size would allow.

"Now, some follow-up questions. Where did you grow up? Why did you decide to become a mercenary? Do you have any family? Go on, say them."

Though in a foul temper, I repeat after her. "Why are you making me do this?"

"Because you're terrified of talking to people. Sometimes knowing what to say ahead of time helps."

I feel my brow furrow. "You do this? Think over what you're going to say ahead of time?"

"If it's a boy I've got my sights set on? Always."

"I don't have my sights set on him! I was just admiring him— and it was only for about two seconds!"

"Never mind that. Now we will both have something to occupy ourselves tomorrow."

"What do you mean? What are you going to be doing?"

"Flirting with Petrik, of course."

I brush the dirt from my hands. "I didn't think he was your type."

"He's not, but he's not showing the slightest interest in me, and I'm taking that as a challenge. Besides, you should be thanking me. I'm distracting him from asking you questions about his book."

"I should be questioning Petrik about magic to figure out ways to destroy the sword. Not flirting with the mercenary!"

"I've got it covered. I'll ask him about it in between my longing looks and comments about his strong arms."

"You're unbelievable."

"I think the word you're looking for is *amazing*."

CHAPTER NINE

The evenings are mild, just cold enough to need a single blanket. Temra and I sleep under our own tent. Petrik has a tent. Kellyn prefers to sleep by the fire, the tall trees keeping the rain off him.

I've always been a poor sleeper. It often takes me hours to find oblivion, my mind unable to stop thinking about all the things that are troubling me. And now that I'm on the ground, with only a thin bedroll between me and the dirt, it's even more difficult. I toss and turn, unable to get comfortable.

The nights are really getting to me, and this morning, a sleep-deprivation-induced headache pounds at my temples. All I want is my house. My bed. My forge. My blankets. My room.

But I can never return to any of it.

Temra and the mercenary appear perfectly rested. Petrik and I seem to be the only ones affected by sleeping outdoors.

"I could carry your pack for you today," Temra offers to Petrik.

"No, thank you," he says simply.

"What do you have in there anyway?"

"Aside from the necessary traveling supplies, books."

"Those must be heavy."

He hoists the pack higher on his shoulders. "They're a comforting weight."

She keeps up a steady stream of conversation. Occasionally, she throws in a comment about how smart he is or how strong he must be to carry so much over so long a distance. The flirtations are subtle, an art all their own.

The familiar well of envy takes me over, but I'm brought up short by Temra's meaningful glance between me and the mercenary, who takes the lead of our party several feet ahead.

Go, she mouths.

I shoot her a dirty look in response, but she ignores that, going back to talking to Petrik. She's holding Reya's lead, which leaves me and my hands free.

I stare at the mercenary's back, willing him to vanish into thin air.

Temra nudges me with her arms and mouths, *Ogling*.

She's threatening me again.

My hands tighten into fists, and Temra shoves me a few feet ahead, nearly causing me to collide with Kellyn.

The mercenary turns his head in my direction, and I could strangle my sister as I now keep pace with him.

Oh, damn it all.

"Kellyn, tell me about yourself," I say. As soon as the words are out, I feel goosebumps rise on my skin. My mind panics and my body sizzles like a lightning bolt has struck just under my skin.

This is horrible. Why is this happening? I hate her. I hate this. I hate everything.

After the initial surprise on his face, Kellyn says, "What do you want to know?"

"Where are you from?" I spit out, remembering the words Temra forced me to rehearse last night.

"A small village called Amanor in Prince Skiro's Territory. I grew up on a farm with my family."

Okay. I can do this. Follow-up questions. What do I want to know?

"Does your family still live there?"

"Yes, I am the oldest of my siblings, and the only one who is away from home. Everyone else still tends to the farm. Sometimes I return for the harvest to help out."

Really? "Do you make them pay you?"

He laughs. "No. I'm a sellsword. That is all. Besides, you don't charge family."

Hmm. That's a kind thing: helping family out. I hadn't expected it of him.

"What did you do before you were a smithy?" He surprises me by asking a question of his own. Does he actually want to know? Or is he just being polite by continuing the conversation?

And then I can all but hear Temra's voice in my head: *You can fixate later. Just talk to him.*

I want to growl in frustration. Instead, I paste a smile on my face. "Well, first I had to train. So before I was a smithy, I was an apprentice to one. My gift manifested when I was nine. Before that, Temra and I were at the orphanage in Lirasu." My thoughts jumble together, and I don't know where to start. I take a breath and try again. "One day the priestesses took all the orphans for a walk through the city to get some of the energy out of our legs. We passed by a smithy."

I look up briefly to gauge Kellyn's mood, but he seems perfectly interested in the conversation.

"Go on," he says. "Then what happened?"

"The forge was outdoors. I could see the smithy working on a scythe for a farmer. I remember seeing the shape of the tool and the heated metal just lying on the anvil. And I felt drawn to it inexplicably. I parted from the rest of the orphans, walked into the forge, and blew on the blade."

"And?"

"And then the blacksmith, Mister Deseroy, yelled at me because I might have hurt myself. He sent me on my way, and the priestesses rushed me onward. But the next day, the smithy came to the orphanage. It was well-known in the city who my mother was and that she had left two daughters behind when she died. When the scythe showed magical properties—the ability to use the wind to separate the seed from the chaff—the smithy set out to find me, thinking perhaps I was Samika's daughter.

"And then he and his wife offered to take me in. I said I wouldn't go anywhere without my sister, so they brought her along, too. I spent my days in the forge, learning how to make steel and bend it to my will. Mister Deseroy had me start magicking his farming equipment, and he brought in quite the profit. It didn't take long for me to outgrow him. Once I learned the basics, my gift filled in the rest of the gaps on its own. I was creative, and I immediately learned I loved weaponry. By the time I was twelve, Mister Deseroy was ready to retire on all the money I'd made him, and then Temra and I had outlived our usefulness.

"He was kind, though. He gave me some money and all the tools I'd need to get started. I bought back our parents' land, and I started working."

Kellyn is a patient listener. He takes it all in quietly. "That's incredible. What you can do is incredible."

I shrug. "It's not really me. It's the magic that makes me what I am. I can't really take credit for that, can I?"

"Of course you can," he says. "You observed and learned all the necessary tricks of your trade. You're a prodigy. That doesn't make you less talented. It makes you even more impressive, magic or no."

I feel light at his words, like I could drift away if I'm not too careful, and a thrill buzzes beneath my skin.

And then the panic comes, because I have no idea what to say next, and the silence stretches on.

"I always knew I wanted to be a mercenary," Kellyn says. "When I was little, one came through the village. He was so big, arms wider than a tree trunk. He let me hold his sword, before my mother saw, and though it was heavy, too much for my six-year-old hands, I remember how right it felt."

"How did you learn to fight?" I find myself asking.

"There was a retired palace guard living in the village. I

begged him to teach me after I finished my chores each day. Ma didn't like it, but Da talked her into it. Said it was only a good thing if I knew how to defend myself. I love them both dearly, but I always wanted to see the world. I left as soon as I was old enough to take on work. I visit regularly, though. I can't stay away too long. I get homesick."

I've been gone from my forge just over a week and already I'm homesick. I feel this kinship with Kellyn. It's nice to hear someone else admit they miss home.

"Thank you for telling me," I say.

"Thank you for asking," he says. He turns his golden gaze on me. "You're all right, bladesmith. For a while, I thought you might be too uptight."

"I thought you might be too unlikable."

"I had a good night's sleep," he says, as though that explains anything. "And just so you know, I rarely drink. I was celebrating my birthday. Turned twenty."

Well, doesn't that just make me feel like a monster for abducting him on his birthday. "Happy late birthday."

"Thank you. To be honest, I think I like how that day ended." His eyes do a sweep of my body, from the top of my newly shorn hair to the base of my boots.

Everywhere his eyes touch, I feel like I've been lit on fire.

Why is he looking at me like that?

When Kellyn meets my eyes again, I don't know what he sees there, likely the panic. He looks over his shoulder, notes that Temra and Petrik have fallen way behind.

"Pick up the pace, scholar!" he shouts. "And try not to trip on your dress."

Petrik looks up with a familiar glare that seems to be reserved only for Kellyn. "I told you, these are robes! And you try not to fall over from the weight of your head."

Kellyn laughs, and I join him.

When we break for camp, Petrik separates himself from Temra. He grabs what appears to be a notebook and quill from his pack before seating himself on the log I've occupied.

Dinner is cooking, some sort of stew that makes my mouth water. The mercenary is off doing who knows what, and Temra pouts in Petrik's direction.

"I've noticed that your horse carries a bundle of weapons. Are they your making?" he asks me.

"Yes," I say cautiously.

"May I ask what they do?"

"You took your time before approaching me with your questions."

"I didn't want to bombard you. You're clearly hesitant to talk about your abilities."

"I'm just hesitant about talking in general."

"You spoke to the mercenary earlier."

Because my sister was blackmailing me.

"Do you want me to answer your questions or don't you?" I ask, a hint of irritation creeping into my tone.

"Yes, please."

"In the weapons bundle, there's a shortsword named Midnight. It turns black when those who mean you harm are nearby." I've looked at it no less than two hundred times since Petrik and

Kellyn joined our party. It has remained the natural gray of steel, so that gives me some comfort.

"Can I ask about its origin? How did you make it?" He scribbles something into his notebook. "I'm looking to understand how your magic works."

I do not like this line of questioning, but I realize this may be just the conversation I need to carefully enlist Petrik's help in destroying the blade. "It was the first thing I made after Temra and I bought back our parents' home. Mother and Father were killed in that house, the culprit never found. We were alone, just the two of us, and I wanted to feel safe. It was a shortsword, because I wanted something that Temra could lift, should she need to. She was only ten. Anyway, the sword picked up on what I was feeling, and it gave me a way to know I was safe so long as the blade remained gray."

"The magic is tied strongly to your feelings," he notes.

"Yes."

"What other weapons did you bring?"

"The Sanguine Spear. It seeks blood when thrown. It will always hit the nearest fleshy mark, even if it's thrown way off course."

"How fascinatingly morbid. And how did this one originate?"

"That one was actually an accident. I cut myself, and a few drops fell on the spearpoint."

"Wow, the weapon actually contains a part of you. Your own blood. That is very likely why it's so much more powerful than the aforementioned shortsword. This is wonderful." He licks the tip of the quill before scribbling madly some more. "What else? I think I saw another sword in there."

"Yes, a broadsword." I drop my gaze down to my interlocked fingers. I release the pressure, my fingers having gone red from the death grip.

"Secret Eater," Temra says, coming up beside the two of us, taking the attention off me. "It reveals the secrets of those it cuts."

She's so clever, as always. Putting the focus on one of the sword's abilities while completely ignoring its invulnerability and incredible range.

"And how did you make that one?" The question comes from behind us, and I flinch at the unexpected sound.

The mercenary joins us by the fire. He's worked up a light sweat, likely having just finished an exercise with his sword.

He waits expectantly for my answer.

He doesn't know. How could he know? And yet he's the one who asked the question.

"I whispered my secrets to it while making the blade."

"What kind of secrets?" Petrik and Kellyn ask at the same time.

Petrik wants to know for his book. Kellyn wants to know because he's nosy, and I just ignore the both of them.

"Like stealing taffies from the larder," Temra says, crossing her arms.

"Ah," Kellyn says. "Such secrets you keep." He grins in my direction.

My face heats impossibly at the real truth. How I wanted to touch Kellyn, who stood so far away, and the sword gained long-range abilities.

"Can I try it?" Kellyn wants to know.

"What?" I ask.

"The sword. Secret Eater. Can I try it out?"

"And just who do you plan to cut with it?"

Kellyn immediately looks at the scholar.

"No," Petrik says. "I'm no good with blood, and I refuse to be party to your ill-conceived ideas."

"Fine," Kellyn says, put out. He turns to me instead. "You use it. On me."

"You want me to *cut* you? Why?"

"Curiosity. I want to know what it would tell you. I want to know if it really works."

"No," I say at the same time Temra says, "Okay."

"Of course it works," I say, ignoring Temra, "but I'm not about to slice you open."

"I'll slice him open," Petrik says.

"You said you didn't like blood," Kellyn says.

"I'll close my eyes."

"Absolutely not," I say.

Temra leans into me. "This could be good," she whispers. "You wanted to know whether or not he could be trusted."

"He'll notice the sword doesn't actually touch him when it cuts him," I whisper in response.

"So we'll make him look away."

"And Petrik?"

"You heard him. He hates blood."

"Fine!" I snap, probably louder than necessary. I stomp over to Reya, who swishes her tail at me.

I return to the fire with Secret Eater. Temra sits next to Petrik. Kellyn has rolled up his sleeve. He looks at me expectantly.

"Look away," I order him.

"I'm not scared of being cut."

"I don't care. I can't do it with you watching. So if you want me to cut you, you better look away."

He rolls his eyes but turns away.

I throw a quick glance Petrik's way; he has his eyes squeezed shut and two fingers pinching his nose, as though he's afraid he'll smell the blood from there.

Temra gives me an encouraging nod.

Kellyn doesn't so much as blink at the pain when a thin well of blood appears on the littlest finger of his nondominant hand. He must be used to all the injuries that come from his line of work.

"How does this work?" Kellyn asks. "Do you ask me a question and I answer? Does it compel me to be honest?"

"It doesn't work like that," I say, but I lose my train of thought as the mercenary's voice floods my mind.

I've always wanted to go back to Thersa. It's beautiful, full of waterfalls and warm weather. Really, it's like these girls are paying me to take another vacation. They'll be safe with me.

The bladesmith is so gentle and quiet at times. You really can't help but feel like you want to protect her. The sister is feisty and pretty, to be sure, but this one has a more calm beauty, something I feel drawn to inexplicably.

I drop the sword and step away from it, as though it might say something else offensive.

Offensive? That's not quite the right word.

Kellyn eyes me, and I feel my cheeks heat like the sun.

Uncomfortable. Awkward.

Yes, those fit better.

"What do you mean it doesn't work like that?" he asks.

I can't answer right away. "It reveals some of your thoughts. Usually the more relevant ones to whoever is holding the blade."

Kellyn smirks. "And just what did it tell you, bladesmith?"

I start coughing for no reason. Probably to prolong my words for as long as possible. Temra sees right through this tactic, but I hope the mercenary doesn't.

Finally I catch my breath and say, "You're excited to go back to Thersa. You said we're practically paying you to take a vacation."

"True," Kellyn says. "Was that all?"

"You said we'd be safe with you."

"Also true. Anything else?"

"N-no."

"Did you know you get a blush on your cheeks when you're lying?" Kellyn asks.

I look to Temra for help.

"He's right," she says. "You do."

Panicked, I say the first thing I can think of to get the attention off me. "He thinks you're pretty and feisty."

Temra lets out a noise somewhere between a scoff and a laugh. "Both are true, but you're not my type, mercenary."

Kellyn claps a hand over his heart in a mocking gesture. "Alas, most ladies just can't handle a paramour who is better-looking than they are. These features"—he runs a hand over his face—"are a blessing and a curse."

Temra laughs. "Whatever you tell yourself. Petrik, let's check on that stew."

Kellyn's eyes land on me once more, and I look away hurriedly.

"Maybe one day you'll tell me your secrets, bladesmith, now that you know some of mine."

He thinks you're a beauty.

He thinks you're a beauty.

He thinks you're a beauty.

The thought is on repeat in my head. It's all I can think about while I try to sleep that night.

"I think there's something wrong with him," Temra says.

"The mercenary? Of course there is."

"No, Petrik."

This finally pulls me from my thoughts. "How do you mean?"

"I'm not getting anywhere with him."

"You guys talked for hours today."

"So? He hasn't complimented me once! It's like I don't even exist. He just wants to talk about books and magic and how he grew up. Which, admittedly, I mostly find interesting, but he is showing absolutely no interest in me."

"And that means something's wrong with him?"

"Obviously."

"Some people just aren't attracted to other people in that way."

"That's not what I mean. I would be fine if that's what it was! But he clearly said he wasn't celibate."

"Maybe he likes men."

"He doesn't. I already asked that."

I have to cover my mouth with a hand, but my muffled laughter comes through anyway.

Something whacks my head, and I register it a moment later as Temra's pillow. "How dare you laugh at me!"

I laugh outright now. "Poor Temra. Hordes of men fall at her feet, but she can't get one scholar to adore her."

"Oh, I will. He's just making me work for it, is all."

"Why do you care so much? Do you even like him? Do you even want him?"

"No, but it's the principle of the thing! I don't know how to handle a man who doesn't want me."

"Maybe you should set your sights on the mercenary instead."

She retrieves her pillow from where it landed beside me. "I would never do that. He's yours, Ziva."

"He's not *mine*."

"Still, I'm not pursuing him."

"That's your choice."

"Yes, it is, and I've already made it."

A howl rips through the camp, and another howl answers it. We've heard a few coyote yips at night along the trip, but these are much different, much closer.

Much more dangerous.

Temra shoots to her feet and pulls back one of the tent flaps.

I can see that the fire has died, but Kellyn is up and alert, his sword in his hands.

"Stay in your tents!" he calls out.

Temra dashes outside.

"What are you doing?" I shriek after her.

I've no choice but to follow.

Reya is frantic; I can hear her hooves pounding against the ground as she strains against her rope. She neighs in distress.

Temra goes to her, and I'm right on her heels. I snag the rope and pet the space between her eyes, muttering soothing sounds. I expect Temra to stroke her back. Perhaps jump on so we can ride away. Instead, she goes for the weapons bundle.

She frees Midnight from its sheath, the shortsword just as black as the night sky.

The howls grow louder, and now I can hear rustling in the foliage.

A spark appears, followed by blinding light. Kellyn has relit the fire. I watch in confusion as he rips off his shirt, ties it tightly around one of the large branches stacked beside the camp for cooking tomorrow's breakfast, pours a hefty helping of oil from the jug onto his shirt, and thrusts it into the flames.

"Wh-what's going on out there?" This from Petrik's tent.

Kellyn pulls back the makeshift torch and spins around just in time to face a wolf launching itself out of the trees.

I scream—I can't help it. I've never been attacked by anything before, and watching Kellyn fight off a drooling beast is terrifying.

It lands just short of his feet, and Kellyn swipes at it with the torch before slamming the point of his longsword into the wolf's back.

"Stay in your tent, Petrik!" Temra shrieks as more wolves pour out from the trees. They nip at Reya's shins, and she goes up on her back legs, sending me careening to the ground. Temra puts herself between the three wolves and the horse, slashing at the beasts with Midnight.

One wolf leaps at her, and I force myself not to shut my eyes as I watch her shove the shortsword right through its gaping maw. The tip splits through the back of the beast's head, and Temra loses her sword as it falls to the ground.

"Here!" Kellyn yells, and he throws the torch at her. She catches it effortlessly and spins to swipe at the next wolf. Meanwhile, the mercenary wields his longsword in two hands, spearing wolves left and right with it.

I watch in awe as my baby sister defends our horse and herself against wolf after wolf with . . . *practiced ease.* She presses the end of the fiery torch against one wolf's shoulder. It howls in pain before retreating through the trees.

And then the torch goes black, the oil running out, Kellyn's shirt scraps snuffing out with the barest breeze.

A final wolf sprints through the trees, rushing at my sister's back. I throw myself at her, shoving her to the ground and spinning just in time to catch the full force of the beast. Sharp claws dig into my shoulders, and long teeth snap at my throat. I barely manage to get my hands around the wolf's neck, pushing with all my might to keep it from making contact.

Goddesses, but it's heavy. I can barely breathe, spittle and rank breath fill my nose and mouth. I try to roll, to kick, but I can't find any purchase.

And then the weight is gone.

Kellyn literally kicks it away from me. He jumps over me to follow the creature and finishes it off with his weapon.

And then the clearing goes silent. Nothing but heaving breaths and the sputtering of the little campfire.

"I-is it safe to come out now?" Petrik asks.

I think Temra says something in response, but I don't hear it, because a shirtless Kellyn is leaning over me and touching my neck.

"Are you hurt?" he asks.

And just like that, I can't breathe again. I'm staring at the muscles in his abdomen, the way they ripple with his exerted breaths, the way the flames send shadowy light across them.

I am on the verge of hysteria, and I need him to give me some space. I don't want to be rude by shoving him away. Words. I need words.

"My shoulders," I manage to get out. I can tell the wounds aren't deep, but they'll need to be cleaned.

He puts his hands under my arms, helps me to stand as though I were a child, but right now I think I need it.

"I said to stay in the tent!" he suddenly yells at me once I'm upright. "You could have died!"

"I only left because Temra did! Why aren't you screaming at her?"

"Because she can defend herself. You cannot!"

At that reminder, I round on Temra.

"How can you fight like that?"

She swallows and has the common sense to look guilty. "Just came naturally?" she tries.

Unimpressed with the answer, I cross my arms and wait.

"You know Ankon and Ceren."

"Yes, you've snuck out many times to meet up with them."

"Right, and you always thought it was for romantic reasons? They're actually training to be part of the city guard, and I've been learning from them . . . for a few years now."

My mouth drops open. "But you didn't say—you let me believe—"

"I didn't think you'd approve, and I didn't want you to worry about me."

She's been . . . scuffling with city guards? Honing these skills. "Why?" I ask. "Why did you want to learn to fight?"

She shrugs. "I'm good at it, and I really love it. I thought I might want to be a guard someday."

"But that's dangerous!"

"And that's why I didn't tell you. I knew you'd react like this."

I stare openmouthed at her. All the sneaking out. It was so she could practice fighting in secret?

"You should be glad," Kellyn says. "She was a big help just now. Especially since you divided their numbers by coming out of your tent."

"You stay out of this!" I hiss. Then I turn back to Temra. "I can't believe you didn't think you could tell me about this."

"Because you would have forbidden it! It's my choice what I do with my life."

"You're damned right I would have! It's my job to look after you." Mother and Father would be so disappointed if they knew. Not just about this, but how I failed to protect Temra. From this blasted sword and the warlord and everything else that threatens us.

Petrik crawls out of his tent. He's fully dressed in his scholar robes. He takes in the dead beasts first, then looks over Temra and me—for any wounds, presumably. Then his eyes land on Kellyn.

"You just had to use your shirt, huh?" Petrik says, looking distastefully at Kellyn's torso.

"I didn't have time to ask to borrow your dress."

Petrik shakes his head, like he can't even bother. "I'll make some tea."

CHAPTER
TEN

Temra cleans the claw marks for me in the privacy of the tent, neither of us saying a word. After, we all sit around the fire, Temra and Kellyn with their weapons unsheathed, prepared should the few wolves that fled decide to return.

Kellyn has thankfully donned another shirt.

I tell him, "Thank you for saving us. That was quick thinking about the torch."

"Have I earned my keep, then?"

"I'd say so."

A silence follows, and I feel the need to fill it, but I have nothing to say. Discomfort spreads over me like a scratchy cloak.

"We need to have a discussion about following orders when we're under threat like that," Kellyn says. "I need you all to listen if I'm to do my job properly. Strangely, the scholar was the only one who obeyed."

"I knew I could help," Temra says defensively.

"And now that I know you can, I will use that knowledge next time I give orders." Kellyn turns his gaze to me expectantly.

"I'm not about to stay behind if Temra is in the thick of danger. If I hadn't pushed her away, that wolf would've—" I cut off, unable to finish the thought.

"So it's better that you were hurt instead of her?" Kellyn asks.

Temra says over the top of him, "You shouldn't have thrown yourself at me. That was reckless."

"I'm stronger than you are," I say simply. She couldn't very well have held her own against a wolf barehanded. I barely did—and only for a short amount of time at that. Any longer, and it would have had me if Kellyn hadn't intervened.

Another silence.

"Regardless of how stupid it was, it was very impressive," Kellyn offers. "I've never seen anyone wrestle a wolf like that."

The compliment startles me, and I have no idea how to respond to it.

"Had I known we were all ignoring the mercenary's sage advice to stay in our tents, I would have come out to help," Petrik says, sounding somewhat embarrassed.

"I had my hands full enough keeping these two out of trouble," Kellyn says. "You should be proud that you're such a good listener."

I ignore the men, instead focusing on my brave sister. She was amazing tonight. I was so scared for her, but I realize now that we're safe, and in spite of everything—"I'm glad you know how to fight."

"Really?" she asks, her eyes looking to me with something akin to hope.

"I always want you safe. That is more important to me than anything else. I'm sorry I reacted poorly, and in the future"—I let a hint of sternness creep into my voice—"I expect you to tell me things."

"I promise."

We ought to be exhausted while traveling the next day, but the attack has made all of us hyperaware of our surroundings. I haven't been able to calm down from full alertness yet.

Still, I need a distraction from the constant terror of wolf mauling.

"Petrik, what do you know of other magic users in the world today?" I ask, hoping to move the conversation in such a way as to help me figure out what to do with Secret Eater.

Petrik is delighted by the question. "Though I'm sure there are many magic users in the world who keep their abilities a secret, there's only one other who is widely known like you are: the cotton spinner. While you take the ores from the land and shape them into magicked weapons, she takes the plants of the earth and spins them into illusions."

I've heard stories of cloaks of invisibility and masks of disguise. The merchants and mercenaries who pass through our city bring many exciting tales. I don't hear them myself, of course. I hear them secondhand from Temra.

What I hadn't expected was that there were only two of us who advertised our abilities. I thought surely there must be more, even if I hadn't heard of them before.

"The witch hunts of a century ago really wiped out most of those with magic," Petrik explains, as though reading my thoughts. "Bloodlines known to carry magic were basically made extinct. Now that magic is no longer outlawed, I hope we'll begin to see the ability spread."

I've often wondered if that's who came after Mother and Father. Someone with a violent hatred of magic. But that doesn't explain why they killed Father.

Or why they left Temra and me alive.

"In all your studies," I say, "have you ever read about anyone else with an ability like mine? Aside from my mother?"

"I have not, I'm sorry to say. I've read about those with control over many of the planet's natural resources. Clay, plants, water, wood, minerals, animals—even the people themselves." Petrik grimaces at the last one. "While others before you have used metals and minerals in other ways, you're the only one I know of to combine magic with forging.

"I came across an old children's book that talked of a man who could skip rocks great distances over the surface of the water," Petrik continues. "There was a witch back in the day who could bend silver into any shape she wanted. She was the one to create a common currency throughout all of Ghadra, shaping the metal into coins. There are tales of an old woman who could call grains of sand to her. She could move them where she liked, make them form together to build extraordinary things: a house, a fence, the wall around a city.

"I'm afraid no one interviewed your mother or recorded her abilities. That is why I'm doing this. Life can be fleeting, and we don't want any more knowledge lost."

"I'm sorry if our mother's death was an inconvenience for you," Temra suddenly bites out.

"Oh, I didn't mean—Temra, I'm sorry! I shouldn't have phrased it so carelessly. I only meant that what happens in our world is precious and should always be remembered. Your mother should be remembered."

Somewhat appeased by his words, she says quietly, "I wish I could remember her. I was too young when she died."

In my memory, she was nothing short of perfect. Beautiful, soothing, loving. I should tell Temra this, but my eyes sting just to think of her. My most vivid memory of her was shortly before she died.

I was so angry with Temra because she was playing with one of my dolls.

"I hate her," my five-year-old self said. "We should get rid of her."

"You want me to get rid of your sister? What should we do with her? Put her out in the street? Toss her out with the garbage? What do you think would happen to her?"

I remember feeling a little guilty, but I still thought life would be better without someone taking my things.

Mother bent down to my level. "You listen carefully, Ziva. A sister is the most special gift you could ever be given. Better than any doll. She will be a best friend you can take with you through life. Someone who will love you no matter what."

Those words stuck with me, and they turned out to be true.

When Mother and Father were gone, I was beyond lucky to have Temra with me through it all.

I'm pulled back to the present, realizing I've missed the turn the conversation has taken.

"We were very lucky Ziva's ability manifested itself when it did," Temra is saying. "Else we might have been stuck in that horrible orphanage for years more."

"It wasn't horrible," I say.

"The staff didn't hate you as they did me."

"You pulled pranks on them. Put mud in their boots and hid their teaching supplies."

"They asked for it. You saw the way Miss Bekis would look at me, like I was some unruly heathen of a child."

"You *were*!"

"Just whose side are you on, Ziva?"

The back-and-forth feels so normal that for just a second, I forget about everything else. I can pretend we're out in the yard, enjoying a warm summer day.

"I, too, was raised in a public house," Petrik says. "I spent the majority of my life in the library, stuck with the same tutors day after day. I can relate."

"Did you like growing up in a library?" Temra asks. "Sounds boring."

"I loved it." The two of them start sharing life stories, Temra's full of pranks while Petrik's life was built on rigorous study.

They're so very different, but those differences seem to connect them in constant conversation. Temra is fascinated by everything Petrik has to tell her, and he in turn hangs on her every word.

I leave them to it, tugging on Reya's reins when she tries to stop to eat leaves from a low-hanging tree.

"Was it difficult, being alone while also having to look out for someone younger?"

I startle at the mercenary's voice. I hadn't heard him step beside me.

"Of course it was."

"I'm sorry about your parents."

"Thank you, but you needn't be sorry. It's not your fault."

"No, but I hate to imagine you all alone. Raising your little sister while you yourself were a child."

Sometimes he says just the right things to endear him to me a little more. I have never been friends with a boy before. But I think I might just be forming friendships with these two as we travel on the road.

He thinks you're a beauty.

The thought comes unbidden, sending a flash of panic through me like a whiplash.

It shouldn't matter. It's not as though he knows I know. Yet the thought still seems to make me uncomfortable in his presence. I can't control it.

Maybe it's the fact that Secret Eater came to be because I thought him beautiful. And then the sword shared such a similar word regarding Kellyn's thoughts about me.

Beauty.

Such a silly, superficial thing, and yet, so much danger was created because of it.

The days grow into weeks on the road. With Temra's new fighting ability revealed to the group, she's somehow talked Kellyn into sparring with her in the evenings before we turn in for bed. Since there was nothing I could do to prevent it, I watched from the sidelines once, but after snapping at Kellyn when he shoved Temra backward, she begged me to leave.

I watch them from afar now so Temra doesn't know I'm spying.

She's incredible. She has a natural grace in the way she swings, and I'm so impressed by the strength she manages to force into each thrust of her sword. Kellyn barks instructions to her, but I'm too far away to hear.

"She's really good," Petrik says from where he crouches down beside me, his eyes also on the sparring pair.

"She is."

We watch as Kellyn pauses to get behind Temra and correct a stance. She snaps something to him good-humoredly, and he grins in response.

"What do you think they're saying?" Petrik asks.

"They're flirting."

Petrik takes his eyes off them to look at me. "Surely not." It doesn't surprise me that Petrik wouldn't pick up on this. After all, Temra has been flirting right at him for days, and the scholar has failed to notice.

"I know my sister. She's very good at it. And, well, just *look* at him."

I feel my cheeks heat as soon as the words are out. I just admitted I find him handsome. Stupid.

But Petrik doesn't seem to care about my slip. "It wouldn't

work. They're too similar. And they don't like each other like that."

"How do you know?" I ask.

"You can tell by the way they move around each other. They don't touch except when necessary. They're being playful with their words to dispel any awkwardness. It's not at all like the way the mercenary is with you."

I nearly lose my balance in my crouch. "What?"

"You don't really look at anyone except your sister. Even now when I'm talking to you, you're looking at the ground. It's okay. I know it's just how you are, but you don't notice the mercenary as a result. The way he is with you."

I force myself to meet Petrik's eyes. "How do you mean?"

"Just pay attention. You'll see."

The weather grows warmer and wetter the farther we go. The trees gradually change from those with needles to those with leaves. The canopy becomes thicker, blocking out more light and the rain, which makes for easier travel. Fewer plants grow aside from the trees because very little light gets down to the ground. Only the road remains open to the alternating sun and clouds.

We risk traveling on it again at Kellyn's behest. We're close to our destination, everyone eager to reach it as quickly as possible. We cross paths with a few other travelers. Kellyn and Petrik are friendly, making impressions, while Temra and I are silent, drawing up our hoods.

Petrik's words have been like a hammer in my mind, beating

against my skull, making it impossible for me to think about anything else.

Pay more attention to the mercenary, as if he would—

I happen to glance over at Kellyn, and when I do, my eyes instantly meet his. I look away hastily, before I can see any sort of expression cross his face.

He was watching me. Staring at me?

Yes, because I'm the bladesmith. I possess magic. I'm strange, and it's natural for him to be curious about me.

But a few minutes later, when I catch him doing it again, I say, "Stop that."

Temra is up ahead with Petrik, both of them leading Reya along.

"Stop what?" the mercenary asks.

"You're looking at me."

"You're looking at me," he counters.

"Only because you're looking at me!"

"If you say so."

"It's the truth."

My whole body feels overheated, as if I'm back in the forge. The secrets the sword shared with me are a burden I didn't realize I wouldn't want. I don't like knowing this man thinks I'm beautiful. But there's no way to take it back. One can't unknow a secret.

"It's the sun," he says, pulling me out of my thoughts.

"What?"

"All the sunshine. It's making even more freckles burst across your arms and face."

"So? You've never seen freckles before?"

"They're even on your lips," he says, peering closer.

"Stop looking at my lips." I clap a hand over my mouth to make it impossible for him.

He grins, as if he finds my reaction amusing. But then he steps back to his side of the road and keeps his eyes on the path ahead.

Who even pays attention to lips?

And how does Kellyn not have a single freckle on him? His hair is red, after all. Don't those two always go together?

Instead, the sun is darkening his skin, making it glow almost.

I huff.

I am not impressed by him. And his lips are stupid. Look at them. All symmetrical, with the lower slightly bigger than the upper. They pull up into a grin, even though he's not looking at anyone in particular.

"I can feel you staring," he says.

I pick up my pace to catch up with Temra.

We know when we're almost upon the city, because we pass by so many more people on the road. Some are entering Thersa like we are. Others are leaving, manning wagons full of unfamiliar fruits and jewelry and clothing.

The air is so moist that my clothes stick to my skin. It feels as though a light mist blows into my face wherever I turn.

The people are unusually friendly. Everyone makes a point of saying hello as we walk by. They raise one arm high into the air in greeting. Though I think it odd, Kellyn seems unsurprised.

"Thersa is a busy city that relies a lot on trade. The people are sure to greet newcomers warmly. It's what keeps travelers coming this far north. That and the sights."

Before we even officially reach the city, merchants are hawking their wares. The smell of spicy meats is thick in the air, and kabobs are brandished under our noses. Temra finally gives in and buys one for each of us.

"Mmm," she says after taking a bite. "What is this?"

"There are only two things in abundance in Thersa: fish and flightless birds," Petrik says before Kellyn can.

"Have you been here before, too?" Temra asks.

"No. Part of my schooling was to learn about all the major cities of Ghadra. I've always been fascinated by the idea of a flightless bird. Did you know that they still have wings?"

Temra grins at his enthusiasm.

Though there are people everywhere, I rest a bit easier knowing the crowds will hide me and Temra. They will keep us safe. This city is our salvation.

And it's beautiful.

As we travel farther into the market, we can see the fjords. High cliffs tower over the inlet, and waterfalls thunder down into the water below. The sound is soothing, and the sight is unlike anything I've ever seen. Suddenly all the rainfall doesn't seem so bad. Not when these waterfalls are the result.

Black-and-white birds swim through the water and waddle on the shores.

Flightless birds, indeed. So interesting.

I catch Kellyn staring at me again and glare at him. "What is the matter with you?"

"It may be lovely here, bladesmith, but you should be careful. Don't tell anyone who you are. Many in Thersa are superstitious about magic users."

"Magic has been legalized for a long time."

"Sometimes change takes generations," Kellyn says. "And sometimes people disregard the law to pursue their own beliefs."

"But none of the territory leaders have a problem with magic."

"Doesn't matter. This town has a history with magic that supersedes any law or ruler. Do what you want. I'm just letting you know to watch your back now that I won't be there to do it for you. Oh, and don't forget about my sword. I'll be at the Dancing Kiwi until it's ready."

"Here's your promised bonus," Temra says, stepping forward to pay the man.

Kellyn gives me an entirely unnecessary wink before disappearing into the crowd.

That's it? No *goodbye* or *hope to see you soon*? After so much time spent together, talking about orphanages and families and freckles, he leaves me with nothing more than a wink? He thinks I'm a beauty!

Why do you care? You hated talking to him.

Didn't I?

"Good riddance," Petrik says.

"I kind of like him," Temra says. "He got us here in one piece, didn't he?"

For the life of me, I cannot figure out why I feel as though I've lost something once he's gone.

It doesn't take much asking around before we're given directions to the home of the Sotherans, our father's family.

"Sure, I know where the Sotherans live. Their property is just at the top of that bluff there. Can't miss it. You'll find a trail leading to it on the northeast side of town," an older gentleman tells Temra when she asks. "What business do you have with them?"

Temra turns to me, unsure of how she should answer. I nod to indicate she needn't be fearful of the truth. "We're relations."

"How wonderful!" he says. "May the Sisters bless your reunion."

"Thank you," Temra says, not bothering to correct him. This is not a reunion so much as it is a first meeting.

We begin following the old man's directions.

"Should I also find an inn to stay at while you meet up with your family?" Petrik asks.

"No," I say quickly. I feel safer having an extra body with us now. Temra and I have no idea how our new relations will react to us.

Neither Petrik nor Temra questions the hasty response.

"Why is it that you've never met your relatives before now?" Petrik wants to know.

"They live far away," I answer.

"Which is strange to begin with," Petrik says. "Most people don't go far from where they're born. And didn't you say your father took your mother's last name?"

"Yes, but that's not uncommon. Many couples within the princesses' territories do that to honor the matriarchal rule."

"I'm just saying it kind of sounds like your parents wanted to hide from these relations."

"And why would they do that?" Temra asks.

"I don't know," Petrik says. "What if their business is illegal?"

"That might help us," I say, "considering we're on the run from . . . powerful people."

"But what if they try to exploit that and sell your whereabouts to these powerful people?"

"We're not about to tell them we're on the run, now, are we?" Temra says, slapping Petrik playfully on the back of his head. "You worry too much, scholar. Why don't you stick to reading and let Ziva and me worry about our relations?"

Petrik grumbles something under his breath, which Temra either doesn't hear or pretends not to.

Petrik's thoughts don't worry me, yet I get a sinking sensation in my stomach when the house is in sight.

It's a large estate, with many pens holding all manner of livestock. Pigs, goats, and birds almost as tall as I am with vibrant blue featherless heads.

The rain is pouring down by the time we reach the front step, and I'm nearly in a full panic over how we will be received, as though the rain might be an omen from the Sisters.

Which is silly. It probably rains here every day. Still, we've been so scared for so long on the road. It's hard to let those fears go now.

"Here we go," Temra says with a hopeful grin. "I'm so excited!" She knocks on the door, and we wait.

A man who looks so much like my memory of Father opens the door. I feel tears threaten my eyes just at the sight of him.

"Yes?" he wants to know. "If you're here to sell anything, you'd better leave before Volanna finishes her morning prayers."

Before I can think over the words, I say, "Are you Darren's brother?"

The man blinks. "I haven't heard that name in years. Who are you?"

"Darren is—was—our father."

A heavy silence follows, and the man—our uncle—steps back. "I think you'd better come inside."

CHAPTER
ELEVEN

We tie Reya off to a railing. Temra grabs the bundle of weapons to bring inside for safekeeping, while Petrik removes the saddlebags. We wipe our muddy boots on the colorful rug just inside the front door. The spacious receiving room is immaculate, with statues in the likenesses of the Sister Goddesses positioned on decorative tables. Ebanarra is always done in white while Tasminya is in black.

"Please have a seat. I'm sure Mother will be down shortly."

He leaves us standing there, dripping from the downpour outside. We shuck our cloaks and hang them on nearby pegs. We're so dirty from weeks of travel that we don't dare sit on the finely upholstered couches.

"Who are you going to tell them I am?" Petrik asks. "If

the mercenary's cautions about magic are true, we probably shouldn't tell them I'm a scholar studying magics."

Temra thinks a moment. "A cousin on our mother's side."

Petrik blinks. "All right, then."

I fiddle so violently with my fingers that they turn red. Temra reaches out a hand to still me.

"It'll be all right, Ziva. Maybe we'll even get to sleep in real beds tonight. Who knows? Think of happy things right now. I can do all the talking."

It feels like hours before anyone joins us, when in reality I'm sure it's only minutes.

A woman with her hair cut into a gray bob enters the greeting area. She wears a short skirt that doesn't quite reach her knees. Sandals cover her feet, and her sleeveless shirt shows off beautiful tattoos of local flowers, marking her from her wrists to shoulders. Blue eyes flit from Temra to me and back again. Her hand flies up to cover her mouth. "You look so much like your father. You have his eyes. And you his nose." She laughs sadly. "I'm your grandmother, Volanna. Would it be all right if I embraced you?"

Temra runs into her arms without hesitation, and guilt replaces any fear I may have had about this encounter. I didn't realize how starved for comfort Temra was. But it makes sense. We've been on the run for over a month. Before that, it's just been the two of us. No parents or even parental figures.

I'm not one for hugs with strangers, so I do not embrace Volanna when she turns to me. Instead, I plant an awkward smile on my lips.

But Temra captures her attention once again, telling this

woman our names, our ages, where we're from. She introduces Petrik.

When Volanna asks what happened to our father, Temra tells her how Father and Mother passed away when we were young, leaving it at a home invasion gone awry. Temra and I slept through the whole thing, and I found our parents in the morning. At least that's what the matron of the orphanage told me. I have no memory of that day, for which I'm grateful. Temra, of course, doesn't include any of those details. She explains how I've provided for us while Temra has focused on her schooling. Volanna nods politely and squeezes Temra's hand reassuringly through the painful bits.

Then the older woman looks to me. "You don't have much to say, dear. Is there something wrong?"

"Oh, Ziva is just very shy, Grandmother," Temra says.

Grandmother? That was fast.

"No matter," Volanna says. "We have endless time to get to know one another. I'm so glad you decided to seek us out. Come, let's get food in your bellies."

It turns out Father has three brothers. He was second eldest, and all the others work on the estate during the day before returning home at night to their families.

"You have six cousins!" Volanna says over a meal of fresh bread and butter, salted pork, and tropical fruit. "You'll get to meet them later this week at the service. Oh, you will of course wish to join us for church?"

Temra doesn't miss a beat before saying, "Of course."

Our worship of the Sisters has always been flimsy at best. We've never regularly gone to services held in their honor. I can't stand to be around all the people. Temra went a few times for the social aspects, but she eventually quit attending. I don't think she believes in a higher power.

I believe the Sisters are real. The world and all its creations had to come to pass in some way. The Sisters gave me my own sister, and for that I'll always be grateful. But they also let my parents be taken from me.

So I suppose my relationship with the divine is complicated at best.

But Temra and I can feign interest in a religious service if it means earning the protection our father's mother can provide us.

"I just can't believe you're truly here," Volanna says. "Darren disappeared twenty years ago. He left a note to tell us he was safe but his future was in another place. We never met your mother. I don't know if he met her before or after he left or what caused his disappearance. I am relieved to hear he was safe and had a family of his own, but I am grieved to hear of his passing."

She takes a bite of pork. "You're welcome to stay with me for as long as you'd like. I would be overjoyed to have you live with me. With all my boys gone to their own homes and my dear husband passed away, it's been empty in this large house. My faith has kept me strong, but this old woman does get lonely sometimes."

"We'd love to stay, Grandmother," Temra says. "And we're happy to help with the chores however we can. Ziva obviously has many skills. She can repair any farm equipment. Petrik and I are strong."

Volanna looks close to crying. "My son raised you girls right. We'll figure something out. For now, let us enjoy one another's company. I'll show you the city tomorrow. Sunday belongs to the Sisters, so we will spend it in worship and prayer. After that we can decide how best to proceed. Now, why don't we get you all cleaned up and in bed?"

The bath was heavenly, more so since it was the first time I was truly alone in a room for so long. I scrubbed over a month's worth of dirt from my body before changing into a clean night-dress provided by Volanna. She showed us all to our rooms and promptly took our clothes for washing. Temra has taken it upon herself to look after all the weapons, and I don't protest. She's clearly more capable of protecting Secret Eater than I am. I watched her stow it under her bed for safekeeping along with the shortsword, spear, and staff.

I felt rude for not saying much to my father's mother, but I was so overwhelmed by everything, I couldn't find any words to say.

And now. Alone in a comfy bed, all I can feel is relief.

Relief, and a little fear.

What if Kymora somehow knows where we are? Is she tracking us? What if it's not safe to close my eyes? There is no mercenary looking out for us now. And I somehow have to make a magical blade for Kellyn. Just how does he expect me to pull that off when he also cautioned me not to mention to anyone that I have magic?

He thinks you're a beauty.

Ugh.

That thought has a habit of poking its head through my consciousness when I least expect it. I don't need to be thinking about him right now.

It's only been a few hours since I last saw him.

There are much more important things to be thinking about than that mercenary.

Like Kymora and the sword. Like my sister and her happiness.

I worry about Temra. I think she's already attached to Volanna, but should something happen—should Kymora find us—we'll have to pick up and leave again. Leave what's left of our family.

And it will be my fault.

Again.

Volanna takes us to all her favorite stops in the city. A shop that sells fruity drinks. A store entirely devoted to hair ribbons and cosmetics. And finally, a dressmaker's.

"We'll need to find something for you both to wear to the service. No time for something tailored," Volanna muses aloud. "What do you have already made in their sizes?"

One of the workers produces two ghastly dresses with strange frills and lace in uncomfortable places.

Volanna is delighted by the dresses and buys them instantly. I turn to whisper my thoughts on the new clothing to Temra.

"You're just upset you have to wear something fashionable for once."

We head to the fjords after the dressmaker's, find a place to sit, and spend time watching the fish through the clear water—and those strange birds swimming after them.

"They're called penguins," Volanna explains. "They're normally found in very cold climates, but this is a special breed found in the fjords." We quickly learn that Volanna loves animals, and she tells us the name of every fish as we spot them.

We laugh over the birds playing with one another. They push each other into the water, play games of chase.

At one point, Temra excuses herself to find a privy, leaving me alone with Volanna.

"It's all right," she says once my sister is gone. "Your father was the same way, you know. Very shy. A man of few words. More comfortable when he was on his own. I didn't think he'd ever go off and leave me, let alone marry. I'm happy he found someone to share his life with." She gives me a warm smile. "All I'm saying is, you can say as little or as much as you'd like. I understand and don't hold it against you either way."

"Thank you," I say, and I offer her my first sincere smile.

I hadn't known that about my father. I don't remember him being shy or soft-spoken. What I remember is him throwing me high into the air and catching me. I remember him dancing with me, having me stand on his toes while he'd twirl me around the room. And I remember him telling me stories, though I can't recall what they were about.

"I am glad to be here and to have met you," I say. "I hope you don't think differently."

"Not at all. I can't wait for us to grow closer." She leans over to hand me a smelly sack full of dead fish. I reach in with my fingers, pull one out, and toss it into the water. I watch in fascination as two penguins race for it.

Before the day's end, I set out to find the nearest smithy in the hopes that she'll let me borrow her tools and forge. Temra waits outside with Volanna while I enter the shop. Temra obviously knows I need to make arrangements for Kellyn's longsword, but Volanna thinks I'm commissioning something.

Stepping into the forge is like stepping into a hot bath. I breathe in the smells, take in the familiar tools. I feel relaxed at once.

Wornessa is nearly two feet shorter than I am, but her arms are so much broader than mine. She and I quickly decide on a price for the use of supplies and her shop. I let her know everything I'll need, and she promises to procure it for me by the beginning of next week so I can get started. I'm careful not to mention my abilities.

Talking to Wornessa isn't like talking to anyone else. I know smithying better than anything, and it doesn't make me uncomfortable to discuss it. I wish conversations were always like this. So effortless and enjoyable.

My anxiety recedes over the next few days as I get to know my grandmother better. She's fond of basket weaving and cooking. She bakes Temra and me delicious cakes each day, and she shows us how to make a few meals, since we're both hopeless cooks.

Petrik is polite, giving us space and hovering at the outskirts.

He spends a lot of time in his room working on his book, questioning me in the evenings before bed about my abilities.

"Have you read any occurrences of magicked items being destroyed?" I ask casually one night, having tread so carefully to work the conversation so the question would seem natural.

"Sure," he says without missing a beat. "If the item is simply broken, the magic often breaks with it. I'm sure you've come across that on your own with some of your weapons."

"I have." But that's not what I meant. I try again. "What if an item was magically incapable of breaking, though? Do you know any stories about those being destroyed?"

"An item magicked not to break." He chews on his lip while he thinks. "Why would someone want to break it?"

"What if it was cursed with bad magic?"

"Oh, I see. I know some magics die with their caster, but not all. For example, there was a man who could move water. He would sing to it, and whole rivers would change their course at his command. But when he died, the water reverted back to its natural state. Flowing with the land. Your items, however, are physical and likely wouldn't lose their magic after you die."

Well, that's terribly unhelpful. Not that I want the answer to my problem to be for me to die.

"Why do you ask?" Petrik wants to know.

I dreaded this question, but I also prepared for it. "There are bad people in the world. Someday one of them might possess magic. I was just curious."

"As magic becomes more common, I'm sure it will undoubtedly find itself in the hands of those who would misuse it. Let us hope that the bad will always be outnumbered by the good. By people like you, Ziva."

"Thank you, Petrik." A sharp pain pricks my heart, for I'm the reason magic almost found its way into the hands of a bad person. And I can't fix it. All I can do is try to keep it away from her.

With a newfound family that seems to accept me, and everything in order to prepare Kellyn's weapon, I start to relax. For the first time in a while, I feel safe.

And then Sunday arrives.

Volanna makes us sit in the front row, and in that moment, my regard for her dims. She does, however, shoot me a sympathetic look. Did my father also struggle sitting in the front row? Did he hate public places as much as I do? I'll have to ask Volanna about it the next chance I get.

With her sons and their families positioned on Volanna's left and Temra and me and Petrik on her right, we take up the entire center pew.

I can feel the stares of all the people sitting behind me, which is *everyone* in the church. My skin itches, and I think I pull a muscle in one of my fingers as I fiddle with them, but that doesn't stop the nervous tick.

By the Twins, I'd rather be anywhere else right now. Facing the warlord. Back on the road. In the tavern with Kellyn.

That last thought surprises me. Even more so when I realize it's actually true.

But I can do this. My newfound family likes to sit in the front row, so I will sit with them.

We arrived early, so it is several more minutes before a priestess takes the stand at the front of the chapel.

Two lifelike paintings, one of each Sister Goddess, hang on the walls to either side of her. Ebanarra has golden-white robes. Her lips are curved up in a smile, looking at something we can't see. Tasminya is in ebony. Her face is unreadable, but she stares straight ahead, catching the eyes of all who would look upon her.

The priestess herself wears a simple skirt and blouse combination, white on top, black on bottom to represent the Goddesses. She smiles as she looks down at the congregation. "I see we have some new members in the audience with us today. Why don't we start with a refresher for their benefit?"

I sink a little lower in my seat. That's what this day was missing: being singled out.

"In the beginning, there were two sisters born into the vast universe. The first was called Ebanarra and the second, Tasminya. While their looks were identical, their spirits were as opposite as night and day. But they both shared a fondness for creation.

"Ebanarra made the stars, while Tasminya formed the moons. When they created worlds together, Ebanarra would make the land, the plants, and the skies. Tasminya, the waters, animals, and winds. Together, they made the first woman, who gave birth to the human race.

"Ebanarra was always careful and meticulous with her creations, nurturing them, guiding them, watching them grow. While Tasminya was a little more reckless, not striving for perfection, but uniqueness. She rarely stayed to care for her creations, more interested in what they would make of themselves.

"Today, we give thanks to the Sisters for every good thing in our lives, and we pray to them both when we're in need."

I relax somewhat in the telling. Everything in Thersa is new and requires adjustment, but it's nice to be met with something familiar. The Goddesses are the same here as they are back home.

"The Goddesses have set an example for us since the beginning," the priestess says. "We should show care and love for this world and the people in it. The church accepts donations for the poor and less fortunate. Those who can't afford to give of their income are encouraged to share their time. The priestesses at the orphanage can always use more helping hands.

"Be kind to all, despite our differences. Pray for those who wrong you. Ask the Sisters to help change their hearts."

I can honestly say it never occurred to me to pray for Kymora. I suppose it couldn't hurt.

"Do these things and there will be a place reserved in the Sisters' heavens for you. A place where there is no pain nor fear nor strife."

There is so much comfort to be taken in the Sisters' teachings. That's why I haven't managed to give up on them yet. I believe we should all be kind to everyone and do our part to help others. I want to believe there is an existence after this one where I don't have to feel scared or anxious anymore.

I'm almost glad I was forced to attend today's service. The comfort of it is a balm to my troubled heart.

"And of course," the priestess continues in the same gentle voice, "above all else, we must eradicate magic at all costs."

That has me snapping my neck up.

"We do not know when it first came into existence—magic

predates the written word—but it swept over this world like a disease, infecting some while blessedly sparing others. We do not know its origin, but we suspect it came from the land. From digging minerals out of the earth, churning the soil for crops, burying the dead. Somewhere, the magic sprang forth, and those who became corrupted permanently destroyed their bloodlines, passing the taint down from generation to generation."

Temra and I share a look before the priestess continues. "At first, the world mistook magic as a blessing from Ebanarra, but all too quickly it became clear that it was a curse. Our own city had the worst of it. Here in Thersa, there was one born with the ability to control the minds of others. Magic came from the land, and the Goddesses formed the first woman from the dust of this world. We are of the land, and so this magic user could control the people around him. Craynd was his name. He used his ability to control this city. To make all people do his bidding. We were enslaved. All newcomers became captive to his spells. We were unable to even pray to our Goddesses for aid, as we were incapable of recognizing our own enslavement. His rule lasted until he died, an old man of eighty-seven. Only then were we freed. This was some five centuries ago.

"Then came the rightful time of the illegalization of magic and the extermination of those who were sickened with it. The world cleansed itself of this blight by any means necessary. The bloodlines bearing it were wiped out. And the world was made whole once more.

"On occasion, a latent line of magic will bear a new magic user, and when this happens, it is our duty to stamp it out. To keep the healthy peoples of the world safe."

The priestess turns her attention right on me in the first row and smiles. "We are so happy to have you join us in our divine duty to this world."

I swallow in the silence that follows. Petrik gives me the side eye, while Temra reaches out to clasp my hand in hers.

"What a lovely reminder of our history," Volanna says as we walk back to the estate. "Did you enjoy yourselves, dears?"

"Yes," Temra lies. "Though I was surprised by the bit about magic in the sermon. We've never heard such an account. Do you really put all magic users to death?" Her question is phrased innocently enough, but I still worry that Volanna will see right through it.

"Magic played such a horrible role in our city's history. We can't risk it happening again. Those with magic aren't really human. They're something else entirely. Such executions are just and necessary." She nods to emphasize her point.

That answers that question: If I'm discovered, they'll kill me, family or not.

"Did my Darren not teach you such things?" Volanna asks.

"We were too young when he passed to remember, Grand-mother," Temra lies. Obviously Father didn't have a bias against magic if he married Mother. I think I can guess why he left Thersa without any trace. "We have a lovely chapel back home, but it is nothing compared to Thersa's," she adds, changing the subject. "Your priestess seems most wise and capable."

Volanna grins. "Thank you, and do not worry over the new-ness of Thersa. You will understand such truths soon enough.

Now, let's head home and we'll have a nice luncheon with the family. We'll discuss the sermon further over food."

Volanna gets caught up in conversation with her other grandchildren, who are all much younger than Temra and me. The three of us fall behind in the procession so we can't be overheard.

"What are we going to do?" Petrik asks.

"Nothing," Temra says. "There's no reason to worry. Volanna hardly seems violent, regardless of what she believes. Besides, legally the church can't do anything to Ziva. Magic isn't outlawed, despite what this sect believes."

"That does very little to comfort me," I say. "Kellyn said some might take the law into their own hands. I could be dead before any lawmakers are involved."

"Maybe we should consider running," Petrik says. "If they find the books in my room, the ancient magical texts, who knows what they'll do? Never mind if they actually learn that Ziva is a magic user."

"You're overreacting," Temra says. "We have nothing to fear. Some of those texts aren't even in a language most people can read. They'll never know what they contain. And Ziva isn't about to use magic, so why worry?"

"Because I promised Kellyn I would make him a weapon," I say. "Or have you forgotten he's staying in town until I complete it?"

"So we'll buy him off. Pay him the cost of one of your weapons. He's not about to turn away money."

"But that wasn't the arrangement."

"He seems an understanding fellow. I'm sure he'll be open to discussion."

"So what if he is? I can't go the rest of my life without making another weapon. It's what I do. It's what brings me joy and comfort. I can't not be who I am."

Temra shakes out invisible wrinkles from her horrible dress. "Not forever, of course. Just until Grandmother really gets to know us. Then she'll accept us no matter what. I'm sure of it."

"Temra, I know you've already grown fond of her, but she's part of a sect that believes killing magic users is not only acceptable but a divine calling. That they'll be blessed for doing so. Can't you see how that scares me?"

Temra stops walking and rounds on me. "Can't you see that we're finally not running for our lives? We've been alone for so long, and now we finally have a family that wants to love us and protect us. Why are you trying to take that away?" Her voice has risen considerably.

I feel my face turn red. "Why are you already choosing them over me? Temra, they'll *kill* me. How can you be all right with that?"

"That's not what I'm saying. Can you learn to relax a little and stop being scared of everything? You're so pathetic all the time. You can't even see a good thing when it's right in front of you! I followed you clear across the continent. But enough is enough, Ziva!"

I look down at the ground, feeling tears drip down the sides of my face.

"Temra," Petrik says. "How could you say that?"

"Oh, shut up," she says to him. "Figures you'd take Ziva's side. She's the special one after all, isn't she? The one worthy of being written about in your book?"

Temra runs ahead, pushing through the hordes of relatives until she reaches Volanna's side and takes her hand like a child.

"I'm sure she didn't mean—"

"No, Petrik," I say. "Don't defend her. She meant every word."

Am I so pathetic that I'm blind to safety and happiness? Is she right?

We're approaching the house, but the last thing I want to do is go inside.

"I'm going on a walk," I tell Petrik. "Can you hide my absence and keep an eye on Temra?"

"Of course."

"Thank you."

CHAPTER TWELVE

I never walk the streets alone, not if I can help it. Even back in Lirasu, I wouldn't go anywhere unless Temra was free to join me. I can't help but be wary of everyone and everything. Because no matter what, it all feels like a threat.

I startle at every sound and have to eye every stranger I pass, ensuring none of them is Kymora. And damn this town, but everyone is *too* friendly, saying hello whenever I pass them by.

I don't want to talk. Why can't everyone just keep to themselves?

Careful not to get lost, I finally get the courage to ask for directions to the Dancing Kiwi Tavern. Turns out a kiwi isn't just a fruit but yet another kind of flightless bird. I stare up at the image of the squat bird with a long, thin beak painted on the sign above the door.

He's probably not even inside. It's not like he's going to spend his days just sitting in the public area all day. No, he'll be off enjoying the city. Although it is lunchtime. So maybe he's eating?

Honestly, I can't tell if I want him to be inside or not. I sort of want to talk to Kellyn, but I'm also equally terrified of it.

But I need to talk him out of a weapon, and I can't do that if I don't actually speak to him.

Pathetic.

Pathetic.

Pathetic.

That word rings in my ears in Temra's voice. She's usually so supportive of my weaknesses, but I can't help but think that was all a lie and she's finally told me how she really feels.

If it were Temra, she wouldn't think twice about going to talk to a boy. She would be confident, smiling, ready to take on anything.

For just a second, I pretend I'm her, and I enter the tavern.

My first objective is simple: Don't panic, and find an empty table to sit at.

It only takes one quick perusal to confirm there are no empty tables.

I can't sit next to someone I don't know. That leaves the stools near the front counter. There are seven of them. There's a person in numbers one, three, four, and seven. Which means no matter which stool I sit in, I'll be next to someone.

That won't work, either.

Panic sets in.

I can't stand here, and I can't sit.

Walk out.

I should definitely walk back out.

But what if someone saw me walk in here, saw me panic, and then turn around?

It shouldn't matter. They're all strangers. Who cares?

My face heats up like I've just gotten the most wicked sunburn, my palms are shaky, and I swear everyone in the room is looking at me.

I hear laughter coming from one of the tables. It's probably directed at me. This was so stupid. Why did I—

"Bladesmith."

His voice cuts above all the other noises in the tavern, and I find myself relaxing at it.

"Mercenary."

Kellyn comes into view. He's clean. Obviously, he took advantage of a bath and fresh clothing. He smells nice. Like lemons and grass. Some sort of local soap?

He's also shaved. His beard was darker than his golden-red locks on the road, a burnt red. But now he's fresh and smooth. It's impossible to miss his smile.

"What are you wearing?" he asks, barely concealing a laugh.

I glance downward and feel my stomach turn over.

I'd completely forgotten I was still in this hideous dress.

"I promise it wasn't my first choice." And right now, I honestly wish I were back in my dirty traveling clothes rather than this.

But blessedly, Kellyn doesn't say another word about it. "There's no way you've finished my weapon already," he says.

"I haven't."

He nods, sticking out his lips in thought. "Care for a drink?"

I've never really cared for alcohol before, but—"Sure."

He heads over to one of the tables. It's empty now. I didn't even notice he was the one sitting in it when I did my cursory glance. Kellyn pulls out a chair, presumably to sit in it, but he looks to me expectantly.

What is happening?

He doesn't mean for me to—

Before I can finish the thought, I'm sitting in the chair.

He's being polite and courteous. As if we'd planned to meet together. As if he'd asked to take me out.

I should say something, I think as soon as he takes his own seat. I'm the one who came to him. He'll expect me to initiate conversation. Why is this so hard?

Pathetic.

Pathetic.

Pathetic.

"Did you meet your family?" he asks.

After my initial surprise, I answer, "I did."

"And?"

"I don't think I like them."

"I'm sorry to hear that."

At the next pause, I blurt, "The problem is that Temra loves them."

"Ah."

A drink is set before me. I didn't even notice Kellyn ordering it. The serving maid gives the mercenary a very unnecessary smile before striding off on swaying hips.

I stare at the cup, glad to have something to hold to keep my hands busy.

Am I being selfish? Am I making everything about me? Am

I so pathetic that I don't know how to be happy when a good thing is presented before me?

At the silence that follows, I say, "You're probably wondering why I'm here."

Kellyn looks at the bottom of his cup as he takes a drink. "Not really."

"What do you mean?"

"You don't have a job for me to do, and you haven't finished the one I gave you. So you're here for social reasons."

Oh my Goddesses. I am. I mean, I do have something to discuss with him, but I haven't even brought it up yet. I'm currently being social.

Don't think too hard about it. Just keep talking.

"Our new home doesn't feel safe," I say. "I had to get out. I don't know anybody in this city." And I don't want to.

"But you know me. So I was your only option."

I tilt the cup in my hands so I can stare down into the dark contents. "I could have shut myself in my room."

"Or made small talk with the scholar. Or did he take your sister's side?"

"My sister's side?"

"You had an argument, did you not? Why would you be here if you had your sister's skirts to hide behind?"

I'm so shocked by his words that I nearly lose my grip on my tilted drink. "Excuse me?"

Kellyn rubs the side of one finger against his forehead. "That came out wrong. I just meant that you are attached to her. You can't really start a sentence without looking to her to finish it."

I feel my brow shoot up to my hairline.

"I didn't say it was a bad thing. Just that you're awfully dependent on her, and maybe it's good for you to get out on your own every once in a while. Bladesmith, I'm trying to say I'm glad you came to see me."

I can't even begin to unpack those words. Should I pretend to take a drink from this cup I have no intention of actually consuming?

"I don't like getting out," I say.

"I know."

"I hate most people."

"I know."

"I don't even drink."

He grins. "I guessed as much. You just like having something to hold in your hands, right?"

At that, I lock eyes with him. How has he guessed so much about me?

He thinks you're a beauty.

My cheeks redden. This whole exchange is humiliating. If I ran out of here, would he chase me?

"What just happened?" he asks.

"What?"

"You were fine for a moment, and now you look ready to bolt. Did I do something?"

"No. It's me." It's always me. "I'm not good at talking."

"You're doing perfectly."

That's kind of him to say, but I'm almost certain he's lying for my benefit.

At my silence, he asks, "Are you ever going to tell me the rest of what that sword revealed to you about me?"

I look down at the wood grain of the table, twisting the cup in slow circles. "No."

"Oh, come on. How can you not tell me my own secret?"

"It's too humiliating," I whisper.

His jaw clenches. "I did some things in my past that I'm not proud of. I want to know which one the sword told you about."

At that, I backtrack immediately. "I didn't mean humiliating for you! I meant humiliating for me!"

He relaxes visibly, understanding settling in. "I find you attractive."

My chest grows tight, and I involuntarily hold my breath.

"I think it's adorable when you stammer. I like that you don't open up to most people. It makes it more of a challenge when I finally get you to trust me. You're the perfect height. I barely have to bend down to be at eye level with you. When you fiddle with your hands, it makes me want to take them into my own, and—"

"Would you stop it!" I hiss between my teeth as loudly as I dare.

"Were any of those what the sword told you?"

"And then some!" I say rebukingly.

I can't look at him. Doesn't he realize how uncomfortable he's making me? Is he amused by how unsettled I am? Was that his goal?

"I'm sorry," he says. "You could even the score, though. Tell me some of your secrets about me. Then we would be even."

"I don't have any secrets about you."

"Really? Then why did you come to me instead of staying with your family?"

In a voice barely above a whisper, I say, "They'll kill me if they find out what I am."

A heavy silence descends over the table. Meanwhile, the rest of the tavern is as busy as ever. Carrying on as if my whole life hasn't fallen apart. As though I'm not the most scared I've ever been.

"They're part of a religious sect that believes in exterminating magic at all costs. That's why I'm here. I need to ask you if you would consider more money in exchange for me not making you a magicked longsword. I can't risk revealing what I can do in this town. You were right about this city and these people. I fear for my life and my sister's because of her relation to me."

Kellyn sets down his drink. "I didn't realize it was so serious."

"It is, and I'm scared."

Maybe it's foolish to admit to him, but it's the truth.

"Is it impossible to mask when you're doing magic?"

I shrug. "Depends on how the magic turns out."

"You don't perform the magic until near the end, and it's a one-time occurrence, yes? It's not like glowing light is coming from your fingers the whole time or whatever?"

"Right. But what if someone sees?"

"I could come with you," he offers. "Be with you in the forge while you're working. I wouldn't let anything happen to you."

I swallow, try for honesty. "I don't know if I could work with you watching."

"Me specifically? Or anyone watching in general?"

The answer is somehow both.

But I'm still warmed by his words. He'll protect me? He'll

spend his days just sitting in the forge with me? Keeping me safe? No one but Temra has ever done that.

"I'll even scare away anyone who tries to interrupt you," he offers when I don't answer his question.

I look up into those golden-brown eyes, framed by golden-red hair. How does this boy understand me so well so quickly? Is he really so observant all the time? Or is he somehow just so observant with me? Or does he just really, really want that sword?

That's far more likely.

But that doesn't change the fact that I've come to feel slightly more comfortable around him. It's not perfect. He still makes me nervous at times, but I chose to come here, didn't I? That's huge for me.

And despite not enjoying being around people, I like him.

I almost forgot about all the other bodies in the tavern while we were talking. Kellyn has that way about him. A way of making me focus on him and forget about everything else.

But I notice when the doors to the tavern open and a figure comes running inside.

Petrik does a sweep of the room before his eyes land on me, and he races over. He's juggling the bundle of weapons, Secret Eater among them. He has his pack full of books on his back.

"We—have—to—hurry," he says between heaving breaths. Did he run all the way here from the estate?

"What is it?" I ask. "Is Temra okay?"

"We—have—to—save—her."

At that, my heart stops. The world goes quiet for two beats, before everything starts back up, seemingly faster than before.

"What happened? Does she have her?" My voice cracks at the last word.

Petrik takes a few quick breaths before spitting out, "Yes, your grandmother. She's convinced Temra has magic. They're going to kill her for the Goddesses."

"What?" When I said *she*, I actually meant Kymora, but I'm glad Petrik mistakes my meaning.

"Volanna has your uncles helping her. I saw them confront Temra and then take her away. I suspect they're going to the church. I knew I couldn't stop them on my own. I came as quickly as I could and brought these to help."

"Let's go." I race after Petrik but stop after a few steps.

The mercenary isn't following.

"What are you doing?" I snap. "I said *let's go*."

Kellyn has a pained expression as he looks at me.

"We can't take on so many people by ourselves," he says. "It'd be suicide."

"We'll worry about that when we get to the church!" I say.

He stares into my eyes for a few more seconds before sighing. "I normally get paid for this kind of idiocy."

It takes me a moment to process his words, I'm so outraged. Then I reach into my clothing, find my coin purse, and hurl it at him. It hits Kellyn in the head before landing on the floor.

I don't watch to see if he'll pick it up. I follow Petrik through the streets, running as fast as I can. I hear steps behind me shortly, and I allow myself a moment of relief as I realize Kellyn's following. Petrik fumbles with the weapons stash, so I take it from him. It's awkward with the staff and spear sticking out so far on either end.

"Petrik, take the staff and spear."

He does so, running with one in either hand.

I toss the shortsword to Kellyn, who catches it and doesn't ask any questions as I tie Secret Eater around my waist. I have no intention of using this cursed weapon, but I'll be more useful if my hands are free. The weapon pulls heavily at me, but I only push my legs harder against the extra weight.

Then I take the shortsword back from the mercenary.

We race across town, not caring who we step on or send careening to the ground. If they're in our way, they get plowed over. I don't care. Nothing matters except Temra.

She can't be hurt.

She can't be—

She *has* to be okay.

I send a prayer up to Ebanarra, to Tasminya, to whoever might be listening. *Save my sister and I'll do anything.* Anything.

The steep incline is the worst part. The ground rises as we run away from the fjords, toward the east end of the city. But I welcome the pain, the burn in my legs. I'll take any punishment if it means I get to keep my sister.

"What's the plan?" Kellyn asks.

"The plan is to save her."

"I know that, but we're outnumbered, and you and Petrik can't fight. So it's to be me versus how many?"

I do not want to hear how outmatched we are. Why can't he just—

"It's unlikely any of them are skilled with weapons," Petrik says. "They're farmers. And Volanna is an elderly woman. It's just her three sons."

"Are they small lads?"

"Uh, no," Petrik says.

"Great. If you get me killed, bladesmith, I will find a way to cross back over to the land of the living and haunt you forever."

"As long as you save my sister in the process, I don't care."

We don't bother checking the estate first. Petrik said they left in the direction of the church, so that's where we go. It's on the far end of town, near the outskirts of the city.

When we reach it, we note a small crowd gathered around the outside. Bodies are packed together, trying to get a look over one another's heads.

We plow straight on through, pushing people out of the way. When one big man doesn't budge, I poke him with the sheathed shortsword. Kellyn parts people, shoving with his enormous shoulders, and Petrik trickles behind him in the path he makes.

When we finally get inside the chapel, we find all the pews filled, people standing in the spaces between, all staring up at the stand.

Where Temra is bound and gagged.

Pain rips through my chest at the sight. This is all because of me. Because of what I can do. I brought us here. I did this.

The priestess says something, but I can't make it out over the pounding of my heart. Some sort of horrible drivel, I'm sure. Making an example of my sister and the horrors of magic.

Volanna and her sons stand next to the priestess. My uncles are resolute, but Volanna looks almost sad by the turn of events. As though it greatly pains her.

But not enough to stop this, apparently.

The priestess holds a wicked dagger in one hand, the blade curved, perfect for eviscerating and watching things die slowly.

No.

We're still running. Still shoving. Trying to reach the top.

The priestess gesticulates with the blade. Punctuating her remarks. Each time it inches toward Temra I think I'll lose my mind.

We're not going to make it to the front in time.

"Stop!" I shout at the top of my lungs.

The priestess and my relatives look up, trying to find the voice in the crowd.

"I'm the one with magic. You have the wrong sister. I'm the one who needs to be sacrificed!"

Kellyn turns to me. "What are you doing? Shut up. Are you trying to make this harder?"

"Let her through!" a voice rings out. And the bodies shove aside, leaving a path up to the stand.

"Never mind," Kellyn corrects. "Carry on, bladesmith."

There's no way we can fight everyone in this room. I had hoped it would be only Volanna and her sons, but of course the priestess would want to make a spectacle of this. We've no hope of fighting a hundred or more city folk.

"I make magical weapons!" I shout. "Look, here they are!" I raise the shortsword higher, which is black as night when I loose the blade. "Take me and let her go."

"We can't be sure she's telling the truth," the priestess says as the three of us finally reach the front. "We should take them both, just to be safe. We can't risk the blight of magic infecting this city once more."

"The missive we received was that one of the sisters was carrying a magicked weapon," Volanna says. "Perhaps if we just confiscated the weapon and let the poor girls go—"

"Out of the question," the priestess says.

Temra is straining from her bonds, shouting underneath the gag, her words unintelligible.

"It's going to be okay," I tell her, stepping forward.

"Oh, like hells," Kellyn says from behind me. "Here's what's going to happen. You, wicked priestess, are going to hand over the feisty one, and we're going to leave the city, never to be seen again. No one's committing murder tonight. The law forbids this. Now let her go."

The priestess clutches her dagger more firmly, her knuckles turning white. "No. The Goddesses demand that this filth be purged from our midst. We will not sin against their wishes."

"The law has legalized magic. You are sinning against the realm," Petrik volleys back.

"The realm has become corrupt. We must take a stand. It must stop."

Kellyn sighs and draws his longsword. "It's not murder if you're defending your life, and I'll be glad to rid this town of you." Kellyn points the considerable length of his sword toward the priestess.

"Take one more step and she dies!" the priestess shouts, holding the blade to Temra's throat now. "Sotherans, grab the other."

"No!" Volanna says, but her sons start toward me anyway.

Kellyn puts himself in front of me, blocking their path. I almost make the mistake of feeling gratitude before I remember how he didn't immediately agree to help me save my sister.

From beside me, Petrik asks, "Should I throw the spear?"

"No, it might hit Temra. It'll hit any flesh. That won't work."

For all of two seconds I consider the usefulness of Secret Eater, but that won't work either. Temra can easily get injured if I start swinging that around. And so can Petrik and Kellyn. It's a weapon of mass destruction. Utterly useless if you're trying to protect someone other than yourself, unless you have the training to use it with precision.

Midnight isn't helpful right now. That leaves . . .

"The staff, Petrik. Give it to me."

"What? Why?"

"Now is not the time for your endless questions!"

He swaps me the staff for the sword.

I have impeccable aim when it comes to swinging a hammer, but throwing a projectile is another matter. Still, if it hits Temra, it won't kill her.

I take aim and throw for all I'm worth.

The metal cuffs on either side of the wood cause it to turn end over end, and the magic gives it even more strength.

But I still have to direct it.

The staff misses the priestess completely, as I'd intended, but I shove into Petrik hard, altering the path between me and the spinning weapon.

Because when the staff starts turning end over end, back

toward its caster, it hits the priestess in the head on the return. Her eyes roll into the back of her skull as she slumps to the ground, dropping the knife. The staff twirls back toward me, and I catch it round the middle.

"Boomerang staff?" Petrik asks in wonder.

I forgot that I never told Petrik what the staff did. Kellyn interrupted the conversation by demanding Secret Eater be used on him.

I set Twirly—Temra named it—on the ground and grab the shortsword from Petrik before racing toward my sister. Now that Petrik knows how the weapon works, I trust him to use it wisely.

And so he does.

I watch it spin out of the corner of my eye. Volanna's sons are in a line, trying to reach Kellyn. The staff clonks all three of them, turning over itself, hitting a different one on each rotation. The first takes it in the stomach; the second, the head; the third, the crotch.

Kellyn doesn't pause before stepping forward to finish dispatching the men, knocking each one out with the pommel of his sword. He dodges the staff as it flies back toward Petrik.

I reach Temra and use Midnight to cut her bonds. She removes her gag as I work at the ties on her ankles.

"I'm so sorry for what I said," Temra says. "Ziva—"

"Later," I say.

When Volanna tries to advance, I hold out the shortsword.

"I swear I didn't mean you girls harm. This was out of my control. I couldn't ignore the threat of magic."

I shake my head in disgust. "You failed us. Just as you failed your son. Our father was so ashamed of you that he ran away so he could marry Mother, knowing she had magic. They were happy. And so were we. Now you've lost us. We won't be seeing you again."

"Bladesmith!" Kellyn shouts, and I turn to see the whole room of devotees standing from their pews, getting ready to charge.

"There's a back exit," Volanna says. "Through there. Go!"

We could be trapping ourselves, but our only other option is to push through the horde of bodies.

We run.

CHAPTER THIRTEEN

Volanna did not lie, it turns out. So we've one small thing to be grateful for. As soon as we step down from the alabaster steps of the church, we take off.

The angry mob follows.

I suppose the good news is none of them carry weapons, but faith appears to count for a lot.

I hand the shortsword over to Temra, since she has a knack for it, and keep the spear for myself. Not that I can actually throw the weapon, because then I'd have to go back to retrieve it. But Petrik has no problem throwing the staff as hard as he can, taking out waves of Thersans in the process. They fall down in the road, tripping the others next to them. The staff whizzes back to Petrik's outstretched hand each time, like a lodestone drawn to iron.

Bit by bit we gain some distance.

Then they start throwing things.

The first rock catches Kellyn in the shoulder. The second, square on his back.

"I see how it is. Aim for the biggest target. That does it." He plants his feet, refusing to run any longer. The rest of us slow our pace but don't stop.

"Kellyn!" Temra shouts over her shoulder. "What are you doing?"

With the tip of his blade, he draws a line in the dirt road, from one tree line to the next, covering the whole width of it.

He shouts in a voice I've never heard from him before, "Anyone who crosses that line is going to have their head separated from their shoulders!"

The city folk come to a halt just before the line, but one large man near the front tosses a rock up in the air and catches it in his hands in an obviously threatening manner.

"Try it," Kellyn says. He runs through an impressive series of slashes, showing off his sword's length and speed. He becomes someone I've never seen before. A hulking giant with death in his eyes.

"Abomination!" someone in the back of the crowd yells.

"The Goddesses demand blood!"

"Destroy the blight of magic!"

The crowd is tense, toeing that line Kellyn made.

"Oh, the Goddesses will get blood," Kellyn says. "It's just up to you whose they get. The first volunteer may step forward."

I hold my breath, waiting to see how bloody it's about to get, prepared to shut my eyes against it.

One person at the front of the line retreats, apparently deciding we're not worth it. I pray the others will follow suit.

And then there's a ripple in the crowd, as though people in the back are pushing toward the front. Kellyn, with his superior vantage and height, swears.

"City guards!" he calls, and turns tail.

Ah, they *will* have weapons.

He soon surpasses the rest of us with his impressive leg span, and he veers from the road instantly, plunging into the trees. Quick thinking, since we've no guarantee of outdistancing trained guards. Our only hope now is to lose them in the forest.

I hear their shouts behind us as leafy branches scratch my cheeks. My boots sink into the wet earth, slowing me down. Secret Eater throws me off-balance, the weight of my secrets pulling me to the left.

We twist and turn, Temra and I hiking up our skirts to prevent them from getting caught. Petrik has the best of it; his blue robes were replaced by fancy dress pants and a frilly shirt for the morning's service.

Kellyn turns his head over his shoulder regularly to make sure we're all still behind him, and I look back to see where the city folk are.

Not nearly far enough away.

As Kellyn returns his attention to what's in front of him and rounds another tree, he windmills his arms, trying to slow his momentum. "Stop!" he shouts, but it's too late.

A decline lies ahead.

Barely better than a drop, really.

We tip over the edge and slide downward. I lose my feet, going onto my rump as the mud slicks underneath me.

In fact, part of the earth seems to tumble down with us.

Mudslide.

Petrik is falling end over end to my right, and Temra is on her side, her dress coming up to her hips with the slide.

I think I'm screaming. I know Petrik is. I wait for the solid ground that has to follow, surely, and wonder how bad the impact will be.

Instead, everything disappears.

No ground. No mud. No sliding.

I'm falling.

I hear a waterfall churning somewhere nearby, can barely make sense of the noise over all the sensations coursing through me.

And then my knees buckle as my feet crash into the surface and water fills my mouth. At first I can't tell up from down. Then my body slams into a rock, orienting me and bruising me at the same time.

I manage to get my feet under me and kick up toward the surface.

But Secret Eater will have none of that.

The sword is heavier than ever. Each time I swim a few feet upward, it drags me back down. In a full panic now, I twist my fingers around the knot holding it to my waist, but the leather won't loosen now that it's wet.

Something brushes against me in the water, and I shove away, imagining large fish and birds and who knows what else.

Until a hand wraps around my arm and hauls me up. I kick for all I'm worth, and my savior does the same.

When I finally break the surface and take my first drag of blessed air, I think I'll find Kellyn grasping my arm.

But it's Temra.

"I've got you," she says. "I'm not letting go."

We kick to the shore, where I see Kellyn dragging Petrik out of the water. They're screaming at each other, so at least I know they're both breathing.

"—grown man doesn't know how to swim?"

"I was raised in a library! There were no lakes or rivers or damned puddles in the library!"

Once I crawl onto solid ground, I roll onto my back to breathe. Mud and rocks and even small trees still plunge into the lake from where we fell, the slide not done yet.

The guards are blessedly absent, finally, deterred by the dangerous drop.

We made it.

Kellyn urges us up and finds the nearest road leading out of the city. The visible threat may be gone, but it could easily return.

After a few hours, we finally rest. Kellyn clears a path through the trees, and we slump onto the soft mosses on the ground, each of us out of breath, a hundred or so feet from the road.

"Everything's gone," I say. "Our spare clothing, all the supplies, the horse."

"Poor Reya," Temra says.

"They won't hurt the horse," Petrik assures her. "She'll likely have a very good life on that estate. You needn't worry."

"At least we have the weapon. Weapons," she clarifies to avoid specifying the sword. "And we have money, don't we?"

Temra turns to me. "You always carry a large purse on you. Just in case."

At that question, I turn my accusatory stare to Kellyn. "No, we don't have any money. Not anymore."

"Did it fall in the lake?"

"No," Petrik supplies. "The mercenary wouldn't come help us save you unless he was properly compensated. We would have been there sooner if Ziva hadn't had to *convince* him to come."

"You're exaggerating," Kellyn says. "That's not what happened."

"Really?" I cut in. "What would you say happened?"

"I said taking on the whole town would be stupid. I meant we needed a plan before jumping in!"

Petrik is shaking his head before Kellyn finishes his sentence. "You only came once Ziva handed over everything she had on her. You're despicable."

"You all wanted me to take on a hundred villagers! Excuse me for hesitating! Besides, it's not like you didn't pause to grab your books before coming to alert Ziva."

"They were already packed! It didn't even take a second to sling them over my shoulders! I had to grab the weapons, anyway. I knew we would need them in the fight. Don't try to put this on me. You're the one who didn't leap to Temra's defense immediately."

"Never mind that now," Temra says, breaking up the argument. I'm impressed by her sensible tone. She should be furious. *She's* the one who almost died. "We need a new place to lie low, and we need supplies."

Temra, Petrik, and I huddle together, exhausted and wet. "I have some food in my pack," Petrik says. "We can gather fruit to take with us. There's no helping sleeping on the ground at night, but if we stick together, we should be all right."

Temra nods. "We need a destination. Someplace to start afresh."

"We're already headed in the direction of Lisady's Capital," Petrik puts in. "The big city would be a good place for you two to start over and hide."

Oh, I do not like that idea. "We could just as easily lie low in the woods. Away from people and things. We could live off the land."

"We don't know how to hunt, Ziva, and I don't think either of us fancies living off fruit until the end of our days. I'm with Petrik. We should hide in the capital. There will be job opportunities there. We can find a little place to rent and call our own."

"To rent a place, we'd first need money. We don't have any." I can't help the look I slide Kellyn's way.

Before he can speak, Temra says, "We'll sell one of your weapons. The spear. None of us has the skills to use it. This way it'll be put to good use."

I want to argue. I feel a shiver go down my spine just at the thought of living in the capital. But Temra's logic is sound. There's no way for me to talk around it.

"What is happening?" Kellyn asks from behind us all. "You think I'm just going to take your money and run? I'll get us supplies. I'll get you to the next city. We'll be fine. Besides, I'm not going anywhere until I have that magicked longsword. Where the bladesmith goes, I go."

The three of us lower our heads together once more. "I don't like it," I say. Specifically, I don't like *him*.

"Me neither," Petrik agrees.

"Doesn't change the fact that we need him," Temra says.

"You're an excellent fighter," Petrik says. "We'll get by."

"As excited as I am for you to finally acknowledge something about me, I'm not enough fighting power, and you both know it. What happens if we run into more wolves? Or bandits? Or our pursuers?"

She's right.

I hate that she's right.

"Fine," I say. "You tell him he can come."

Now that the immediate threat has passed, I feel myself close to collapsing. Before I can break down in front of everyone, I excuse myself. I count sixty steps before I stop and slump to the wet ground, not caring that my skirts soak up the mud. I'm still mostly damp from the lake anyway.

I almost lost my sister.

Forever.

Everything else may be gone. The money. The horse. The forge. My home.

But it all pales in comparison to the fact that I almost lost the most important thing to me in the world.

I let the tears fall. Allow myself the comfort of crying. I lean my back against a tree and wrap my arms around myself.

How could it all go so wrong? How could I let this happen to us?

My thoughts grow darker and darker as the sun fades, until I hear Temra calling for me.

"Over here," I say. My tears have long since dried. She crouches down beside me, and I hug her to me. "I thought I lost you for a moment."

"I'm all right. You came for me."

"I'll always come for you."

She runs a hand over my hair. "Even when I'm awful to you."

"I forgive you."

"Ziva, what I said, I didn't mean any of it. I was just so relieved to know our family and to feel like there might be a new place, maybe even a better one for us. I just wanted to feel safe, and you were taking that away. You were pointing out the facts, and I didn't want to listen. I put *you* in danger by not listening. I swear to you that I will never do that again. You're my sister, the only family I need. I won't forget it a second time."

"Thank you for saying that."

Now she's the one hugging me, offering me comfort. I feel guilty taking it from my little sister. I'm supposed to be the one protecting and comforting her. I nearly got her killed twice now. I wonder again if she wouldn't be better off separated from me.

"I hate that mercenary," I say after a while. "He's dishonorable. Are you sure we can't send him on his way?"

She doesn't grant my question any weight by responding.

I bury my face against her shoulder. I have to scoot my body to the side to manage it with my superior height. "He slowed us down, Temra. He actually started talking about money while you were in danger. What kind of person does that?"

"He is what he is. We shouldn't expect anything more from him. The one thing we can rely on is that he will always do what we need of him if he wants something from us. That should give us some relief."

"It doesn't." The embarrassing part is that I almost thought we were friends. Someone I could finally tolerate having around who wasn't my sister. I've *never* had that before.

And then he did this.

We may need the mercenary around for our survival, but I give myself full permission to hate him every step of the journey.

"Is it possible," Temra asks, "that you're overreacting?"

"How could I ever overreact where your safety is concerned?"

"I just want to make sure you're not looking for excuses to push him away."

"What nonsense are you speaking?"

"You were starting to like him. Maybe that scared you a bit."

I sit up straight. "First of all, I was not starting to like him." Lie. "Second, liking someone would not scare me." Probably another lie. "Third, he was talking instead of running, Temra. If he had concerns, then there's no reason why he couldn't have brought them up while we were running."

"I don't think he's used to befriending his charges. Bargaining is second nature to him. It's his job, Ziva."

"Will. You. Stop. Defending. Him? I want to be angry!"

She raises a hand to cover her mouth. "All right. You be angry. We hate Kellyn. He's the worst, and if we didn't need him for protection, we'd send him packing."

"Thank you." I inspect her face. "Are you trying to cover up a laugh?"

She keeps the hand in place over her lips. "Never." The sound comes out strangled.

I return my head to her shoulder, letting the lie slide. A comfortable silence sits between us. I relish in the feel of her alive and breathing beside me.

"I want you to know," I say, "no matter what happens, I'll take care of us. You don't have anything to worry about. I'll find work in the capital. We'll rent our own place as quickly as possible. A small apartment, perhaps."

"*We'll* find work," she corrects me, "and then we'll rent a bigger apartment. Or perhaps a small townhome at the city's edge."

"You don't have to—" I start.

"Oh, hush, Ziva. I'm going to work, too. You won't be able to work as a smithy anymore. You won't be doing what you love or receive as lofty of an income. It's going to be tough, but we'll manage it together. Stop trying to take care of me. I'm not a little girl, and you only insult me when you suggest that I won't be helping with anything."

I'm so proud of her, even though her words make my heart ache. "Understood."

I know she's right. What she suggests sounds perfectly reasonable, but I can't help but feel as though I'm failing her in some way.

As though I'm failing my parents.

CHAPTER FOURTEEN

There is now a distinct *us* and *him* separation in our group. Petrik, Temra, and I walk a sharp distance behind Kellyn, staring at the horrible man's back as we walk.

I can't believe I once thought him handsome. He is now more ugly to me than any other person ever could be.

From his pack, Petrik pulls out what meager food we have when we make camp. One round of soggy bread. Some oats that miraculously stayed dry in their leather pouch, and dried meat.

That's it.

"It'll last until we can barter with other travelers on the road," Kellyn says, for once the optimistic one. Is he trying to get back in our good graces?

It's not going to work.

"How far is it to the capital?" Temra wants to know.

"Just over a week."

We get a fire going, and Petrik boils some oats before pulling out his books.

Temra and I stare at the sodden tomes on ancient magic. Though the pages are bloated, the ink still looks mostly intact.

One silent tear slides down the scholar's cheek. Without a word, Petrik sets to turning the pages close to the fire, letting them dry while he waits for the food to cook. I go to help him. I know what it's like to lose my life's work.

Kellyn takes a whetstone to his blade. He opens his mouth occasionally, as though he wishes to say something, then thinks better of it.

Temra approaches the snake, drawing her shortsword. "Let's go, mercenary."

"Are you challenging me to a duel?" he asks without humor.

"It's time for another sparring session."

The whetstone makes a piercing *scritch* as Kellyn almost loses his grip on it. "You still want my help honing your skills?"

"Obviously."

He glances over to where Petrik and I sit. "I thought you all had some private pact not to interact with me."

Temra smiles. Smiles at the man! "They're not exactly endeared to you right now, but I need the practice. Prepare me better for the next time I'm outnumbered four to one."

He grunts before saying, "All right. Let's go."

They step away from the fire, finding another clearing a ways off, but they are still within hearing distance.

"When they came after you," Kellyn says, "what happened?" He holds his longsword up in the air, looking at it rather than my sister.

Temra stretches out her limbs, preparing for their sparring session. "I excused myself to my room. I was debating whether or not to go after Ziva. I'd said some stupid things and needed to apologize.

"Volanna came in first after knocking. She was pleasant as always. She started asking questions about my mother, and I knew she was trying to get me to admit that she had magic. But I lied and attempted to divert the topic.

"Then she started searching my room. I tried to talk her down, but she found the weapons under my bed and shrieked. That brought her sons running; all three of them barged in at once. I kept circling, trying not to let any of them get behind me. Volanna tried to call them off, but they didn't listen to her. She eventually gave in and helped them."

Temra bends down to touch her toes, stands, and pulls one ankle up as close to her back as it will reach. "I didn't expect her to grab me. That was foolish. Even so, I don't know that anything could have been done against so many."

Kellyn's face is a mask of indifference as he sets down his sword. "How did she grab you? Show me."

Temra steps forward and clamps her fingers around Kellyn's forearm like a vise.

"It's instinctual to pull away, but it's far more effective to strike." He shows her a series of moves, bringing the flat edge of his free hand down on Temra's forearm to loosen her grip. He has her grab him again in the same way, then leans into her and mock-knees her in the stomach. "Use the enemy's closeness against them," he says.

After several minutes of going through different motions, Kellyn says, "Even I have trouble being outnumbered. When that happens, you have to intimidate or outthink your opponents. That's harder to teach."

Eventually they raise their swords and take swings at each other. Listening to Temra's explanation of what happened has made my chest grow tight. She must have been so scared and alone. I never should have left her.

Petrik doesn't take his attention off his books. I think he's trying very hard not to cry anymore. "Thousand-year-old books, and I let them fall in a lake." His voice cracks at the end. "I've never felt more of a failure."

"No, Petrik. You didn't fail. You saved Temra. Thank you for coming to get me the moment you knew she was in danger."

"I know I set out on this journey for my book, but we're friends now. Of course I'll look out for her. For you both. I know I'm not good for much, but I'll be here as long as you want me."

He looks over at the sparring pair then, and as I watch him watching my sister, one thing becomes perfectly clear.

He likes her. He's never let Temra see it, but right now I can tell clear as day.

Does he know that the second he shows interest, she'll stop flirting with him? She'll get her victory and become bored. Is that why he holds back in front of her?

He's more clever than I gave him credit for.

When I'm alone again with my thoughts, I can't help but think of my father, since I just left his family for good. I miss him. The sound of his deep voice. His big arms around me. I don't remember much of anything he said to me. But I remember how he made me feel safe.

And I realize now just how much he must have loved my mother to leave everything he knew behind and start a new life with her.

I wonder if that life caught up with him.

Was it religious zealots who broke into our home that night and killed my parents? Did Volanna lie about never knowing what became of her son?

I might be plagued with unanswered questions forever.

That night, Petrik stays up writing in his book by the fire while the rest of us go to sleep. I think he's tracing all the notes he's made, reinforcing the watered ink so it won't fade. No matter how much I tried to convince him to get some rest, he said he'd go to bed when he was ready.

I lie on the hard ground, missing the blankets and bedrolls and tents that were abandoned at the Sotheran estate. My feet are pointed toward the fire, and Temra is curled up against me. My thoughts usually keep me awake, but tonight I feel myself drifting until Temra rises and leaves my side exposed to the night air.

After a few beats of silence, I hear her voice over the top of the crackling fire. "I didn't get a chance to thank you, Petrik."

"Thank me?" he asks.

"For grabbing Ziva and Kellyn and coming after me."

"You don't need to thank me for that. I'm sorry I'm not

skilled enough to have put a stop to them taking you in the first place."

"That's a silly thing to say," she says.

It's quiet for a bit, and then I hear the faint whisper of paper. Is Petrik turning a page or putting down the book? I'd have to sit up to see, and I don't want them to know I'm eavesdropping. Kellyn's snores from across the way prove he's out cold.

"Why did you?" Temra asks.

"Say a silly thing?"

"Bother to save me?"

I think Petrik must be stunned by the question because he doesn't answer for a moment. "I don't understand."

"I'm not the one with magic. You don't need me. You could have taken Ziva and ran without having to deal with overzealous city folk. You probably would have had plenty of time to even go back for the horse and the supplies before fleeing the city."

"As if your sister would ever leave without you."

"You could have lied to her. Told her I was already dead."

My heart hurts to hear such things, but I realize she's right. Petrik didn't have to do any of the things he did.

"It didn't even cross my mind not to save you," he says after another beat of silence.

"Smart and kind. Thank you for being you, Petrik."

I think Temra might start to rise from beside the fire, but Petrik stops her. "You think too little of yourself. Has it ever occurred to you that there's a reason you love the sword? Maybe you were always meant to protect your sister." He pauses. "I know who hunts you. I know the warlord was in town. I saw her stop by the smithy. I'd been biding my time, hoping to approach

Ziva. You guys left right after a visit from Kymora and went to the tavern. I don't understand why you're running, although I imagine it has to do with the fact that Kymora would want to bend your sister to her will. But my point is, I think the Sisters took great care in putting you and Ziva in each other's lives. Your value is just as important and vital as your sister's. You are just as special."

I wish I could see the way they're looking at each other. Or not looking at each other. I want to read the situation and maybe hug Petrik for saying just the right thing.

And knowing that he's chosen to stick with us despite knowing who hunts us—and keeping the secret from Kellyn as well—it endears him to me even more.

Without another word, Temra lies back at my side.

I pretend to be asleep.

We pass many travelers on the road, including—thankfully—a clothing merchant. The second Kellyn spots the tailor, he runs ahead of our group and talks with the man for a while. The conversation ends with Kellyn handing over some coins. The merchant jumps down from his cart, waves away the mercenaries hired to guard his wears, and opens the back of the wagon.

Kellyn climbs in and disappears out of sight.

When he returns some time later, he has several bundles under his arms. He tosses one to each of us.

"They were fresh out of dresses," Kellyn says to Petrik.

"Oh, har!" Petrik says without humor. He veers off to one end of the road to change while Temra and I take the other.

"He feels bad," Temra says as she peels off her hideous dress. I know she means Kellyn.

"As well he should," I say, freeing myself from my own garments.

"He knows he messed up. He's trying to make things right."

"He's going to have to do a lot better than scraps of cloth."

Although, the clothing is quite good. He didn't go stingy, choosing durable leather boots and soft cotton tunics. I pull fabric bracers over my wrists for added warmth, and the belt pulls snugly against my waist to keep everything out of the way.

Temra turns to me once she's done dressing, and her mouth drops open.

"What?" I ask self-consciously.

"Do you see my clothes?" she asks.

"Yes, they're fine. Why?"

"They're too big."

"So? Now's not really the time to be picky."

"*So*, yours fit like a glove! And he chose blue to match your eyes."

"I'm not following."

"He sized you up *exactly*. He obviously has not taken the same care with me." She grins, as though this means something. "Never mind. Let's head back."

When we return, I note that Kellyn has also bought something for himself. He's in emerald, which looks remarkable with his hair. He likely knows it, too, with the way he smirks at me when he catches me watching.

"You look nice," he says.

I don't respond.

Petrik emerges from the trees, dressed in pants and a tunic, like the rest of us. I watch my sister do a double take.

Turns out the scholar had been hiding quite the physique under those robes. You couldn't really tell in the loose-fitting outfit Volanna had him in for the service, but in regular travel clothes that are just a hair too small for him?

He's got a fair amount of lean muscle on him. His dark skin looks remarkable against a white tunic and black pants. The tunic parts in the front, showing a little V of skin.

"I don't suppose you could have found anything bigger?" Petrik asks.

"Self-conscious about your ankles, are you?" Kellyn goads him.

Petrik's boots cover his ankles, but I suspect the pants don't go all the way down to his feet.

"You look great," Temra tells him.

Petrik stops complaining.

That night, when I go to lie on one of the new bedrolls Kellyn purchased for us, I find a bouquet of wildflowers on my pillow.

I turn to Temra. "Did you—"

"Nope." She smiles to herself.

I continue to cherish my nightly routine of sequestering myself away. If arriving in the capital will be anything like Thersa, I will get precious little alone time once we're in another big city.

I've found a sturdy tree to lean against. A small brook provides a comfortable background noise. The air is full of the heady scent of large red flowers with pointed petals and protruding stamens.

I hold my hands out in front of me, stare at the faded calluses on my palms. I long to wrap my fingers around a hammer, to feel the reverberations of steel meeting steel pound up my arm. I miss the smell of smoke and the color of liquid metal.

Even as the self-pity sets in, the isolation refreshes my mind. It energizes me in a way nothing else does, not even sleep. Things seem less bleak. I can do this. We will survive. Temra and I can still have a good life. Maybe someday we won't even need to look over our shoulders anymore. It will never be what it was before, but that doesn't mean I'll hate the rest of my life.

"Petrik says food is ready. He sent me to find you."

Kellyn.

My whole body tenses at the sound of his voice.

"I find that hard to believe. Petrik would send Temra, not you."

"All right. So maybe I volunteered." He crosses his arms over his chest, leans against one of the trees, hooks one foot behind the other.

As though he means to stay and chat.

"I'll be along in a moment," I say.

He doesn't move.

I look heavenward. "That was the polite way of me telling you to leave."

"And I was politely ignoring it." He moves closer, daring to crouch down right in front of where I sit.

"Go away. I don't like you. I don't want to see you." I don't care if I sound childish or petulant. I'm going for clarity.

"I thought we had a real connection for a moment. At the tavern. I want to . . . I want to get back to where we were. It was nice."

"I'm not the one who ruined it," I say, barely thinking over my words first. In a whisper, I add, "I will never forgive you for almost costing me her life."

Kellyn stands back up in one fluid motion. "I—I made a grave mistake. I know that now. I'm not used to jumping into things, especially when there's so much danger to consider."

"You still demanded money from me before helping."

"I did not. You threw money at me as I was standing up to join you. I didn't actually ask for it."

"And yet, you didn't return it."

"It's not for me. I need it to—" He cuts himself off, a look of frustration making a line between his brow. He won't finish whatever it is he started to say.

"I shouldn't have expected anything more from a mercenary. You're attached to no one. No place. Nothing. You only care about yourself. About how much money you have. It's disgusting, and you should be ashamed of who you are."

He looks down at the ground for a moment. "This is how you see me?"

"You haven't shown me anything else." Not entirely true, but I don't take back the words.

A pause sits heavy in the air, and I look up in time to see Kellyn stagger backward. His hand flies to his cheek. "What the—" His jaw cracks in the other direction, as if something struck him.

He immediately takes a fighting stance, thrusting his arms out in front of him. His fingers close tightly into fists.

"Do you see anything?" he shouts to me.

"N-no. What's happening?"

In a decisive movement, he unslings the scabbard from his back before drawing the giant longsword, holding it in both hands before him.

For a split second, I think I see something move in front of him. Just a shimmering outline of a shape. Then a bastard sword materializes in the air before Kellyn.

Just the sword, floating in the air. No wielder.

"The hells?" Kellyn says. Then he has to move as the sword comes arcing toward him. The two blades connect audibly in the near quiet of the woods. "Are you seeing this?" he asks me as he dodges and swings at seemingly nothing.

"Y-yes."

"Is this one of your weapons? Something that strikes all on its own?" Kellyn dodges a blow, leaping backward.

"Definitely not," I answer. "I think you're facing an invisible assailant. Not a floating sword. Ow!" A sharp yank at the back of my head snaps my neck in that direction. There's a force against my scalp, my hair being grasped and pulled.

Then I'm being dragged.

"Kellyn!" I shout. I reach my hands up, my fingers catching on cloth-covered wrists, but through my watered eyes, I can't see anything. The pain is quite real, but there's no one there. Or they are, but I can't see them.

The pain intensifies as I'm pulled backward. I dig my heels into the dirt, but all that manages to do is increase the pain at my scalp. I think I briefly catch sight of Kellyn trying to make his way to me, but then he's forced to face his attacker again. He can't help me.

I cry out again as my heel catches on a tree root, the burning sensation in my scalp escalating. The tension loosens only briefly as I feel something strike at my leg, causing the root to lose its grip on me. Then I'm being forced backward once more.

If I could just get my feet under me. Get some leverage to—

I can't help the whimper that escapes my throat as a more intense burst of pain radiates from the back of my head. I feel clumps of my hair come free as I flip over, landing face-first on the ground.

But then the pressure is blessedly gone. I get my feet under me, ignoring the pain. I look up to find—

Temra. She's there, wielding Midnight, the blade a dark ebony, and circling to find whatever it was that held me.

Just as before, another sword materializes, this time in the new assailant's hand. Temra doesn't even flinch at the appearance.

"Temra, run!" I shout.

She blatantly ignores me, and before I can do anything else, she leaps toward that floating sword, slashing just below it. The bastard sword curves down to block her strike, but Temra doesn't pause. She spins to get more momentum behind her swing and sends it upward, toward where a head might be.

The attacker finally finds their own rhythm, sending a volley of strikes at my baby sister.

I gasp in terror as I watch her block blow after blow, before sending her own at the attacker with battle cries and impressive footwork.

Kellyn still deals with his own invisible assailant.

How is this even possible?

I search the ground for something I can use, and my eyes land on a sturdy tree branch. I place myself behind the floating sword as it advances toward Temra and swing. The branch connects, and I feel the strike bounce up my arms. Temra uses the distraction I made to thrust her blade forward.

A cry rises from the invisible person, and Temra draws back her blade, the point now stained with blood. There's a *thud*, and then a red stain floats above the ground, moving forward and backward slightly.

With the strained breathing of the injured person.

Temra removes their weapon before running to help Kellyn. Meanwhile, I lean forward, grab a fistful of cloth, and tug. It catches on something. I feel around until I find a clasp at a throat. I sense fitful movement before everything stills and the rest of the garment comes free.

Beneath is a woman bearing the warlord's colors, her glassy eyes unseeing. And the cloak I removed materializes once it's no longer being worn. It's a finely stitched cloth bearing a striped pattern of tans and beiges. I would think it completely unremarkable if I hadn't seen what it could do once worn.

The assailant's forearms are also invisible, and I remove her gloves, which likewise materialize, bearing the exact same stitching as the cloak.

I turn around in time to see Kellyn make contact with his attacker just before Temra reaches him. His strike connects with flesh, bone, sinew—each of these is revealed once the material of the cloak rips with the force of the blow.

And then an arm appears on the ground. I stare at it a moment, unable to process what happened while deep screams fill the air.

Once I realize that Kellyn *cut it off*, I immediately start gagging. Temra silences the attacker's cries with a well-placed thrust through the heart.

No one moves as we listen for any more attackers. But all is still. No more bastard swords appear, which must clearly be the preferred weapon among Kymora's men. Temra and Kellyn are both breathing heavily, and I tenderly touch my scalp. Feels as though I've got a bald spot about the size of two finger pads in the back.

Now that the danger is gone, I round on my sister, prepared to give her the tongue-lashing of her life for not fleeing when I told her to.

Instead, I come face-to-face with an enraged Kellyn.

"Do you want to tell me what in the twin hells just happened?"

I blink.

"Invisible assassins are where I'm more than allowed to draw the line. Those weren't sent by your family. One of the assailants tried to drag you off. This is what you were running from back in Lirasu. Who is hunting you and why?"

Temra and I share a look, and I still don't know whether or not to trust Kellyn. If this had happened before his poor behavior at the Dancing Kiwi, maybe I wouldn't hesitate, but now that I know what he's really like—

"We're on the run from Warlord Kymora Avedin," Temra says, making the decision for us both. I suppose keeping him in the dark isn't really an option should he threaten to leave.

"Kymora," he deadpans, "as in the former leader of the kingdom's armies? Currently the most dangerous person in all of Ghadra? Unbeatable swordswoman. That Kymora?"

"Yes."

Kellyn's eyes widen, as though he hadn't actually expected Temra to confirm it.

"She's after me," I hurry to explain. "Because of what I can do. She wants me to make weapons for her army so she can overthrow the territory leaders and rule all of Ghadra herself."

"How could you possibly know that?" Kellyn says.

"She cut herself on Secret Eater. I heard her."

Kellyn looks between me and Temra, as though he's not sure where to settle his eyes. "And just how do invisible assassins fit in?"

Temra stands by me, offering her strength during this confrontation. "We honestly don't know anything about that."

"Wait," I say as something occurs to me. "The cotton spinner. The only other girl with magic. She must be working for Kymora. She's made cloaks and gloves that render the wearers invisible."

"Great," Kellyn says. "So there's the potential for more invisible assassins coming our way."

In the silence that follows his statement, a few birds overhead start chirping to one another. The trees sway in the wind, and the shifting clouds finally let the sun shine down through gaps in the canopy.

And then there are hurried steps on the forest floor. Temra and Kellyn raise their weapons once more, turning toward the threat.

Petrik is running as fast as he can, brandishing the staff in two hands. He stops once he reaches us, looks down at the bodies on the ground. "Everyone all right? What did I miss?"

Kellyn shakes his head. "Did you know about this? That the warlord is hunting them?"

"I suspected," Petrik answers after his initial surprise. Then the ground captures his attention. The severed arm still wears a glove, so it's invisible from just below the elbow to the tips of its fingers. Either Petrik's totally unaffected by the gore or he's so blinded by his fascination with magic, because he bends down, feels around the invisible arm, registers that it's a glove, removes it, and then goes searching for the rest of the magically enhanced fabric. He gathers it all and folds the blood-soaked garments to his side.

Kellyn shakes his head at the scholar as he returns his sword once more to its scabbard. "I'm out."

"What?" I blurt.

"I'm not about to piss off a warlord. If she knows I'm protecting you, my life is over."

"You—you can't abandon us!"

"You didn't tell me what was happening. If I had known the full facts I never would have taken this job."

I'm shaking my head, not wanting to believe what he's saying. "You can't be that selfish! We need you."

"It was selfish of you not to tell me everything," he counters. "I should have known what I was up against, what I was risking."

"You risk your life every day being a mercenary!"

"That's different than going against a warlord and her private army, and you know it."

I look down at my feet, a little ashamed, but mostly angry. At Kellyn. At myself. At everything.

The silence stretches and stretches, no one moving. I'm torn between running and staying right where I am so I don't draw attention to myself. I feel like crying for some reason.

Kellyn growls, and I look up to find him glaring at me. No one else. Me. "I will get you to the next city as I promised, but after that I'm done."

CHAPTER FIFTEEN

I have a restless mind, one that fixates on the things that bother me the most.

And right now that's Kellyn.

I remember him drunk and fighting against another mercenary. I remember the way he slaughtered a pack of wolves, kicked one off me before it could go for my throat. The way he looks at me when he tries to understand what I'm thinking.

And over and over again, the way he hesitated before saving my sister.

Fighting invisible assassins.

Buying me new clothes.

Putting flowers on my pillow.

He thinks you're a beauty.

The next night after Kymora's assassins attacked us, Temra

and Kellyn are laughing during her sparring session over something. I think they're reliving the high of the other night's battle.

Petrik and I scowl from the sidelines.

How can she act like nothing is the matter? Like nothing is changing? Kellyn is abandoning us.

When I manage not to think about the mercenary, I watch Petrik and Temra together.

"Let me help you with that," she says while he cooks. She stirs the pot while Petrik adds ingredients. Their fingers brush when Temra hands the spoon over to Petrik so he can taste the food for a flavor check. She watches his lips while he swallows.

And though he keeps a carefully neutral face, there's some extra color on his cheeks.

And I can't help but feel like an outcast all of a sudden.

I hadn't anticipated this happening.

Petrik has definitely become one of us. If his help in the beginning hadn't been the deciding factor, then him saving my sister's life by running for help solidified it.

I shouldn't feel as though Petrik is taking my sister from me. He's not. And yet—

I begin to feel like I don't quite fit here anymore.

Which is probably ridiculous, but I feel it all the same.

I wander from our camp, as I so often do when my help's not needed, but damn it all, Kellyn's following me. I see him out of the corner of my eyes, keeping his distance yet watching over me.

"You're hovering," I say.

"We were recently attacked, and there's every reason to expect more ambushes."

Oh.

I'd honestly forgotten his whole purpose was to keep us safe. And he's doing just that. He's protecting me. Not trying to get me alone.

What am I supposed to do? Just pretend like he's not there? As if.

I want to say something. Maybe apologize for not telling him about Kymora? But I'm still angry at him, and the whole conversation would only be uncomfortable anyway.

But isn't silence worse?

He surprises me by talking first. "I don't want to leave things as they are now."

"Me neither," I answer. Then I blurt, "I'm sorry for not telling you about the warlord. You had a right to know."

"I did." His voice has grown incredibly soft.

"I didn't mean to put you in danger. I was only thinking about my sister. I needed to keep her safe. I should have taken the time to think about who else I might be hurting by letting them aid us. I'm so sorry. I don't hold your leaving us against you."

After a pause, he says, "I'm sorry about your sister. About what happened in Thersa. If I can't make it right, then how can I make it better?"

I turn to face him; the sun is sinking, and I can barely make out his expression through the space between us.

But it's so sincere, so open, it nearly takes my breath away.

"Why do you care?" I ask. "You're leaving us. We'll never see each other again. So why does it matter?"

"If I did stay, would that make it better? Do you want me to stay?"

Why do I feel like that question is asking more than one thing?

"Would you stay if I asked?" I honestly want to know.

He's quiet, but he meets my eyes. My every instinct is to look away, but I force myself to hold steady. Not just to prove to myself that I can do it, but because I need to convey my seriousness.

"If it were just you and just me, then yes, I would."

"But it's not," I say. There's Temra and Petrik. Why does that matter? What does he mean by that?

"But it's not," he repeats.

I don't say anything, but Kellyn's footsteps grow closer.

"You remember when I brought up my family?" he says.

I nod.

"They're who I have to consider."

Oh. Oh, of course. It's just like how every decision I make has to take Temra into consideration. Because I made this sword, she is in danger from Kymora. If Kellyn were to help us, his family would be in danger if Kymora tried to use them against him.

"I understand," I say.

Kellyn raises a hand, lets one finger drift through the hair to the side of my face, and I think I stop breathing. When his finger gets to the end of my almost-shoulder-length hair, he gives the strand a gentle tug.

"If I'm passing through Lisady's Capital in the future, could I stop by?"

I can't think words right now. I think that's why I have to ask, "Why?"

"To see you," he says simply, taking back his hand and letting it drop to his side.

"Why?" I ask again, because I *really* cannot think of any other words, and my skin is crawling with anxiety. I want it to go away. I want to have this conversation with Kellyn. I think.

"Because I like you, and I want to see you again."

I laugh without humor. "You can't like me. I can barely talk around you. I'm very awkward, and I don't like people."

"You talk just fine when you're angry or when you manage to keep yourself from overthinking. You're not awkward. Only you think you're awkward. As for not liking people, that's fine. I don't really like people, either. Maybe we could not like people together."

His words are preposterous, and I can't agree. I want to, but it's too terrifying. And *Temra*. I have to remind myself he almost cost me Temra.

Didn't he?

Yes, he hesitated.

Is it possible that you're overreacting? Temra's words from before resurface. *I just want to make sure you're not looking for excuses to push him away.*

How could I be overreacting? Petrik was also furious with Kellyn for hesitating!

But Petrik likes *Temra, so of course he would overreact. And he's always actively looking to point out Kellyn's mistakes.*

Maybe Kellyn only hesitated long enough to think the situation through.

"What if I wrote to you?" he asks, interrupting my thoughts. "Could we exchange letters?"

Letters? Letters aren't scary. I get to think over everything I want to say before I write it down. Don't have to worry about him searching my face for hidden meaning.

"All right," I say before I can think twice about it.

"Then I'll write to you." He nods once, as though satisfied with the way this conversation turned out.

"And I'll . . . I'll see if I can find a way to make you that long-sword. You can pick it up the next time you come through the city. Temra will get it to you."

He looks like he's fighting a smile. "Thank you."

As far as capital cities go, the one in Princess Lisady's Territory isn't as large as I feared it would be. In fact, it doesn't look much bigger than Lirasu. The streets aren't packed with people like they were in Thersa. I can actually walk the road without bumping into anyone. To the south end of the city, I can see the newly erected castle, where Princess Lisady resides. It's the largest structure in sight with pink flags at the top of the towers.

I can live here. Here is fine. I just need a place to call my own. A place to feel safe, where no one can see me. For now, a room at an inn will do.

But first, we need to sell this weapon without drawing attention to ourselves. We find the nearest pawnshop, and now the four of us huddle in the gap between the building and the chandler next door.

"It's simple," Temra says. "I'll go in and sell the spear."

"You can't," Petrik says before I can. "Neither you nor your sister can be seen with a magical weapon. Any of her spies will be on the lookout for women carrying Zivan blades."

"I agree," Kellyn says. "Kymora already knows we were

headed in this direction. If your relatives didn't tell her, then the sudden loss of her invisible soldiers would have clued her in. There could easily be people in the city looking for you."

"It's my weapon," I say, ignoring them. "I'm the most qualified to sell it and get the most money from the sale." It will be uncomfortable. I loathe negotiating, but selling this spear will set us up for months. I can do this for us.

"If I can't be risked selling it, then neither can you," Temra says with finality.

"I could take it in," Petrik says.

Temra, Kellyn, and I all eye Petrik. He's so uncomfortable outside of his scholar's attire. And the way he holds himself—he looks nothing like a fighter.

"If you walk in there, the vultures will eat you alive." The mercenary shakes his head. "And you were seen by their family." He points to Temra and me with his thumb. "By now the warlord could know you're with them. You shouldn't be the one to enter."

"But that leaves—" I start.

"Me," Kellyn finishes. "It has to be me. I'm the only one not under suspect. No one will think twice about me selling a magical weapon because I'm *actually* a mercenary, and I look the part."

"Absolutely not," Petrik says. He grabs my arm to pull me aside. "I don't trust him. He'll run off with the money from the sale and leave us behind."

"I can still hear you," Kellyn says.

"Ziva, let me do it," Petrik says.

"Just let me do it," Temra puts in. "I'll be in and out in two minutes, tops."

If we weren't in such a hurry, perhaps I would take the time to ponder the fact that everyone is deferring to me. When did my decision become the final say in the matter? When did I become the leader of this poorly-stitched-together group?

"Ziva—" Petrik starts.

"Enough," I say.

I put my fingers to my temples, as though that will help me think. I'd rather be the one to take this risk. If anyone is going to get caught, it should be me.

But if I'm caught, I'll leave Temra on her own, protecting that Twins-forsaken sword.

"Kellyn will do it. He hasn't gone back on his word. Not once." I force myself to look him in the eye. "Do you promise to sell this spear and return the earnings to us?"

Kellyn steps forward. "I do."

I believe him, and I think he knows I do, but seeing Petrik's hesitancy, Kellyn slides the massive longsword scabbard from off his back and tosses it to Petrik, sword and all.

Petrik fumbles with the weapon before dropping it.

"Why don't you keep watch over that for me until I return? If you can manage to hoist it at all." Then he takes the spear and dashes to the front of the pawnshop.

And we wait.

"If I can manage to hoist it," Petrik says in a laughably mocking tone of Kellyn's voice, but Temra and I manage straight faces. Petrik bends down, wraps both hands around the scabbard, and heaves.

He holds the weapon triumphantly in both hands, but after a minute, his arms start shaking. He tosses the sword aside and side-eyes Temra, as though hoping she didn't notice.

Seeing that she did, he sighs before fixing his attention on the back of the shop.

"What are you doing?" Temra asks him.

"Like I said, I don't trust him. I want to make sure he doesn't try to run out the back with our money."

I roll my eyes. "And leave his precious longsword behind? He wouldn't."

Temra says, "With that much money, he could buy a new one ten times over."

"Yes, thank you, Temra, that comment is definitely helping things," I snap.

"I'm just saying."

"The mercenary was the only choice. Now let's just wait before we start getting cynical."

There's some foot traffic on the main street behind us. The smell of fresh rainfall was present throughout the entire journey, but now that we've arrived in the capital, the city has covered it up, replacing it with body odors and horse manure.

Those in the city wear leathers with fur embellishments at their cuffs and collars. They appear to be quite the community of hunters, I observe, as I watch a cart of antlers go by. Many in the street have bows slung over their shoulders.

Though the rain lessened the more we traveled southeast, it hasn't stopped. Even now our boots are covered in mud clear up to our knees. The baths we had in Thersa were a lifetime ago. We're hungry, we're wet, we're cranky.

And we're going to have to stay in a public house until we find a place of our own. I try not to grimace.

"Is that him?" Temra asks shortly after I hear a door slamming.

She's not pointing toward the front of the shop, where Kellyn entered, but at the back, where a tall figure is walking away.

"That's not him," I say. Kellyn doesn't look like that from behind. I would know. I spent so much time glaring at his back. He's broader, holds himself straighter than whoever this fellow is.

"There's not many guys that freakishly tall," Petrik says. "Kellyn!"

The figure turns.

And there's no mistaking that it's the mercenary.

Kellyn winks at me, jingling a heavy purse of money in one hand, before he takes off like a pack of hungry beasts is behind him.

Temra, Petrik, and I freeze for one moment. Confusion takes over. I was so sure that wasn't Kellyn until I saw his face. Temra and Petrik recover before I do, leaping after the mercenary, but it isn't long before I surpass them with my longer legs.

"Trust the mercenary," Petrik says. "Might as well trust a starving lion!" He falls behind Temra and me quickly, despite his best efforts to keep up.

My face turns beet red, but it has nothing to do with the exertion. Kellyn just made a fool of me. Both Petrik and Temra will blame me for this. We can't lose our money. Not again.

There are so many threats I'd like to hurl at that long, muscled back. First among them is to halt before I unsheathe Secret Eater and detach the mercenary's knees from the rest of his body. I could do it so easily.

It's a fanciful thought, but one I would never carry out. I'll leave the violence to Temra.

Kellyn pushes people over in his haste, angry shouts following in his wake. He leaps over a parked wagon, slides around a shop corner, barrels into a merchant's cart full of fruit. I hear Petrik slip on a rolling orange from behind me. Temra loses ground as she has to veer around the overturned cart.

And I'm hot on the mercenary's heels, having jumped the obstacle.

That good-for-nothing wastrel. That lying, scheming, self-obsessed, worthless little worm of a man. When I get my hands on him, I'm going to yell until I lose my voice.

He's heading farther and farther out of town. Does he mean to traverse back to the road out of the city? He won't have anywhere to hide then!

Not that he's been trying to hide. He made a point of slamming the door out of the pawnshop, after all, did he not? And he brandished that bag of coins at me. Taunting me, even. Daring me to chase after him.

Almost as if—

I stop in my tracks. Temra bashes into my arm, not stopping in time. The panting sound behind us must be the scholar.

"What are you doing? He's getting away!" Temra screams.

"Something's wrong," I say.

"You can tell me while we run," she says, yanking my arm and trying to physically pull me after Kellyn.

"He left his sword," I say.

"I already mentioned he could buy a new one."

"But that one was special to him. He loves Lady Killer. And he's—well, it's like he's leading us somewhere."

Kellyn disappears around a bend in the road, just where the houses of the city end and morph into trees, where the noises of the market fade into animal calls. Secluded. Private.

"If he wanted to run off with the money, he wouldn't have made so much noise about it," I say. "He would have been sneaky. Quiet."

"He's an arrogant—bastard," Petrik says between breaths. "This was exactly his style."

"No, I don't think—"

The foot traffic had been thinning, but all of a sudden about thirty people step onto the road. People in red with falcons on their chests.

And Kellyn.

Kellyn is among them.

Standing there like he knows them.

Only, he still looks off to me. He's holding himself differently. And his stature isn't quite right.

What has happened to him?

"You!" Petrik bellows across the road to where Kellyn stands among all of Kymora's soldiers.

Temra is speechless. For while she thought him capable of running off with our money, she didn't think he'd do this.

Neither did I.

"But Secret Eater," I say quietly to my companions. "I cut him."

He must have changed his mind. Maybe Kymora got to him in

Thersa, convinced him to lead us to a place where she had more forces stationed. I suppose if she offered him enough money—

But Kymora isn't among her soldiers. If she knew we'd be here, then where is she?

"Ziva Tellion!" a woman who is almost as tall as I am shouts. "Hand over your weapons or prepare to have them removed from you by force."

"Eat dirt," Petrik says.

Temra nods at him in approval. "Yeah, shove off, lady. You can have them when you rip them from our cold, dead fingers."

Petrik snaps his neck in her direction. "Perhaps we need not take it that far."

"When you're vastly outnumbered," Temra says through clenched teeth, "sometimes you have to rely on intimidation."

"And the mercenary also said he'd be right back with our money! So clearly he's a great source of wisdom!"

"Shh," I tell them. "Let me think."

"While you do that—" Petrik cocks back his arm and flings his staff. It flies end over end toward the closest of Kymora's guards, a big man with a mud-colored beard nearly down to his navel.

And while the weapon worked splendidly against untrained city folk, this man catches the staff in one hand.

But the staff has to return to its wielder, so the guard is dragged forward as the staff jerks back toward Petrik. His feet make long trails through the mud on the road as he wrestles with the stick, trying to find purchase.

Petrik's face is horrified as the guard grows closer and closer. Kymora's soldiers seem mildly perplexed as they do nothing but watch the scene with interest.

The bearded guard has his full focus on the staff, as though now it's become a personal struggle between himself and the stick. He clearly doesn't think us an actual threat.

Which is why his face flits to surprise when Temra sticks him with her shortsword.

A heavy breath escapes his lips before he falls, and the staff finally reaches Petrik once more. He wastes no time before casting it again. A second guard catches it, but she's smart enough to let go before she can be dragged by the weapon. When Petrik throws it a third time, Kymora's soldiers are finally ready. The third guard has his bastard sword out and nicks the staff as it reaches him. Making contact, the spear flies back to Petrik.

That's when the enemy finally advances.

Twenty-nine guards left. They all but ignore Petrik and come running for me and Temra. My sister is prepared, her sword ready for the onslaught, but she can't take on that many trained soldiers.

And I'm useless in a fight. Temra is far too close for me to pull out Secret Eater. I'd risk hurting her or Petrik.

"Get behind me," Temra says, stepping forward to block my body with hers.

I'm both touched and infuriated by the gesture. "They won't hurt me. Kymora wants me alive to build weapons for her army. You get behind me!"

They're almost upon us. Petrik sidles closer, preparing to throw again.

And then we're surrounded. The three of us put our backs to each other, eyeing the soldiers. Kellyn is among them, forming ranks as if he's trained with these men and women.

We must make a truly pathetic spectacle. Two guards grab me by the arms, easily separating me from the rest of the group. A third takes Secret Eater from my side.

No, not the sword!

I kick and yank with my arms, but it does no good. They're firm with me, yet they don't retaliate with any strikes of their own.

I watch as another soldier tries to wrest the staff from Petrik. He tosses it straight up into the air and then sinks to his knees on the ground, waiting for the stick to come back and strike the guard right on the head. But it isn't long before another red-breasted soldier takes the weapon from him and cracks the stick in two across one knee.

"No, you fool!" the woman barking out orders says. "Kymora ordered them and their weapons brought back to us. One of these girls is the smithy gifted with magic."

Realizing his mistake, the guard takes off running.

Is Kymora's wrath so terrible as to send a grown soldier fleeing from a misunderstanding?

My captors drag me toward the soldier in charge. *One of these girls*, she'd said. They don't know who is who.

"I'm the blacksmith," I say hurriedly. "You don't need my sister. Let her go. I'll come quietly."

Temra has already been disarmed, though she certainly didn't go quietly. The men around her are covered in cuts and scrapes.

"Let her go," I say again. "Please."

"We don't need the spare," the soldier responds, "and we're not about to leave witnesses."

That fact sinks low in my chest.

"I'm the spare," Temra and I say at the same time.

What is she doing? "That's Ziva," I say, pointing to her.

Temra shakes her head. "I'm the little sister. That's Ziva right there."

As we start talking over each other, the commanding soldier's voice silences us. "I'm not amused," she says. "And I have no problem taking you both so that Kymora can deal with you herself. Let's go." The surly soldier looks out over the last of her force. "One of you, kill the boy. We don't need him."

Petrik's face goes still, and Temra and I scream our protests. I try to free myself, try to go for a weapon, for Petrik, anything.

The guard holding our weapons walks toward a row of saddled horses I hadn't noticed before, tied to the trees along the road. The soldier nearest Petrik draws his sword.

"Kellyn," I say, twisting my head toward him. "Please, don't let this happen. You're better than this. You have to be."

But the mercenary doesn't even turn at the sound of his name. He watches as the guard advances, an unmoved look upon his face.

Petrik says something to the advancing soldier while holding up his hands. I can't hear what he says, but there's no shame at all in trying to bargain for one's life.

The soldier about to kill him rears back his weapon, preparing to thrust.

I close my eyes. I can't watch this.

CHAPTER SIXTEEN

I flinch as I hear it, the sound of a weapon sinking into flesh. A cry escapes my lips, but a strange sound comes out of Temra's.

Was that . . . a relieved laugh?

My eyes fly open. Instead of finding Petrik skewered, I see Kellyn with his longsword plunged into the soldier's gut.

That can't be right. He left his longsword with us. And he was standing right next to me two seconds ago.

He still is.

My neck turns from one Kellyn to the next, trying to make sense of it.

"The cotton spinner," I whisper. She's somehow made a mask of Kellyn's face. I knew something was off about the Kellyn next to me. He's not tall enough to be Kellyn, and he's leaning with all his weight on one hip. I've never seen the mercenary do that before.

Temra hears my words and puts it together herself. Then she shouts, "Took you long enough!" to the real Kellyn.

"I had to figure out which way you went. Thanks for leaving me behind!" He draws his sword out of the stomach of the man he just killed. "You could have yelled for me or something. Let me know someone was taking you aw—"

His eyes land on himself. Kellyn tilts his head to one side, then the other. "That's uncanny."

"You failed to mention you had a twin," Petrik says from beside him.

"I don't."

"Don't just stand there!" Kymora's commanding guard says. "You five, take care of the boys!"

The rest stay behind to watch over Temra and me: their precious cargo. The others sprint for Petrik and Kellyn. Petrik holds up his fists, as though he has any clue how to use them in hand-to-hand combat. Meanwhile Kellyn brandishes his longsword.

"They're outnumbered," Temra says to me.

"I know."

"They're going to die."

"I know!"

"Do something!"

What am I supposed to do? I've got a soldier in red on either side of me, pinning my arms. Temra has twice as many guards surrounding her. Trained soldiers everywhere. Horses behind us. Weapons on every side.

One of Kymora's men is holding all our weapons, about to attach them to the horse just a little to my right.

I'm terrified. I know these men will hurt me if I try to break their hold, but I have to try. For Petrik.

For Kellyn.

The guard at my right has a bastard sword sheathed at his waist on the left. I wedge my knee between the scabbard and his leg.

Then I jerk it upward as hard as I can.

The guard gasps and wheels backward from the pressure of the pommel digging into his stomach. At the same time he releases my arm, I place the flat of my boot against the guard on my left and shove.

And I'm free.

I know it'll only be a second before the guards respond, so I race for the horse. I snatch Secret Eater, feel its horrible weight in my grasp.

And with all the strength I possess, I throw it, scabbard and all.

As soon as it leaves my fingertips, rough hands grab me, yank me back, but I watch the sword fly. It spins in a circle through the air, sailing over heads, traveling faster than the running guards.

Until it lands far to Kellyn's left.

Doesn't matter.

The guards have already reached him.

"Petrik!" I scream. "The sword. Get Kellyn the sword!"

Understanding, the scholar bolts for where it landed, leaving Kellyn to deal with the soldiers alone.

"Great. Just bloody helpful of you!" Kellyn screams to Petrik's back. With two hands, the mercenary flies toward the first guard, cutting him just below the armpit, where the chain mail doesn't extend. He goes down.

Two more reach him at the same time. Kellyn sweeps his blade back and forth in front of himself, not letting them advance. He loses his balance on the next pass, and as one of the guards takes the opening, I call out.

But it was only a feint.

Kellyn takes off the guard's arm and spins in the same move to get behind the second one, stabbing him in the back.

The lead guard growls. "Will someone please do their job and end those two?"

All but the guards restraining Temra and me take off into the fray. The one shouting orders backs toward us. "Get them saddled." Temra and I have our arms wrenched behind our backs, and we're yanked toward the horses.

And then Petrik has the sword. He tosses it to Kellyn, who has to drop a hand from Lady Killer's hilt to catch the broadsword.

"I already have a weapon, you idiot! What good is this thing?"

"Kellyn, use it!" I shriek at him as someone hauls me into a saddle. "And, Petrik, run! Get as far away from Kellyn as you can!"

To my amazement, both listen. Kellyn drops his longsword and puts Secret Eater in his good hand. With his left, he reaches up to remove the scabbard and tosses it to the ground.

I can hear the magic humming to me from here. Maybe it's my imagination that the sword glows at being released from its confines after so long, but I swear I see it sparkle in the sunlight, and Kellyn adjusts his grip at the unexpected weight. It's only a broadsword, after all, designed with the potential to be held in one hand.

Meanwhile, Petrik looks over his shoulder while he runs from Kellyn, waiting to see what's about to happen.

"Start swinging!" I shriek. One of the guards slaps me up the side of the head.

"Not another word," he says.

Kellyn looks around in confusion at the soldiers who haven't quite reached him. "What, now?" I can only imagine what he must be thinking. How could a sword that reveals secrets be of use to him in his current situation?

"Yes, now!" Temra says.

Perhaps because he simply wants to test the weapon out, or because he wants to try to intimidate the oncoming soldiers, maybe he's humoring Temra—I don't know—but Kellyn starts swinging.

The first three soldiers grab at their middles before sinking to the earth, blood dripping from slashes in their stomachs. Kellyn looks at the blade before meeting my eyes. Then I notice his eyes turn inward, as the secrets of the soldiers crowd his mind.

He comes to as another guard reaches him. He holds Secret Eater high in the air and brings it down, cutting the soldier in half from head to toe. The sword continues down, cutting a heavy swath through the earth. Kellyn has to pull it out with a few tugs.

I feel my stomach turn over as I watch the destruction caused by the blade I made.

I want to close my eyes, to pretend I'm anywhere else. But I force myself to watch. I should see this. See what I've done.

The rest of Kymora's soldiers are soon to follow. They fall to

Secret Eater in waves, helpless to get anywhere close enough for a fair fight.

The last soldier tries to hold up his bastard sword against the strike that doesn't even reach him, but his sword splits in two, as if it were made of butter. The strike goes so far that the power of the blade bites into his neck, hitting the major artery. Blood shoots everywhere as he dies.

When Kellyn turns to me, I realize I'm not being held by our enemies any longer. They've run. Same with the ones holding Temra. Only the one in charge remains. She's at her horse, though not mounting.

She fiddles with something before coming up with a loaded crossbow. It fires before I can blink, before I can call out a warning to Kellyn.

And either instinct or something else compels Kellyn to raise the sword high and bring it down. The wave causes the arrow to splinter as it hits an invisible force. The guard tries again, but her second shot is met with the same result. Finally, Temra pulls one of my never-dulling daggers she still had hidden in her tunic and finishes her.

As soon as it's done, as soon as all our enemies are gone, Kellyn flings Secret Eater away from himself. He collapses to his knees and vomits in the grass.

And as if that were the last thing my stomach needed to see, my gut rolls again, and I follow suit.

When Kellyn finally composes himself, he resumes standing and looks toward me. "What in the twin hells is that thing?"

"That's Secret Eater."

"Horse shit."

"It—it has long-range abilities."

The line of Kellyn's throat is so tight, you could run a bow across it and make music. He stares after where he discarded the weapon. "That's what Kymora is after. You lied to me."

I shake my head fiercely. "I never lied. I didn't tell you everything, but I didn't lie. She does want me to make magical weapons for her army, but I also ran off with the one she commissioned. Don't you realize what she could do with it? What anyone could do with it? I had to keep it safe. You were a stranger. We couldn't trust you. What if you ran off with the weapon and left us?"

"Dammit, bladesmith! I told you I needed to know what I was getting into. And now Kymora's men have seen me."

Temra scoffs from nearby. She toes the dead imposter, who still wears Kellyn's face. "Clearly they'd already seen you. Otherwise, the cotton spinner couldn't have done that."

I'm not about to argue that that's not necessarily true. We don't know how her magic works. She could have made the cloth to match the face of whoever the wearer was looking at when putting it on, for all we know. But what we do know is that some of Kymora's soldiers escaped. She'll know soon just exactly where we are. And who is in our company.

"I don't care! I shouldn't be mixed up in all of this," Kellyn says. "I have a life, a *good* life, and I wasn't planning on losing it all while you three tried to play at being heroes."

Kellyn bends over the dead body wearing his face. He moves his hands about the man's neck and pulls upward. Off comes the mask. Once it's no longer on the body, it morphs back into regular cloth. A monochrome of blues from navy to sky form the spectrum of colors on the fabric. Kellyn uses the nearest fallen sword to shred the thing to pieces.

Petrik winces at the destruction of the magical object. Then he looks up to Kellyn in astonishment. "We thought you'd sold us out to the warlord."

"And run off with our money," Temra adds.

Kellyn looks between Temra and Petrik before his eyes settle on me. "And you? Did you assume I had betrayed you?"

My mouth falls open. "I—" No other words will come out. I knew there was something off, but Kellyn's angry stare prevents me from speaking.

"I see," he bites out, fury still written in every aspect of his posture. He unties a purse from his belt and tosses it at my feet. "The money from the spear."

I want to say something. Anything. But what is there to say? I can't make right what I withheld from him. I can't fix that Kymora knows he's been helping us.

I can't even muster up the proper amount of guilt, because he saved us. He was outnumbered thirty to one, and he risked his life for us anyway. He could have easily run off with the money once he saw that we were no longer waiting for him, but he didn't. He came for us. And he's not even demanding more money for coming for us.

I can't help but admire him.

Stiffly, I reach down and pick up the purse.

The mercenary searches among the bodies for his fallen longsword. Meanwhile, Petrik and Temra collect their weapons.

My sister grabs Secret Eater and hands it to me. I find the scabbard and attach the weapon to my side once more.

When we're all set to rights, the four of us stare at one another.

"I'm in this now," Kellyn says. "Whether I wanted to be or not. There's nothing left but to stick with you lot until something is done about that." He jerks his attention to the sword at my side. "What's the new plan?" His tone is furious, biting. I flinch from it.

"Let's get moving," Temra suggests. "Then we can strategize on the way."

"Our only option right now is the road to Briska," Kellyn says. "Otherwise it's back down to Lirasu, where we know the warlord will have men stationed."

"Then we'll take the road to Briska," she says.

CHAPTER SEVENTEEN

We help ourselves to the warlord's horses. There's no sense in leaving perfectly capable and trained beasts behind. Stored among their tack is plenty of food and supplies. So much that there's no need for us to purchase anything extra. We take everything we can fit onto four beasts and then mount.

It's only when Temra and I are squared away that I notice Petrik still on the ground, leading his mount by the reins.

"What are you doing?" I ask him.

"Leading the horse."

"Why?"

He doesn't answer.

Temra tactfully places a hand over her mouth until she

can square her features. "Do you know how to ride?" she asks him.

"Certainly. I've read a number of books on the subject."

"But have you ever done it?"

He doesn't answer. Kellyn looks about to say something, but I catch his eye and firmly shake my head. *Don't you dare.*

"Here," she says, holding down her hand. "You can ride with me until you get the hang of it. We'll attach your horse to mine, and he can follow."

Petrik still seems unsure.

"You'll slow us down otherwise," she adds gently.

With that, Petrik grudgingly puts his foot in the stirrup and hoists himself up behind Temra. His riding posture is beyond terrible. He's unbalanced and clearly terrified.

"Put your arms around me," Temra tells him.

He does, wrapping them around her waist. His face relaxes minimally. He lets out a squeak when Temra urges the horse to walk on.

She asks, "What did you say to that guard, Petrik? He was about to stab you, but then he hesitated, right before Kellyn got there and killed him."

Petrik thinks for a moment. "I don't remember. I was so scared, I don't think I knew what I was saying."

The guard hesitated before killing him? I had my eyes closed tight during the moment.

"I'm just glad Kellyn got there in time," Temra says.

"Me too," I say, trying to meet Kellyn's eyes, but they're focused squarely on the road ahead of us.

"The plan," Kellyn prompts, keeping us on track.

"We need to get rid of the sword," Temra says. "That's our job. The world isn't safe with it in it."

"It can't be destroyed," I add. "I've already tried. It's indestructible."

Petrik turns his head in my direction, from where it's leaned against my sister's back as he holds on for dear life. "That's why you asked me all those questions about destroying magicked items. Ziva, if you had told me sooner about the sword, I could have helped."

"Can you help now? Do you know what we should do?"

His hands tighten on my sister as the horse goes up an incline. "It can't be destroyed, and Kymora can never get her hands on it. That's what we know for sure." He's thinking out loud, rather than looking for any of us to respond. "We need to take the sword somewhere it'll never be found."

"That's why we tried to take it to Thersa. We didn't think the warlord could find us there."

"That was foolish," Kellyn says. "She's the most powerful and influential person in the world. Her network of spies is vast. Her army is so large it beats almost all the region leaders' combined! And you wanted to hide in the tropics?"

"Now is the time for *helpful* suggestions," I say.

"The ocean," Petrik says out of nowhere.

"What?" Temra asks.

"We get on a boat headed for the northern continent," Petrik explains. "When we're halfway there, we throw the sword overboard. It'll never be found."

After a beat of silence, I say, "It's a good plan."

"Then I'll get you as far as Galvinor," Kellyn says. "From

there, you can hire a ship. When the warlord tracks you to the edge of the continent, she'll soon realize what you've done. Me and mine should be safe then."

Guilt is a powerful thing, and it consumes me as I remember that while I've been doing my best to keep my family safe, I've been putting other families at risk.

We don't make camp until late into the night, when we've put a significant distance between ourselves and the capital. Petrik settles into his usual routine, about to make a fire, when Kellyn warns him against it.

"Let's not risk a fire until morning. We don't know how near our enemies might be."

Petrik is clearly mournful at the lack of a hot meal after a day in the saddle. He returns his pans to their pack, walking around at a near waddle, like some of the birds back in Thersa.

"Here," Temra says, "let me show you some stretches to help with the pain. You'll have to be ready to ride again tomorrow morning."

Petrik groans at the thought, but he still indulges her, bending as Temra does and blushing when her rump is tight in her pants at the next stretch. He looks away.

I smile softly at the two of them.

And then, as though all the events of the day are finally registering, a wave of exhaustion comes over me.

I need a moment.

I brush branches out of my way as I find a path through the trees. The ground is covered in leaves and mulch. My boots sink a good inch into the ground with every step. My arms ache from how they were roughly handled, and my knees go weak as I finally get out of view of everyone else.

Behind my closed eyelids, I can see Kymora's soldiers surrounding us. Every horrifying moment is repeated over and over again in my mind. The sword lunging for Petrik. Temra being carried away. The destruction caused by Secret Eater.

And then the attack comes.

Not an outward one, but one from within.

My breath speeds until the shrill sounds are all that fill my ears. I brace my hands against the bark of the nearest tree as I feel my mind falling. It plummets to a dark and empty place, devoid of hope. There is no ladder or rope to climb back out. There is no end in sight. No light to guide my way.

I am nothing but fear and panic.

On and on time speeds or maybe it stills, stops completely, leaving me behind while the rest of the world goes on.

"There you are!" a voice says from somewhere nearby, the tone furious. I spin toward it, horrified Kellyn is catching me in the midst of an attack. "We need to talk. I cannot believe you've forced me into—Bladesmith?"

I make a shooing motion with my hands while I try to breathe. Kellyn ignores the gesture completely, stepping up behind me. His hands curl around my arms gently, but firmly. His deep voice rumbles, "I've got you. You're safe."

I don't try to get away, but neither do I lean into the touch. I'm shocked into stillness by the contact.

"Ziva, it's okay."

Kellyn stands there, waiting out the attack with me. I'm

mortified that he's witnessing this, but I can't do anything to make the panic subside.

I'm falling.

When will it end?

Please end.

Breathe.

When it finally alleviates, I don't move from my position. I can't.

Because if I do, if I pull away, he'll see the tears now streaming down my face. Being caught like this, by *him*, is bad enough as it is.

Maybe if I just start talking, it won't be so weird that I'm letting him hold me.

"You never call me by my name. It's always 'bladesmith.'"

"I didn't want to get too attached."

"And now?"

He mumbles something that sounds a lot like "too late," but I can't be sure.

"I thought it was over," I say. "I thought the warlord had us. I thought I would lose my sister, that I would be a slave for the rest of my life, knowing that I had brought about the destruction of the world.

"I thought for just a moment you'd left us to that fate," I continue. "I saw you running off with our money . . . But I also knew it wasn't you. You didn't look right, and you betraying us didn't make sense. But it was your face! If I'd just put the truth together—"

"Kymora's men would have caught up to you eventually," Kellyn says. "It was only a matter of time. They knew where we were, and if their trick didn't work, they would have found a way to surround you later on. By then, I might have been long gone and unable to save you."

I swallow, and the sound feels as loud as thunder in the quiet.

"Why didn't you use the sword before when we were in trouble?" he asks.

"I didn't want you to know what it does. I'm not a skilled swordswoman, I fear hurting someone I don't mean to with it. And . . . I don't want to kill anyone. It's not the kind of weapon that can only wound. I never want to wield it. That might make me weak in your eyes, but—"

"No. Not wanting to kill is in no way a flaw, Ziva. I hope you never have to."

He's rubbing my arms gently, spreading heat back into my limbs.

I ask, "Why did you come after us? You had the money. You had no further obligation to us. Why would you save us?"

He gently turns me. I swipe the moisture away from under my eyes. He sees the motion but says nothing of it. "Because I said I would return the money to you. I promised. I had to save you to keep my word."

I make myself look him in the eye. "You were so outnumbered. You had to think you wouldn't win. So why would you endanger yourself? If it was just about keeping your word, you could have dropped the money when you caught up to us and taken off running."

He rubs the back of his neck with one hand. "They were about to kill the scholar. I felt sorry for the man."

"Right."

A lengthy pause.

"And I saw them holding you. They were trying to take you away. I didn't think. I acted. I didn't care how many men were in that clearing, because I didn't even see them. All I saw was you in danger and so I fought."

A delicious, light feeling sweeps through my veins. It starts at my heart and bursts toward my fingertips.

But then it disappears, and I panic, struggling to think of a single thing to say to him in response. The pause goes on too long; I'm sure it does. I step back out of his reach.

"That sword," Kellyn says, "you should have told me about it."

"It's so dangerous. The fewer people who know about it the better." I fiddle with my fingers, popping the joints and twisting the skin. I look down. More quietly, I whisper, "Knowing about the sword wouldn't have stopped Kymora's men from discovering you're helping us."

"I know."

"But that's not what you're upset about. It's that I didn't trust you with it."

"Yes."

"I-if it means anything to you, I trust you now."

I hear the breath enter his lungs. "It does mean something to me."

I bite the inside of my cheek at the next break in conversation. Maybe I need to show him that I trust him? "Do you want to carry Secret Eater on the way to Galvinor? You're the only one I'd trust to wield it."

"I'm never touching it again," he says before the words have quite left my mouth. "It feels . . . wrong when I hold it. Like it wasn't meant for me."

"Okay."

At the next pause, I can feel the tension between us, thick as a cloud of smoke. I want it to abate.

He wants to forgive me. I want to forgive him.

But is it all irreparable?

"I can't change the fact that Kymora will soon know about you," I say. "But how can I make things better?"

Kellyn once said something similar to me. I wonder if he catches that.

When he doesn't answer right away, I look up.

He was waiting for that. His eyes latch on to mine. "I want nothing else kept from me. No more lies. No more secrets. Is there anything more I should know?"

"Nothing," I say.

But then I realize that's not quite true. "Except, well . . ."

He raises a brow. "Well?"

I groan.

"What?" he asks.

"I really don't want to tell you."

"Ziva, no more secrets. You said you trusted me."

"It's not that I don't trust you. It's that I *don't want you to know*."

"Why?"

"It's embarrassing."

"I'm sure it's not that bad. Whatever it is, you can tell me, and I'll try not to react poorly."

I groan again, attempt to gather my courage. "You're connected to the sword in more ways than you think." I bury my face into my hands and mumble the story. "I saw you before we met when you came into my shop. I was in the forge, working on Secret Eater. I hadn't added the magic yet when you walked by on the street. And then . . . it was magicked."

"I'm not following."

"I may have said something about you aloud. A secret. And the sword ate it."

"What did you say?"

"I don't remember the exact words."

His hands curl around my fingers, pulling them from my face. "Yes, you do. What were the words, Ziva?"

I glare at him. "I'm only telling you this because I feel bad about putting you in danger against your will."

He's trying his best to keep from grinning, waiting.

"You have to understand, I don't like people," I say.

"You've said this before."

"No, I mean, I don't *like* people. I've never been attracted to anyone before." Though he has my hands out of my face, I stare at his neck, unable to look any higher. "I've never met anyone who didn't terrify me to the point of wanting to run the other way. I have these attacks, like the one you just witnessed. I panic a lot, and I'm scared all the time for reasons I can't even really explain, except that the fear is always tied to people.

"But then I saw you, and you were beautiful. And for the first time in my life, I wanted to be close to someone physically. And that longing—combined with the spoken desire to touch you—it gave the sword its long-range abilities." The last words come out as a whisper. But then, louder, I press on. I can't allow him a chance to respond to that. It's too humiliating. "Now you know everything. Is there anything you'd like to tell me?"

I still won't look at him. I don't want to see his expression.

"Didn't the sword tell you everything about me?" he asks.

"Only some things. I'm asking if there's anything else. Now that you know what's at stake and everything we're running from and protecting. Is there anything I should know?"

"No. We're good, Ziva."

I let out a breath of air, finally allowing myself a look at his face. I expect to be met with a haughty expression.

Instead, Kellyn is looking at me like he's never seen me before.

As though he likes everything that he sees.

He takes my hands in his, just holds them in between us. Before I can decide whether I want to pull away, Kellyn rubs his fingers over my knuckles as he says, "I heard their secrets. All the men and women I killed with that sword. One was cheating on his wife. Another was thinking of defecting from Kymora's service; she just couldn't decide where to hide, considering a life in the mountains. One was stealing money from his fellow soldiers. One of the women fancied another soldier in the ranks. Almost all of them were afraid of death. I heard it. Their fears. It was horrible. It was too much, so much that it made me sick.

"I'd never held it before," he continues. "The sword is . . . heavy."

"It's weighted with my secrets. They're what give it power."

Suddenly, the contact between our hands is making me anxious. I carefully pull away, and as soon as I do, I regret it.

His presence goes from being welcome to unwanted, back and forth, like my mind doesn't know what to make of him. My body doesn't know how to react to him. One moment, I like that I'm touching him. The next, I wish he were far away.

My life is a world of opposites. One instant I'm safe in my forge; the next I'm on the run for my life. One second I'm fine, and then I'm lost to despair and panic.

I can't control any of it.

And I hate that.

I am more than my fears and weaknesses, but so much of the time, they're all I can think about.

"Could I have some time to myself?" I ask him.

"Of course."

It's only after he's gone that I realize he didn't make one comment on the fact that I find him handsome. That I wanted to touch him. He simply took my hands, as though he only wished to give me what I wanted.

Petrik groans every time he moves. "My knees hurt. My feet hurt. My backside. My back. My *neck*. How is that possible?"

Today was his first time riding in his own saddle, and when we dismount, Petrik lands on his feet—but they quickly give way, and he collapses into the dirt.

Temra comes to his rescue, putting her hands beneath his arms and scooting him out of the way, while Kellyn and I take care of his horse.

"You need to take your feet out of the stirrups and give them time for the blood to rush back in before dismounting," she says to him. "For next time."

"I'm never getting on a horse again!" he whines.

"We still have a long ways to go."

Something akin to a whimper comes out of his mouth.

We unsaddle the horses and give them long leads so they can roam for grass and have easy access to the nearby river.

Temra unpacks the bedrolls. Petrik unwraps the food. I check the horses' hooves for rocks, and Kellyn sets up the tents we stole from Kymora's soldiers. There were enough for each of us to have our own, but I asked Temra if we could continue to share.

I sense eyes on me as I bend over and lift my mare's front right hoof. Kellyn has been trying to meet my gaze since our last private conversation. When we touched. When I admitted the truth about the sword's origins.

But I don't return the look, and I've avoided being alone with him.

In fact, I've been terrified of even the possibility of it.

Because since that—that touching, my mind has wandered to other things.

When I feel his eyes leave me, I risk my own casual glance in his direction. I stare at the long muscles in his arms, the way his biceps move as he maneuvers the tent poles into place.

And I think about what it might feel like to curl my fingers around one of his arms.

He's so big. I'm used to being taller than most men, but Kellyn has inches on me. How far would he need to bend down to—

I startle at the thought.

To kiss me.

At first the thought is terrifying, but the more I try to imagine it, he and I so close, my curiosity piques.

What would it feel like to have another set of lips touch mine? Not just any lips. But his? Would that grin smooth out long enough to become caught up in a kiss? Or would he smile through the whole thing, considering it a victory?

I try to imagine details, but I can't. I've of course seen people kissing before, but I usually look away quickly, because such a scene makes me uncomfortable.

I can't quite imagine how our mouths would move in unison. But I do know that I want to wrap my hand around his arm, maybe slide it across his chest, or touch his hair.

All at once the scene in my head turns from petrifying to thrilling.

But when Kellyn starts to turn back in my direction—

Fear.

Fear takes over.

CHAPTER EIGHTEEN

We see the towers long before we arrive in Briska. The city is *tall*: The homes are thin and built straight up into the air with five or more stories. Kellyn tells us that these are apartments that fit multiple families on each floor.

A shudder goes through me at the thought. As if it weren't enough to have people on either side of you. Now they're being placed above and beneath.

I can't even imagine how many people must be crammed into this city if it's so vast and the buildings are also growing *upward*.

It's okay. We're not staying here. We're just passing through to get to Galvinor.

But my mind is spinning out of control at the thought of having to stay overnight here. I'm certain I would rather die than stay here.

I'd rather be covered in red ants.

Or rolled down a hill in a barrel full of nails.

Or covered in honey and thrust into a bear den.

"Ziva," Temra says cautiously, like she needs to talk me down from a ledge.

She just might.

I swallow, unable to take my eyes off the towerlike homes in the distance.

"Okay, and we're just going to turn this way for a moment." Temra grabs my reins and turns my mare around, back toward the road we just traveled on. "And breathe, Ziva."

"Stop coddling me," I snap. Then, "No, I didn't mean that. I'm sorry. It's just so big. And—"

Kellyn steers his horse in front of me so I'm forced to look at him. He eyes my face carefully before asking, "What are you afraid of?"

"Don't act all surprised. You've seen me at my worst before." So embarrassing. The way he witnessed my fit in the woods.

"I'm just wondering what's causing it. I want to understand."

Why? "It's the people. I don't want to be surrounded by so many."

He quirks his head to the side. "They're not going to hurt you."

"If it was a rational fear that I could just explain away to myself, believe me, I would have done it by now. This isn't something I can control. It's nothing you can fix. It's just something I live with."

Kellyn opens his mouth, but Temra interrupts him. "I have a fear of spiders. I know most of them aren't poisonous. I know most of them don't even bite. I know I'm way bigger than they are. Doesn't matter. I see a spider and I lose it. We all have something like that. Don't you give Ziva a hard time because you don't understand hers."

Again, I think the mercenary tries to defend himself, when Petrik says, "I don't like being alone in the dark."

Kellyn snaps his head in the scholar's direction. "Because monsters might come after you?"

Petrik ignores him. "One time I was in the library all alone, and someone blew out the candles, not knowing I was still reading. I had to feel my way to the exit." Petrik takes a deep breath, trying to dispel the thought.

Then we all look to Kellyn expectantly.

"What? I don't *have* any irrational fears."

"Liar," Temra says. "Everybody has one."

"Well, I don't."

Petrik turns to me. "I think someone has an irrational fear of being vulnerable." He almost sings the last word.

Kellyn narrows his eyes. "I do not."

"Oh, he definitely does," Temra agrees.

I can't help it, I'm grinning like an idiot. I needed these people on this journey. I couldn't have done it without them. Was there a higher power who knew that? Were the Sisters involved? Or was it fate?

I don't feel any better about the city in general, but just knowing these three are with me gives me strength.

I turn my horse around.

✝

No one tries to talk to us or welcome us into the city. People go about their business and keep to themselves. A young gentleman walks two dogs on a lead. An older woman carries bags of groceries toward her home, and no one offers to help her.

I like it.

Until I notice children begging for money in the streets. Temra breaks away from us for a moment to buy them all a meal from one of the vendors.

With a bigger city also comes more poverty and garbage. The streets are filthy, covered in human refuse and rotting food and muddied scraps of parchment.

"Oh, not that way," Kellyn says, steering us to the right fork in the road instead of the left.

"Why?" Petrik asks. "What's down there?"

"Less reputable businesses."

"You mean, like a den of prostitutes?" Temra asks.

"Among other things."

Temra stands in her stirrups and glances down the other road, as though that will help her catch a glimpse of something.

"Stop that." I grab her arm and yank her back down in the saddle.

"What? I'm just curious!"

"If you thought the street urchins were sad, you don't want to see the gaunt faces of those who work down there. Trust me," Kellyn says.

"How come you've been down that street?" I ask skeptically.

"I took a job once for a man I didn't know was seedy until I'd already agreed to the work. Thankfully, all I had to do was escort a delivery. Then I got out of there."

Just a part of me wonders if he's telling the truth. What if instead he frequents one of the brothels? Or maybe he specializes in seedy deals?

But I quickly shake the thought away. That's not Kellyn.

I freeze, my hands tightening on the reins, and the obedient horse comes to a full stop.

Not Kellyn?

Since when do I think that I know Kellyn?

I make a clicking noise to signal the horse back into motion before anyone notices I stopped, my thoughts still troubling me.

Temra and I don't know exactly where we're headed, but Kellyn has a place for us to find rooms for the night. Tonight we get a real bed. That thought encourages me to press on through the throngs of people.

"Is it just me," Temra asks a few minutes later, "or are we being followed?"

Kellyn does a casual glance behind himself while Petrik blatantly begins to turn. Temra grabs him by the shirt to stop him. I glance out of the corner of my eye and definitely note that we've attracted a few stares.

Normally, I catch that sort of thing right away, so aware am I of all the people around me, but I was distracted by my own thoughts.

"You're right," Kellyn says. "There are figures watching us from the alleyways."

Petrik makes a strangled sound, and he jumps off his horse in front of a wooden board. There are all manner of flyers attached to it with iron nails. Missing persons notices. Apartments for rent. Lost pets.

The rest of us unsaddle to get a better look at what captured the scholar's attention.

The most prominent and eye-catching item on the board is a single square of parchment bearing four neatly arranged faces.

Reward: 10,000 ockles per capture. Alive only. All weapons in their possession to be handed over. Notify Warlord Kymora.

And then I see all our faces painted.

No, not painted. What I'd thought at first was parchment is actually cloth. Our faces were stitched onto the advertisement in color. In startling accuracy. Each face is so realistic, it looks as though it's breathing.

The cotton spinner is now making Wanted posters in our likenesses.

"No," Kellyn breathes.

I'm so distracted by my face staring back at me that I don't remember we're being followed until they're already upon us.

Someone yanks on my arm, while another person sends their fist smashing below my left shoulder blade. I lose my feet before I can right myself from the blows. Hands grab my arms and wrench them behind my back, but then another figure reaches one of my feet, trying to yank me away from the first.

"Back off! I saw her first."

"Not bloody likely."

"Those are my ockles!"

I catch a glimpse of two men lifting my sister into the air by her arms. She plants her feet against the wood of the display board and launches herself and the men onto the ground.

Kellyn doesn't even get a chance to reach for his sword. He's overrun by men much smaller than him, but superior numbers count for a lot. They tackle him to the ground, use their weight to keep him in place. Someone brandishes a rope and stalks over to the mercenary.

I would panic, but I can't seem to see through the pain. Someone gets their hands in my hair, and I feel a kick in my side. Everything goes fuzzy at a blow to my head.

A loud whistle shrieks in my ears.

One set of hands lets go, then another. I flop painfully on the ground, my hands gripping my abdomen where the kick landed.

"Sod off, the lot of you. If anyone is going to be turning in these criminals, it's me."

I manage to adjust to a sitting position before eyeing the newcomers. They're in uniform, black tunics with three (or six?) silver stripes running lengthwise from neck to navel.

City guards.

Manacles materialize, seemingly out of nowhere. I can't quite count how many men surround us through my hazy vision, but I think it's at least a dozen. My wrists are cuffed, Secret Eater is taken from my side. I can't even manage to protest as the world sways from side to side.

I don't remember losing consciousness, but the next thing I know, I wake on the ground. It hurts to open my eyes, and every limb aches. When I try to adjust for comfort, pain pierces through my skull.

"Whatever did you lot do to piss off Warlord Kymora?" a gruff voice asks.

When no one answers, another voice says, "Seems to me they

stole her property. She insisted all weapons in their possession be saved for her arrival. You lot really picked the wrong mark to filch."

"Doesn't look like they have a full brain among the four of them. Still, station two extra men outside the prison. I don't want any chance of them escaping before she arrives. Forty thousand ockles is enough to retire on."

"Not in this city."

"Maybe I'll retire to the tropics. Or head south toward the mountains."

"And live without anyone else to boss around?"

Laughter fills my ears.

"Don't like the look of this big brute. Better make it four extra guards outside the prison."

"Yes, Captain."

A creaky door opens and closes. A lock turns. I finally manage to pull my eyelids apart. Even then, it takes me a moment to realize what I'm looking at it.

The cell is filled with inky darkness. I can mostly see shadows where Petrik, Kellyn, and Temra are. My sister is crouched down beside me, her hand not far from mine, as though she'd been holding it a moment ago.

I try to sit up and groan.

The boys rush to my side. Strong arms haul me into a sitting position, and then Kellyn is searching my face.

"Are you hurt?"

"Everywhere," I answer.

"And your head?" Petrik asks.

"That hurts, too." I raise a hand to where the back of my skull throbs, only to find something crusty there.

They made me bleed.

"Where are we?" I ask.

"Briska City Prison," Temra says.

"And the weapons?"

"Right over there." She points, and through the bars, I think I see a mass that could be the Zivan blades atop a table.

"Everything else is gone," Kellyn says, his voice sounding dangerous, like he'd very much like to hit the nearest person. "Filthy guards took our supplies and money. My money. All gone."

"Worry about the money after we get out of here," Temra says. "We have bigger problems if we can't escape before Kymora arrives."

Kellyn steps up to the bars, takes one in each hand, and rattles them for all he's worth. There's a light sound, but not much else happens.

Kellyn growls before kicking at the bars. Then he paces back and forth in our little ten-by-ten foot cell. There's not so much as a window, and the air smells as though it's been stuck down here for years.

"We might want to wait until Kymora arrives," Petrik suggests. "Our best chance for escape may be when they try to move us."

"When Kymora arrives, there will be no chance at all," Kellyn says. "She's the real power in Ghadra, not the royals. Because the kingdom isn't united, she can do as she pleases, unchecked. She's the most formidable swordswoman in the world. When she arrives, the game is done."

"And if she gets her hands on the sword, no one will ever have the power to take it from her," I say.

"So get up," Kellyn snaps. "Don't just sit there. We have to do something!"

"And what is she supposed to do?" Temra comes to my defense. "Smashing your big head against the bars might be worth a try."

"There has to be something in here we can use," Petrik says. "Look around."

The cell isn't large, but when my hand comes into contact with something smooth on the ground, I raise it close to my eyes for inspection.

Then I shriek and jump backward.

"What is it?" Temra asks, coming to my aid.

"A bone!" I say.

"Looks like a human femur," Petrik says after an emotionless examination.

"Charming. Someone died in this cell. And I thought things couldn't get worse," Kellyn says.

"At least they're not recently dead," Petrik says. "Smells and all that."

"Give me that thing." Kellyn grasps the femur, touching it with his *bare* hand, as though it were a flower or sword or something else distinctly not human remains, and paces over to the cell bars. He shoves the long bone between two of them and tries to pry them apart.

There's a *snap*, but it isn't from the bars.

Kellyn grunts in frustration and shakes the bars again for good measure.

Petrik retrieves one of the broken ends of the bone and tries to fit it into the opening of the lock on the opposite side of the door.

"What are you doing?" Temra asks.

"Seeing if we can pick the lock."

"Do you know how to pick a lock?"

"No," he mumbles.

Temra sits next to me on the cold floor and rests her elbows on her knees.

"Could we trick the guards somehow?" Petrik asks.

"Hey, guard! Guard!" Kellyn starts shouting, but after a minute, not a soul surfaces. "That would be a no."

"So that's it." Petrik joins us on the ground.

Kellyn continues pacing, clearly unable to give up.

Hours trickle by at an agonizing pace, and we start to shiver from the chill. Kellyn keeps pacing and pacing; he's worked himself into a sweat. He eventually strides up to the bars and yanks at them for all he's worth.

"Will you sit down? Even you aren't strong enough to move steel," Petrik says.

"That's iron," I tell him automatically.

"That's helpful," Kellyn says sarcastically to me before rounding on Petrik. "I don't see you coming up with any ideas. Aren't you supposed to be the smart one? 'I'm a renowned scholar from the Great Library,'" Kellyn says in a mimicry of Petrik's voice. "'I'm an expert. Look at the length of my robes.'"

Petrik scoffs at him. "I do not sound like that. And excuse me for not reading up more on instances of prison breaks!"

"What good are you? Why are you even here?"

Temra leaves me on the floor to stand between the two men. "Back off," she says to Kellyn. "Petrik has been invaluable on this journey. He's saved us almost as often as you have, and he's a whole lot less volatile. So why don't you check your temper and stop pretending like you're more upset that we're imprisoned rather than that the money is gone."

Kellyn gives Temra the nastiest look I've seen from him yet. "I don't like small spaces." He turns his back to us in an opposite corner.

Ah, so he does have an irrational fear, but now is certainly not the time to poke at the bear.

I rub my hands over my arms in the quiet that ensues. From the other side of the cell, I can feel Secret Eater. The secrets it holds will forever be a part of it, and mine will always call out to me.

The blasted sword has landed me in a prison cell. I'm unsure if this is a new low or my last low. Because I'm quite certain we're not getting out of this cell until someone uses the key the captain took with him.

I stare at those iron bars, and the irony hits me. I can magic iron, and yet I'm stuck behind it. Helpless without my forge or tools. Worthless by myself.

Iron needs heat to bend to my will.

I roll up on my feet suddenly, and Temra protests, nearly falling from where she'd been leaning against me. I don't apologize. I'm too caught up in my foolhardy thoughts.

When I press my forehead to the bars, I can just see the faint pulsing lights in the room. One source from each side of the cell.

Torches on the walls, if I'm not mistaken.

I move to the far end of the cell, thrust my arm through the bars, and reach for the sconce. I can just barely touch the tip of the torch with a fingernail.

"What are you doing?" Kellyn asks.

"Use your gorilla arms to reach for the torch. I can't get it."

He raises a brow at the insult but does as I ask, trading places with me. It takes some finagling, but when he slides his arm back into the cell, he's got the torch in hand.

"Oh, good," Petrik says. "Now we might not freeze tonight."

"Hold it against this bar," I command, ignoring the scholar. "No, the tip. Press the fire to it. I need the metal to heat."

"Ziva," Temra says, realizing what I'm doing. "Is it enough?"

"I have no idea, but it's worth a try."

Temra and Petrik rise, standing just behind the mercenary and me. I can feel their stares over my shoulder as I concentrate on the metal the flame flickers against. The hairs on my neck prickle, and discomfort seizes my limbs.

"Will you two give me some space?" I ask. Petrik and Temra dutifully take a step back.

When the flame has licked the iron for some minutes, I stare at the red-gray metal. Red from rust, not heat. A torch's light is not nearly enough heat to change the color, but is it enough to magic it?

"Break," I say quietly, my gaze boring into the cell bar.

Absolutely nothing happens.

"Break," I say again a little louder.

"Break!" I command.

"I thought you said the metal only responds when you whisper to it. Doesn't it need gentle encouragement?" Petrik asks in his scholarly, know-it-all voice.

"You try being gentle when you know four lives rest in your hands!" I shriek back at him.

A hand settles against my shoulder, and since Kellyn still holds the torch to the bars, I know it belongs to my sister.

"You can do this," she says. "I know you can. You're my big sister, and you always save the day. Just try again."

"I can't do this with an audience. I forge alone. I'm uncomfortable. I'm stressed. It's not going to work."

"Some of your best work has happened when you least expected it," she says. "You forged an air-sucking mace during one of your attacks. This little bar right here, it has *nothing* on you."

Kellyn lowers his head so we're eye to eye. "I believe in you. Your work is so powerful, people all over the world know who you are. If anyone can get us out of this mess, it's you."

"You're a smithy. The master of iron," Petrik says, not to be outdone. "You *have* to do this."

I don't know if their encouragement is helping or making my anxiety worse, but I take a deep breath and shut my eyes, thinking of the times I've magicked metal in the past. I remember the mace Temra mentioned. How I had an attack after an angry customer barged into my forge when he cut himself on his own blade. My hyperventilating gave it power.

I remember the time I broke one of my fingers. It was stupid. I agreed to a walk through town with Temra, and while I was worrying over all the people around me, I tripped and snapped the finger while trying to catch myself on the ground. The next day, when I went back to work, my less dominant hand throbbing, all I could think of was my carelessness the day before, the sound of my finger snapping. That was the day I magicked the daggers that shatter anything they come into contact with.

And then there's Secret Eater. Forged because I was ridiculous enough to admire a boy through the window.

Accidents. These were all instances of accidents. Blades that were magicked when my feelings were overwrought or when I was experiencing something new.

Even at my worst, I can be strong.

When next I open my eyes, I lower my face to the bars, so close the torch almost burns my lips.

"Break," I whisper, my breath brushing against the bar, sending the flame sputtering. I focus on my anger, on how Kymora broke my life and tore me away from almost everything I love.

The sound of metal snapping thunders through the prison. Kellyn jumps back from the bars and drops the torch, which flicks out instantly.

I can hear doors opening and closing somewhere else in the prison.

"Someone is coming to investigate!" I say. At the same time, I pull my sleeves over my hands, reach for the heated bar, find the break with my fingers, and pull the bottom half downward. Kellyn grips the top half of the broken bar, pulling upward.

I turn myself sideways and slither through the two pieces first. I go for Secret Eater immediately, attaching it back to my hip.

In the light of the last torch on the wall, I watch Temra and Petrik slide through the gap. Temra gets her hands on her sword just as a guard gets the door open.

She runs him through without a moment's thought. Petrik steps forward, his hand going to the soldier's open mouth to absorb any sound he might make. He's dead before he hits the floor.

"Let's go," Petrik says to Kellyn.

"I'm stuck," the mercenary says.

Kellyn has one leg and arm on the side of freedom, but his massive chest is wedged in the gap between the bars.

"Breathe out," Petrik mutters.

Kellyn does so, and I grab his free arm and yank with all my might.

With a grunt of pain Kellyn flops to the floor.

Then we flee, wending our way through the jail. When we finally find the outer doors, we slip past the guards, preferring stealth to another fight. They talk to each other with their backs to us, and the four of us tiptoe around the building until we find the road.

With the cover of darkness, none of the city dwellers are able to see our faces. No one calls out to us or steps into our path. In fact, the few Briskans out and about don't even seem startled by the sight of a company sprinting down alleyways at night, which doesn't speak well for the city.

The exercise warms my previously chilled limbs, and freedom warms my scared heart.

The captain will be very disappointed when he visits the prison tomorrow morning. No retirement for him.

CHAPTER NINETEEN

Before delivering us to the prison, the captain and his men stole anything of value we had, and they left Petrik's books lying in the street. We're now on the road for what feels like the thousandth time with nothing except the clothes on our backs, the weapons at our sides, and the company we keep.

After half the night has passed, when we're certain no one is following us, we finally stop.

Petrik bends over and puts his hands on his knees. Kellyn promptly slams his own fist into the nearest tree.

"Whoa!" Petrik says, standing and backing away from the other man.

I rush over to the mercenary and grab his hand to inspect it. He's broken the skin over every knuckle, wells of blood pooling and smearing down his fingers.

"Those posters will be all over Ghadra by next week. Clearly Kymora is sending things faster than we can travel, so she's using carrier pigeons. We won't be safe anywhere! I can't work. I can't *live*."

The anger isn't directed at anyone in particular, but an angry Kellyn is a sight to behold.

"I'm sorry," I whisper as I cradle his hand in mine.

His face softens as he looks at me. "I'm not angry with you."

"I know, but this is still my fault."

"Let's get something straight right now." He moves his injured hand so it's now gripping one of mine. The anger from before still laces his words, giving them extra force. "You are not responsible for any of this. You were doing your job. Something you do very well. The sword is not evil in and of itself. In the hands of a just ruler, it could protect a whole kingdom. What's evil are the intentions of the ones who would use it to do anything other than protect. You do not get to put the fate of the world on your shoulders. You're not that important."

I feel my mouth open and close like a fish's.

"He's right," Temra says unhelpfully.

I step away from Kellyn, thinking over his words. Is it truly not my fault? That the world is at stake? That my sister is in danger?

Is it even possible to take the guilt and blame from me?

I don't know if I can do that, even if it is true. I don't know how. I still *feel* guilty. I still feel responsible for everything that's happened, and it's still up to me to make things right.

We're all quiet now, aimlessly traversing the road. I'm not even sure which direction we're headed anymore. In Lirasu, I could always use the mountains to tell which way was south. I miss that. Such a simple thing, but it grounded me always.

After a few seconds, Kellyn says, "We can't go to Galvinor anymore. You guys would never make it through another city, nor is there any hope you could hire a crew without being recognized."

"Then what do we do?" I ask.

Kellyn purses his lips, shakes his head, lets out a loud breath—like he's arguing silently with himself. "I know a place we can lie low for a while. We'll be safe. We can rethink everything then."

I want to believe him, but we haven't been safe anywhere. Not with our father's mother, not in the big cities, not on the road. Everywhere we go, there's danger.

The safest we'd ever been was honestly in that prison cell.

I freeze in place as an idea comes to me.

"Kellyn, I think I know what to do with the sword. I might know how to keep it safe permanently. I—I need access to a forge."

"Great. There's one in Amanor."

"Amanor?"

"Where my family lives."

Kellyn explains that Amanor is a small village in Prince Skiro's Territory. "It isn't located off any main road. It's not on many maps, either."

"How do you know we'll be safe there?" I ask. "Kymora knows you're involved. Won't she be able to find your family?"

"I don't see how she could. I don't advertise where I'm from. I haven't told anyone where my family resides, let alone that I have one settled somewhere. Excluding you, of course."

"What about your surname? Derinor. Can't she ask around? Is there any chance at all she could track us to Amanor?"

"There's always a chance. But Derinor is a common surname. And she'd be hard-pressed to find anyone who could point her to Amanor. Besides, if my family is in danger from her, I should be there to protect them."

We're only on the main road for another few days before we veer down what looks more like a deer trail than a road. If I thought the forest looked thick from the main road, it's nothing compared to how it is now that we're wrapped in it. The trees are so close together that the only path we could possibly take is the already-made trail.

"I don't like these woods," Petrik says. "There are bears in these woods."

"Right, you're from Skiro," Temra says.

"The capital," Petrik explains. "There are no bears there."

"The capital is right next to the mountains," Kellyn says. "There are cougars. You prefer those to bears?"

"Definitely," Petrik answers. "Cougars are afraid of people, and they hardly come into the city. It's too loud."

"Not if they're hungry enough."

Kellyn takes a strange delight in teasing Petrik. It makes me want to give him a taste of his own medicine.

"Bears are a perfectly natural thing to be afraid of. Unlike vulnerability." A jab at our earlier conversation.

Temra laughs. "He's not afraid of bears because he can swing his sword at them. But Kellyn doesn't know how to protect his feelings."

We giggle, and Kellyn glowers good-humoredly at the two of us. "Perhaps you should learn to swing a sword, bladesmith. Then you'd be less afraid of people."

I scoff. If only it were that simple. If only my fear was of them physically hurting me. No, it is my mind that needs to be protected, and I don't think there is any guard against that.

"Trying to get the attention off you by putting it on me isn't going to work," I say.

"Nope," Temra agrees.

Maybe it's the seclusion of the forest, but I haven't felt this good in a long time. We have nothing, and yet, it somehow feels as though we have everything.

Along the way, we pick mushrooms and berries and nuts that Kellyn says are edible. Though they're not very tasty, they fill our bellies enough. That night, Kellyn assures us no one else will be on the trail, so he and Petrik take turns rubbing a stick between their fingers down onto a bigger stick to make a fire from scratch. We've no blankets or anything else, so we clear the ground of rocks and other hard objects before Temra and I lie side by side on our backs for warmth.

"Don't get any ideas, scholar," Kellyn says to him.

Temra pats the ground on her other side. "You can sleep next to me."

Petrik visibly swallows before listening.

"No, come closer," she says. "How do you intend to keep me warm that way?"

Petrik scoots until he's pressed up right against her.

Kellyn stands alone by the fire, but I meet his eyes, glance down at the spot beside me, then back at him.

I wasn't trying to issue an invitation. I was honestly just taking note of where that left Kellyn to sleep. But he sits beside me on the ground before stretching out with one arm behind his head, the other at his side, accidentally brushing my fingers.

I flinch at the contact before forcing myself to relax. It's not like he purposely grabbed my hand.

Except then he does.

He plays with my fingers, warming them, massaging them. He alternates between sliding his fingers between mine to secure me in a grip and then loosening them to feel my skin.

I can't look at him. I stare straight up into the treetops and starlit sky.

I could stop him if I wanted. It would be so easy. Just move my arm or roll over and put my back to him.

But it's also so easy to just be still. To let myself feel the delicious heat from where our bodies touch without my anxieties getting out of control. Because I don't have to say anything. I'm not being put on display. This is so simple.

Why can't it always be this simple?

After maybe a couple minutes of my heart racing, I find myself starting to relax.

And become brave.

I shrug my hand out of his grip, and he lets me go immediately. I think he's about to roll over to give me my space.

I feel my insecurities wanting to take over. *He didn't actually want to touch you. He's done with you now. He wants to be left alone.*

But there's another voice in my head. *He likes you. He only wants to be respectful of your wishes. You just have to let him know what they are.*

So I take his arm in a firm grip to still him, then let my fingers trail over the skin between his wrist and elbow. The top is rough with hair, but the bottom is so smooth yet hardened with muscle.

A little noise escapes Kellyn. One of surprise?

Or maybe I stepped too far?

No, not that. Because he's suddenly even closer than he was before, so much so that I can't fit my arm between us anymore. He picks up my arm and pulls it across his chest so he can continue to play with my fingers, this time with his other hand.

I let out a long breath as quietly as I can. I'm not going to forget how to breathe just because he's touching me.

Over time, his caresses slow, and his breathing lengthens. He puts his mouth up to my ear. "Try to sleep. We've still a long way to go."

Then his hand stills, holding mine clasped in his.

Is he serious?

I can't sleep with him next to me. Touching me.

Long after I hear Temra's and Kellyn's breathing slow, I'm still staring up at the sky, my body going stiff from being in the same position. Carefully, I take my hand back so I can turn on my side, facing him.

And though he's asleep, he somehow moves with me anyway. He wedges the arm closest to me under my head and pulls me flush up against his side.

And I suspect that he's not sleeping at all, but I'll let him pretend.

†

I don't remember falling asleep or waking up. I'm suddenly just alert.

The first thing I notice is that Temra isn't quite next to me anymore. No, she's rolled over, practically on top of Petrik. They're in a really embarrassing position. Though Temra wouldn't be embarrassed by it, I can imagine how Petrik's cheeks will heat.

Then I realize there's movement above me. A chest moving in and out.

I turn my head.

Kellyn has one arm thrown over me, his head resting on my shoulder, blowing his heated breath into my neck.

At first I think to jump up, but I can't do that. That would be rude while he's trying to sleep.

So I watch him.

I take in what I can see of that long body, those muscled arms and flat chest. His nose is so sharp, his cheekbones so high. And that hair—

A beam of light breaks through the trees and lands directly on those golden-red locks, setting them ablaze.

Dear heavens.

After a few minutes, the beam moves to his eyes, and then he starts to turn his head from side to side.

I hastily shut my eyes and force myself to relax, faking sleep.

I hear his breathing change. He moves slightly, lifting his head, I think.

I wait for him to get up, to nudge me away or something,

anything. But he's still. Watching me. I can feel his eyes burning holes onto my face.

And I don't know how, but I feel the exact moment they drop to my lips.

I remember the fascination, and almost delight, when he brought up the freckles on my lips.

My breath rushes into me, and I have to open my eyes. I probably should put more effort into acting as though I've just woken up, but I don't.

My eyes shoot open and I find him so close, closer than he was before when I was admiring him. He eyes my lips meaningfully, as though asking for permission.

For one second, I think to nod my assent.

But then I remember that Temra and Petrik are just a few feet away. He can't possibly kiss me when they're right there.

So I feign misunderstanding. I smile at him before stretching and sitting up.

It doesn't escape my attention that I was going to let him kiss me if Temra and Petrik weren't right there. It's a sobering thought. One that makes me want to get far away from the mercenary.

Coward that I am, I walk over to Temra and rub her shoulder.

"We should get going," I say once she stirs.

Petrik is still fast asleep, so she reaches over and drags a finger gently down his nose before tapping his lips.

I look away, blushing. How can she be so direct with her flirting? I don't care if it's meaningless or if she's got feelings for the scholar. Either way, she never seems to care if she has an audience—no matter what it is.

I wish I had her fearlessness. I wish I could rid myself of the sinking sensation that feels like falling whenever I'm on display. I wish it didn't become hard to breathe when someone new wants to strike up a conversation. I wish I wasn't helpless in a crowd. I wish my body didn't dictate how I'm supposed to react to things. That I could just tell it, *Behave*, and it would listen.

I wish I could separate myself from the fear, to learn who I truly am.

CHAPTER TWENTY

When Kellyn announces that we've arrived at the village, I'm confused. The landscape looks exactly the same as it has for the last week or so. Beautiful forest country. Wild greenery. Small mammals and birds.

But then Kellyn points to something.

A fence post.

And farther ahead, horses grazing.

Kellyn mentioned that the village consisted of nothing but farming families, but I hadn't quite imagined this. Log cabin–style homes, acres and acres between lots. Trees in every yard. Children playing outdoors. Men and women working with plows and hoes on their land.

Everyone wants to talk. Kellyn is easily recognized, and he takes the time to converse briefly with his neighbors.

After the fourth visit, I whisper harshly, "Isn't it better if no one knows you're visiting?"

"Who are they going to tell? Most of the people here have never left the village. They'll live their whole lives here and die here."

That silences me. For now.

When Kellyn says we're nearing his family's home, he adds, "Please don't say anything about our troubles. I don't want to worry them. You're all friends I'm bringing home for a visit."

"Do you usually bring friends over for a visit?" Petrik asks.

"No."

"Then I'm sure this will go splendidly."

Before the mercenary can respond, a shout of "Kellyn!" reaches us in a birdlike tone.

"Look, it's him!"

"Kellyn's home!"

And then a group of children are rushing him. He holds out his arms, captures all four of them, and then pretends to fall over from the force of their hug.

"We missed you!"

"Did you bring us presents?"

He rights himself and the children, before ruffling the nearest boy's hair. "No presents this time, but I did bring some friends for you to meet."

Three boys and a girl turn their bright eyes to us.

"Right, introductions," he adds. "Ziva, Temra, Petrik, let me introduce you to Tias, age seven; Rallon, age nine; Wardra, age ten; and Kyren, age eleven."

"I'm seven and a half," the youngest boy argues.

"My mistake! How could I forget that half a year?"

"Because you've been gone too long," the girl, Wardra, whines.

"I know. I've been working," he says.

"Can I hold your sword?" Kyren asks.

While Kellyn tries to talk him out of that idea, I'm stuck staring at the little girl. She has golden-red hair the exact same shade as Kellyn's.

"Who are these children?" I ask him.

"My brothers and sister," Kellyn says simply.

"Come, look what we've been doing!" The children drag us over to a little pond hidden among the tall grass. In a section of mud near the edge, there appears to be a small fort of sticks, perhaps one foot by one foot in size. Within is a little green frog.

"We're making him a home," Rallon says.

"And what a fine home it is. He will be the envy of all frogs," Kellyn says.

He's so good with the children. His *siblings*. I've never seen him interact with kids before.

It . . . does something to me.

I find myself wanting to touch him again.

"Where is everyone else?" Kellyn asks after they discuss the finer points of frog houses.

"The little ones are at home with Ma. Da is in the fields with Dynar and Orta." Then Kyren turns to me. "Next year, I get to help in the fields, too. I'll be old enough then."

"But you're so strong already," I say to him.

He smiles before hiding his face against his shoulder. Then he takes off at a run. "Kellyn, I'll go tell Da you're home!"

"Then the rest of us had better go surprise Ma, hadn't we?"

The littlest boy and the girl hold Kellyn's hands as they walk.

Petrik turns to Temra and me. "What happened to Kellyn?"

"He's been replaced with some kindhearted sap," Temra says.

The last boy jumps onto Kellyn's back, and the mercenary doesn't miss a stride as they all keep walking.

"No, I think he's always been like this." Maybe they haven't seen it, but I have. I'm staring after Kellyn so intently that I don't notice Petrik and Temra looking at me until I turn.

"What?" I ask.

"Nothing," Petrik says.

"You're smitten," Temra says at the same time.

I roll my eyes, but I'm embarrassed to have been caught staring.

Mrs. Derinor looks amazing despite all the children she's borne. Her hair is mostly gray, her eyes are crinkled at the sides, and a few lines stand out on her forehead, but she's a remarkably lean and strong woman. Still, she looks exhausted with five little ones hanging off her. She has a child on each hip, one little boy wrapped around one of her legs, another one tapping her tummy to try to get her attention, and a young girl nearby is stirring a pot on the stove.

"Ma," Kellyn says, stepping forward. He wraps her in a hug, careful of the two little ones she's holding. Then he takes one baby and thrusts it at Petrik and keeps the other one for himself. While holding the little one, he somehow manages to dislodge the boy from around his mother's leg.

"Kellyn, you're home! We didn't know to expect you," Mrs.

Derinor says. With her arms free, she steps forward to wrap him in a proper hug.

"Surprise," he says.

"And you brought guests!" the woman says, sounding thoroughly delighted. I don't understand how she could possibly feel that way with her house already overrun with children.

Kellyn makes the introductions, and the woman greets each of us in turn with a big hug. For once, I don't mind embracing a stranger.

"We're so sorry to impose, Mrs. Derinor," Temra begins.

"Nonsense, we're happy to have you! And please, call me Kahlia."

Petrik is holding the baby Kellyn thrust upon him as though he doesn't know what to do with it. The little one starts fussing, and Petrik looks around desperately for help.

"Turn her the other way," Kellyn says, "so she can see the room."

"I don't want to drop her."

Temra shakes her head before stepping forward to help him turn the child in his arms.

"Tias, Rallon, Wardra, go wash up and then set the table for dinner. We'll need four extra plates for our guests."

"Yes, Ma," they say, and tread back outside.

Kahlia helps the little girl at the stove now that her hands are free and finally listens to whatever the little boy who had been tapping on her wants to say.

I lean toward Kellyn. "How many of these children are you related to?"

"All of them."

My eyes widen.

"I have eleven siblings," he says without missing a beat.

"You never said anything about them," I accuse.

He shrugs before stepping forward to chat with his mother, Petrik wanders the house with the baby, and Temra and I help the children set the table. It's a crude piece, with hastily-nailed-together slabs at either end to accommodate all the children. The top has been sanded down and is stained with years of use, but it's even and manages to just barely fit in the kitchen.

We're so busy performing our tasks that we don't notice at first when Kellyn's father enters the house.

But when I see him, there's no mistaking his relation to Kellyn. He's even taller than his son, closer to seven feet than six. His hair is more red than Kellyn's, but their facial features are so similar. He's also a bit broader than Kellyn, with a little more at the waist. I can imagine Kellyn looking like this in thirty more years.

"Son," Mr. Derinor says, and they pat each other firmly on the back while hugging. Kellyn then greets the oldest two children and makes the introductions again, but there are now too many children for me to keep them all straight.

Temra, Petrik, and I are crammed onto one end of the table together. Children are spread out on either side of us while Kellyn sits closer to his parents at the head of the table.

"So, how did you all meet?" Mrs. Derinor—Kahlia—wants to know.

Since we can barely hear the question over the noisy table, Kellyn answers. "I was in Lirasu in between jobs, hoping to commission a weapon from the magical blacksmith there. She was, unfortunately, far too busy to take on a new commission just then. I hope to catch her when she's free another time." Kellyn makes a pointed look my way. "Then I met these three. They paid me to take them to Thersa on business, but we became such good friends that we're still traveling together. They have a job in the capital, so I thought we'd stop by on our way and visit for a bit."

The lie is so smooth, but I think that's mostly because it's filled with truths or near truths, anyway.

"And what business are you in?" Mr. Derinor asks.

"Ziva is a smithy," Temra says. "I'm her assistant. We're traveling to the capital in search of work." Technically not a lie.

Petrik wipes his lips on the back of one hand. "I'm a story-teller."

Also not a lie, but definitely not the whole truth. We're probably safe in this small town that rarely receives news of what's happening outside of it. But if anyone in the village does hear about the warlord's bounty and knows that a scholar of magic and a gifted blacksmith have arrived, they just might put it all together.

"How wonderful," Kahlia says. "You must tell us a story before the children go to bed."

Groans sound around the table. Not in regard to the story, but the bedtime, I think.

"Kellyn," Kyren, the eleven-year-old, says, "did you kill any bandits on the road this time?"

"Kyren, that is not appropriate dinner conversation," Mr. Derinor says.

"Nor is it appropriate conversation at all," Kahlia adds.

"Quite right."

Kellyn winks at the boy, a promise to tell him all about it later.

Kyren turns to the three of us at the end of the table. "When I grow up, I'm going to be a mercenary like my brother."

"You most certainly will not," Mrs. Derinor says. "It's bad enough that I have to spend my days worrying over Kellyn. Horrid profession."

I think Kellyn senses a lecture coming on, because he changes the subject, asking his da about the crops and farming.

We mostly keep silent during dinner. There's too much to observe to bother with talking. At one point, a fight between two boys breaks out, but Mrs. Derinor stops it with a single look.

There are three bedrooms in the house. One for Mr. and Mrs. Derinor and the babies, one for the girls, and one for the boys.

Kellyn assures his parents we will be fine sleeping outside. In fact, the family has a few hammocks set up in the trees. I've never slept in one before, but I find it much more comfortable than the ground.

It isn't until I'm wrapped in homespun blankets and staring at the branches above that I realize I didn't feel panicked once today.

I felt safe.

Children don't seem to spark my anxieties the way adults do, and Mr. and Mrs. Derinor were too kind for me to worry about them.

So many people in that house, and yet, it felt like home. It felt like safety.

I can't imagine why Kellyn ever left.

I rise early to visit the local smithy the next morning.

He seems confused at first by my appearance and even more perplexed when I ask if I can have any leftover scraps of metal he has no use for. Used nails. Shavings. Tools that didn't turn out right.

"You an apprentice?" he asks me. The man is clean-shaven, perhaps in his early forties, and he seems kind.

"Something like that. Would it also be all right if I borrowed your kiln?"

"What exactly are you making?"

"I'm not quite sure. But hopefully, something to keep us safe."

He thinks me odd—I can tell by the rise of his brow and how he turns his face away—but he humors me.

I help tidy his workspace in exchange for his help and materials. This smithy works in iron alone—he hasn't the supplies to fashion steel, but I don't think that will be a problem.

So long as the magic decides to cooperate.

I alternate between days at the forge and days at the farm in the coming weeks. The Derinors need all the helping hands they can get, and I'd feel like a monster if I ate their food without helping with the chores.

Farming is hard yet satisfying work. We wake before the sun

is quite up and go to the fields, where we pull weeds from the dirt, fill in gopher holes, and make sure the water supply gets to the end of the field. We shovel manure from the horses into the soil that's soon to be planted, pluck fruit from the already ripened trees, help tend to the livestock.

As someone who's come from a life where I buy all the food and clothes I need, it's absolutely fascinating to see how a family provides for everything entirely on their own.

Kahlia teaches Temra and me how to sheer sheep, spin the wool into yarn, dye it, and knit it—though for the most part it's just us staring at her in fascination. Knitting is far too complicated to pick up right away.

We learn to make delicious meals with the barest of ingredients, how to stitch up holes in our clothing, how to feed the babies.

There are of course the less fun tasks, such as changing the cloth diapers or hauling water from the river, washing laundry, and such. But we do it all with a smile on our faces. So relieved to finally be safe. To finally feel like we can breathe.

Mrs. Derinor has to be the sweetest soul on the planet. As if it weren't enough that she manages all her children, she also bakes sweets to take to the children of the village widows. She loans out her children to help with household chores for the elderly, even takes in little ones when their parents are out in the fields at times.

In the evenings, Temra and I sit off to the side while Petrik tells stories to the children. He's so well read that he has an endless supply of tales to share with Kellyn's eager siblings. Stories of valiant lady knights saving princes in dragon-guarded towers, stories of mermaids in the sea, or gryphon-riding armies.

Temra is just as transfixed as any of the children.

Getting my hands on bricks, clay, and more iron is tricky. I visit several houses in the village looking for the items. Temra accompanies me to dispel any awkwardness. People are so friendly, not questioning anything. One person hands over a broken hoe. Another finds a cracked clay pot to donate.

I wish I had grown up in a small town. Amanor is lovely. So few people, everyone kind and willing to help their neighbors. I wonder if it's even possible to feel unsafe in such a place.

I borrow the Derinors' shovel to dig a large hole into the ground just outside the forge. I line the interior with clay and brick, leaving no gaps. It's a slow process, stacking the bricks, lining them with clay, visiting more villagers when I run out of materials.

But I love every moment of it.

It feels so good to be using my hands again.

I may not be hammering, but using the kiln, wielding the familiar tools, feeling safe again—I cherish all of it.

Farming. Forging. Farming. Forging. Laughing with the children, listening to Petrik's stories, watching Kellyn interact with his family—I enjoy all of it.

On a farming day, I return from the river with a bucketful of water in each hand. I pass by the storage shed, where the Derinors keep their farming equipment overnight.

Deep voices stop me in my tracks.

"I'm so sorry, Da," Kellyn says. "I had nearly three thousand ockles saved up for you and Ma, but we were robbed on the road, which is why we arrived with nothing but the clothes on our backs."

"I'm only glad you're safe," Mr. Derinor, Garon, says.

"But you would have been able to expand the house, buy more seeds for the next planting season, and—"

"Kellyn, you know your ma and I don't want you doing what you do. We would much rather have you safe than have you continue to send us money. We wish you would give up the sword and settle down. Speaking of which, don't think it didn't escape my notice that you arrived with two young women. Which one do you have your eye on?"

He doesn't speak for a moment, and I hold my breath.

"The tall one," Kellyn answers.

"The quiet one?" his father inquires.

"Yes, she's really quite amazing when she does speak."

"Well, there! Stop swinging that sword around, marry the girl, and settle down. That's how things are meant to be done."

I nearly drop my buckets.

"Da, I don't want to give up the sword. Besides, Ziva thinks I'm a selfish crook who's obsessed with money. She'll never have me."

"Have you made a gesture?" Garon asks.

"Oh, Da—"

"No, you listen here, young man. Your ma was the beauty of the village. Every lad and some of the ladies wanted her. But do you know what I did?"

"You didn't propose first; you proposed the grandest," Kellyn utters, deadpan, as though he's heard the words a million times.

"That's right. I declared my love in front of the entire village. I laid my soul bare to show her just how much I cared."

"People don't marry so young anymore, Da. Besides, this one doesn't like grand gestures. She hates attention. That would never go over well."

"Then think of what would be a grand gesture to her and do it. Women are all about us telling them our feelings and showing that we care. Do that, and she won't be able to say no to you."

"This conversation is making me really uncomfortable."

"Well, good. You should be uncomfortable. Love is uncomfortable at first. It's terrifying and exhilarating. But that will pass. It will become easier and something that you *need* rather than want. And if that doesn't happen, then you're with the wrong person."

"I know, Da."

"Good."

I shuffle away from the pair before I'm seen, my mind whirling with the overheard words. I had no idea Kellyn's father was such a romantic, but that doesn't surprise me as much as Kellyn's first words.

I bring the water into the house for Kahlia before excusing myself. I head for the surrounding trees, near the hammocks, needing time to think. Birdsong mixes with the rushing river in a soothing tone. The grass dents comfortably under my boots, and the trees provide me cover.

But either I wasn't as quiet as I thought or Kellyn saw me tiptoeing over here.

Because he's suddenly there.

He looks troubled. "How much of that did you overhear?"

"Probably all of it."

"I'm so sorry. My da is ridiculous."

"I think he's sweet." But that's beside the point. "Why didn't you tell me?"

He shuffles between putting his weight on his left and right leg. "I'm going to need you to be more specific."

"I thought you selfish. I was so angry at you for taking our money and not jumping into danger when you were needed. But it was all for your family. They desperately need the money, and they can't afford to lose you."

He doesn't say anything, so I repeat, "Why didn't you tell me?"

"Because . . . it was easier to let you think me a villain than to tell you some sob story about my poor and enormous family."

"I asked about your family. You could have told me then."

"I know. I . . . have a hard time talking about personal things."

Vulnerability. That's what it comes down to for him.

"There's so much love here," I say. "Why would you ever leave? It's safe and beautiful, and those children adore you."

He steps forward a few feet to lean his shoulder against the nearest tree. "It's hard for you to imagine, isn't it? Ever leaving somewhere safe? This place is wonderful, and I love to visit. But it's also stifling. I don't want to be a farmer. I didn't like any of the seven girls my age in the village.

"Besides, I wanted adventure. I wanted to see the world and meet new people. I would never have had that here."

We're so different, he and I. He wants to see the world and I want to hide from it. Here he feels stifled. Here I feel safe.

I wonder if he's thinking the same thoughts I am in the silence that follows.

"Wait," I say, looking up. "You talk about personal things. You made a point of telling me ridiculous nonsense about your feelings early on."

He grins wickedly. "You mean my feelings about you?"

My cheeks heat and I look down.

"That's not personal. Besides, it'll never amount to anything because you don't want it to. So why should I feel vulnerable about that? I do it simply to get a rise out of you. To see that lovely blush spread across your freckled cheeks."

"I'm glad making me uncomfortable is so entertaining for you."

He steps forward until he's standing right in front of me. I stare at the triangle of skin beneath his throat, where his shirt is cut into the shape of a V. Then his fingers are on my cheek, and my whole body lights up in flame.

"It's not that," he says. "I hope that one of these times, you might not be uncomfortable. That you'll be brave enough to try something new."

I clench my jaw and look up. "I can be brave if I want to. I just don't want to be brave with you."

His head angles to the side, and his eyes are on my lips. "Why?"

The question is so sincere and so startling that I freeze.

Because he's selfish?

No, he's not. I know that now.

Because he's arrogant?

Yes, but not overly so. I actually kind of envy that about him.

Because he's so big and terrifying?

He's never hurt me, and I know he would never hurt me.

So then, why?

Because this is new. Because I've never done this before. I don't know how. It isn't safe. It isn't familiar.

I can't tell if the next words out of my lips are intentional or not, but out they come anyway. "Because I don't know how." I realize then that my eyes are trained on his lips. I can tell this because they're moving closer as he leans his head down.

"To kiss or to be brave? Because I can help you with the first one, if you'd like?"

The question might sound arrogant on someone else. But he says it so gently, so openly—in such a way that I know he cares about the answer, and I know that the rejection will hurt. Because this time, he's really putting himself out there.

He's allowing himself to be vulnerable. For me.

And if he can do that for me, can I do that for him?

Kellyn's body halts in front of me, just mere inches away. It takes me a few seconds to realize he asked me a question.

It's completely up to me if I want to be brave or not. And he's showing me the way.

"Yes." The word is the barest breath of sound, but he hears it clearly.

CHAPTER TWENTY-ONE

Kellyn is more gentle than I imagined he could be. When he lets his lips touch mine, the contact is so soft and expels the breath from my lungs. I wait for something to happen.

Does one suddenly understand how to kiss? Or does it take several tries before you pick it up? Should I feel swept up in feelings or something?

Because mostly I'm just terrified because I don't know what I'm doing, and he's just standing there. And is this supposed to feel this awkward?

As if he can feel the tension in me, Kellyn's hands go to my face to steady me. No, to angle my head differently. And then his lips surround my upper lip, tugging gently. He pulls back and repeats the movement before turning his attention to my lower lip.

That's when the change happens. Something clicks into place. I feel the tug of his lips all the way down in my toes. My fear evaporates, and there's nothing but me and this boy.

And our lips.

And then I'm kissing him back. Because I get it now. And I understand why Temra always wants to sneak off to do this act. It's wonderful and freeing and removes every other thought from my head.

No worries or fear. Just heat and lips pressed together, which turns into bodies pressed together. Kellyn angles me against one of the trees. And then he's kissing me harder.

And I like that even more.

His hands slide from my cheeks to my arms, down to my hands, where he tangles our fingers and raises them high, pinning them to the tree above my head. The bark should be uncomfortable at my back, but for some reason it only makes this more exciting. Its sole purpose in life is to help me get closer to this boy, who has done nothing but protect me and try to understand me.

I want to protect and understand him, too.

I pull away to say, "I'm going to make you that weapon."

His eyes take a moment to focus. "I didn't realize this was a transaction."

I grin. "It's not. But I want to make you one all the same."

"Only if you can do it while staying safe."

"Okay."

And then I feel stupid. The kissing was great, and then I interrupted it to say something stupid. And now the fear is coming back and the awkwardness and how can I look at him after this?

"Take a breath," he says, not moving a muscle to step away from me. "You don't need to panic."

I bite my lip to keep from saying anything else stupid, but my traitorous eyes are trained on his lips.

"If you're not done kissing me," he says, "you need only lean forward. I can promise I will always return a kiss from you."

Initiate it? Oh, no, I couldn't do that. Is it different if I'm the one starting it? What if I do it wrong?

A breath of a laugh expels from his lips as he leans to the side, near my ear. "What is it like in that head of yours?"

"Busy," I mutter.

"Maybe this will help."

His lips trace the outline of my ear; then he's kissing down my throat. When I make a sound that I don't recognize, Kellyn pauses in place and continues to kiss that spot. He runs the tip of his tongue over it, sucks lightly, nips at it with his teeth before resuming his kissing.

I'm dying. The most embarrassing noises are coming out of me, and I don't know how to stop.

He takes pity on me, lifting his head. I can breathe for all of half a second before I realize he's only moving to the opposite side of my neck to try the exact same thing there.

And then my thoughts are swept away as something else fills their place.

Need.

I wrench his face up to mine so I can taste his lips again. He's smiling against me. I can feel it.

Arrogant.

But I realize I'm smiling, too.

I think I'm up against that tree for hours. Because when Kellyn steps back, it's dark outside. I hadn't even noticed the cold until he wasn't touching me anymore.

"If we don't return to the house, someone will come looking for us," he says between panting breaths.

Something delicious turns in my stomach to know I made him sound like that. Excited and out of breath.

"All right."

But I don't move. I'm stuck to that tree, my head wonderfully cloudy. I close my eyes, savoring what just happened, letting myself feel the memory of it.

And then his lips are there again. One last sweet reminder.

He grabs my hand and tugs me away. My legs feel stiff from disuse, but my lips are tingling.

Kellyn pauses when we're just outside the house. Then he's patting down my hair. *Righting it*, I realize. That only makes my face warm again. He takes my hands and tries to tug me inside with him.

"We should go in separately," I rush to say.

He turns to me. "Because you're embarrassed to be seen with me in front of my own family?"

"No, so that no one suspects what we were doing."

"Ziva, everyone is going to take one look at you and know exactly what you were doing."

"What is that supposed to mean?"

"Your cheeks are stained red, your lips are swollen, and your clothes are rumpled."

That has me backing away from the door. "I can't go in there like this!"

"Do you want me to tell everyone you're ill?"

"Yes, that's a great idea."

He looks up at the sky, and I realize he wasn't serious. "I promise it won't be that bad. Now come here."

He tugs me through the door after him. Everyone is readying the dinner table. The house is warm and loud and full of movement. No one takes notice of us. Until his mother looks up and sees my hand in his. She smiles.

"Well, are you going to stand there or help?" she asks.

And that's that. We separate. I put my focus on hefting food to the table, but everywhere I go, I'm aware of exactly where Kellyn is in the room. Like there's a string connecting us, and every time he moves, I feel the tug.

He sits beside me instead of near his parents tonight. I think maybe everything will be fine.

Until Temra sees me.

She opens her mouth, closes it. Notes how close Kellyn is sitting next to me. But she doesn't say a word as she sits on my other side.

It isn't until Kellyn's father has offered thanks to the Sisters for the meal and everyone noisily digs into their food that she leans forward and says, "Well done."

That night, it truly is impossible to sleep. I'm replaying every moment of the evening in my head, memorizing every movement and every feeling. My mind is so busy that it won't calm. And even when the dawn comes, I'm still staring at the canopy.

When the boys disappear for chores, Temra corners me before I can do the same. "I want to hear every single detail."

So I relive it again, answering every question she asks. It feels nice to share this good thing with her. I don't even seem to feel that tired, despite not having slept.

It's strange to have a mind thinking on good things for a change. Right now, I'm not scared of anything. Not what anyone will think of me, or if I should be embarrassed by anything I've done. Is this how everyone else feels? Those who don't have my attacks because they can't stop worrying?

Everything is happy and wonderful until I see him again.

I spent the day in the forge, constructing more of the mold, while Kellyn worked the fields. I haven't seen him in hours, and I beat him home for dinner. But the moment he steps into the house, I know it. I can't meet his eyes. It's embarrassing. Because I know what he's thinking and he knows what I'm thinking. And Temra does, too, but she's too kind to say anything about it.

How do people deal with this? These moments and these pressures and the constant thoughts that just don't go away?

Being social is hard, and sharing a piece of yourself with someone in this way is even harder.

I sit at the table, and Kellyn leans his long body down into the chair next to me. I feel myself start to panic at his nearness, but either Kellyn knows me better than I think he does, or he's just naturally capable of giving me what I need.

He starts talking. "The little ones joined us in the fields today. They like helping with the orchards. It amuses them to no end to see how high I can hoist them in the air to reach the fruit at the top of the trees. Afterward, Tias spotted a garden snake winding through the tall grass, so we chased it. I caught it, and everyone let it wrap around their fingers for a bit until we released it back to the wild. Then Wardra found a patch of flowers, and she made us all crowns."

When I finally look at him, I see he has a crown of flowers in his hair.

In his other hand, he brandishes a yellow blossom on a long stem and sets it beside me.

His talking puts me to rest. It gives my mind something to process without any pressure, and my heart warms at the sight of the flower.

"I arrived home early enough to help with dinner," I say. "Your mom taught me how to make bread. Turns out these hands are good for more than just beating metal. I hadn't thought dough could be so tiring."

Kellyn reaches under the table and takes my hand in his as I talk.

And everything is fine again.

Soon, I find myself lighting up whenever I see Kellyn, even looking forward to it, instead of dreading it. My mind relaxes, and I revel in Kellyn's presence. I love smelling the flowers he brings me. I love it when he takes my hand and even become brave enough to take his.

I love touching him when we kiss. Curling my fingers over his arm, running the flat of my hand over his chest, exploring the plane of his throat with my lips.

I'm happy.

And everything might just be okay. Temra is safe. I feel safe for once. Kellyn is perfect. Petrik is a favorite among the children, and he spends every second he can with them.

And then the day comes when the mold is finally ready. The last of the clay dries, and I invite Petrik, Temra, and Kellyn to join me at the forge.

"I don't know if this will work," I warn, "but I thought you all would want to be here for this part."

Petrik scrounged up more parchment from somewhere in the village, and he's been working to rewrite all the progress he lost on his book. He has it with him now, and he scribbles like mad from his spot on the ground, where he has a clear view of the hole. Temra is by his side, her arm on his shoulder as she reads what he writes.

"It'll work," she says without looking up. Total faith in me.

I don't think I deserve it.

Kellyn wears Lady Killer on his back. After our initial arrival to his family's home, Kahlia forbade weapons in the house, so we stored everything high up in one of the trees. But I told Kellyn to bring his longsword by the forge so I could take its measurements. I can get started on his magicked weapon as soon as Secret Eater is taken care of.

With my friends watching patiently and the curious smithy side-eyeing me, I heat up all the piles of scraps I've gathered. One by one I pour pots of liquid metal into the mold in the ground, filling it until the molten iron reaches the top.

I have so many eyes on me. For real this time. This is no imagining in my head. People have gathered to see what I'll do.

Even some townsfolk have appeared, wanting to know what's got everyone so intrigued outside the smithy.

I look inward for the strength I found in the prison cell. I've done magic in front of people before. I can do it again. Even if so much more is at stake this time. Not just the lives of four young adults, but maybe all of Ghadra.

It has to be kept safe.

I'm the bladesmith. The only one gifted with magic. I created Secret Eater, *almost allowed it to fall into the wrong hands*, and maybe it's always been up to me to fix it.

I remove the broadsword from my side and unsheathe the weapon.

"Please work," I whisper.

I slowly dip the sword into the liquid metal until only scant inches of the blade and the entire hilt remain visible. The mold does not crack. The liquid metal does not disperse.

I take a deep breath and just stand there, holding the sword in place.

But I need to coax the heated iron to do my will, so I speak to it. "I don't know why I was given this ability. Whether it was a gift from the Sisters or some curse of my birth. I don't know what I was meant to do with it. All I know is that I've spent my life trying to make the world a safer place with my creations. Yet, I somehow managed to put it at more risk with this singular blade. So whatever the reason, I ask this now: Keep the sword safe. Keep it hidden from the world. Maybe it will have a purpose one day. A purpose for good. But keep it safe until someone worthy comes along. Someone with the good character not to misuse its abilities. Someone with the power to keep it out of the hands of those who would use it for evil. Let only that person have the strength to pull the sword from this stone."

Normally, it would take weeks for the metal to cool on its own. It's far too big to quench, so I assumed I would have to find a way to prop the sword in place and camp out here until everything was done.

But the magic has a different idea.

There's a cracking sound and a rumble in the ground beneath my feet.

I jump backward; Kellyn catches me before I hit the ground, and we run.

A crater opens up in the earth, a circle perhaps ten feet in diameter. The mold snaps, breaking off in chunks that rain down, revealing the iron rock, perfectly cooled in place, and the sword held firmly in its grasp.

I turn to the smithy, who has an expression of shock on his face. "May I borrow a hammer and chisel?"

He flees, and I think I might have scared him off completely, but he returns with what I requested.

Jumping into the crater, I hold the tools aloft, pounding at the stone with all my might. Not a crack, not a chip. Nothing I do will crumble it.

And though perhaps it's silly, I wrap my hands around the hilt of the sword and pull straight up. Of course it doesn't move.

I hold out a hand to Kellyn and Petrik and Temra. They each take a turn trying to pull out the blade. It doesn't so much as bend from its position.

"You did it," Kellyn says. He laughs and grabs me under the arms, hoisting me in the air and twirling me around.

"Of course she did," Temra says. She hugs me next.

Petrik pats me on the back. "I'm thinking of writing a second book. Secret Eater's story. Our story. It'll be filled with adventure. And romance." This causes me to blush, but Petrik can't help the glance he gives Temra out of the corner of his eye. "Generations will know what you did with this sword. They will know it is here, waiting for its intended master. Safe until the time is right."

"I wish I knew what the broadsword was meant to do," I say. "But I hope I'm long, long dead when it's pulled from the iron."

"I'm certain it will do great things for a time far ahead of us," Petrik says.

I approach my creation once more, place one booted foot against the rock and try to shift it. It's far too heavy to budge, of course. "If I'd known a crater would open up in the earth, I wouldn't have done this here." I send an apologetic look the smithy's way.

"Leave it," he says. "I think it's fine ornamentation for my business." A pause. "You that magical smithy I've heard rumors about?"

"That's me," I say.

"I'd sure be honored if you'd show me—"

The smithy—I never even asked him his name—grabs his navel, his fingers touching the spear shaft now imbedded there. He falls to the ground, his breathing shallow. I'm staring far too long at him before I make sense of what happened.

When I raise my eyes, I see the horses barreling toward us. Scarlet tunics on their riders. And at the front of the charge—

Warlord Kymora.

CHAPTER TWENTY-TWO

Temra rushes over to where the smithy landed on the ground. She holds the man's hand but looks to me helplessly. "He needs a healer."

He needs to not have a spear in his chest. Why is there a spear in his chest? Why would Kymora hurt him? He did nothing. He was innocent. He helped me protect the sword.

She assumed he was harboring you.

You did this.

My fault. Just like everything else.

Kellyn steps in front of me, putting himself between Kymora and me. He and Temra have both taken action, and I'm still standing there. I don't know what to do.

I watch as the warlord's horse comes to a stop about thirty feet away, her men halting just behind her. How many of them even are there? Far too many to count. Kymora dismounts, takes a few steps toward Kellyn.

She says nothing. Her face shows nothing. And somehow, the nothing is more terrifying than if she were screaming and raging. She's unpredictable, and unpredictable people are the most dangerous.

Her eyes find the sword that bears her sigil at the hilt, the falcon wings at the guard.

"What have you done with my weapon?" she asks.

And though this is a confrontation of the worst kind, I find my voice. Because I did something right. The consequence has caught up with me, but what I did was *right*. "I've protected it from you. Only someone worthy can pull the sword out of its iron casing."

She eyes my creation, her face growing thoughtful. Then, "Could you explain to me why I've had to chase you through half of Ghadra? I offered you protection and freedom. Why in the hells would you run and do *that*"—she points—"to my weapon?"

"Because you were going to use it to enslave all of Ghadra. You would have forced me to make weapons for your soldiers so you could take over the world."

Kymora bites the inside of her cheek as she thinks. "Someone told you this?"

"The sword did. When you cut yourself on it. I heard your thoughts. It revealed your secrets to me."

Her brow rises a fraction of an inch. "You really do have a gift. Unfortunately, you seem just as resistant to helping me as your mother."

Temra steps up beside me, her hand finding mine. I realize I don't hear the smithy breathing anymore. He must be gone.

And somehow, that pales in comparison to what Kymora has just told me.

Red tinges the edges of my vision. I'm squeezing Temra's hand hard enough to hurt. She's shaking beside me. With fear or fury, I can't be certain.

"Leave, Kymora." This comes from Kellyn. "I have great respect for what you have done for our kingdom, but your weapon is gone. Trouble us no more. There's no reason for this to get ugly."

Kymora turns her gaze to the mercenary. "If you hadn't aided these two, I might have offered you a position among my ranks. I've heard you can do remarkable things with that sword. But you've irritated me, and I don't do well with irritations."

Kellyn tries again. "There's no need to fight."

"You're right. There will be no fighting. Ziva will come with me willingly. She may have rendered my original sword useless, but if she built it once, she can do it again." She looks right at me as she says, "When your mother denied me, I didn't know there were two little girls sleeping upstairs. Threatening your father didn't work to make her see reason, but I bet using you would have. I won't make that mistake again. So believe me when I say, *Come with me now, Ziva Tellion, or I will start carving up your sister in front of you.*"

I take just a moment to steady my pounding heart and accelerated breathing before stepping forward. Temra yanks me back.

"Don't you dare," she whispers. "You're not going anywhere."

Kymora seems amused by the exchange, but then, as though

just remembering something, she looks around at our small company.

"Where is my son?" she asks.

Her son?

My eyes do a sweep of the area. All the villagers have returned to their homes, likely running at the first sign of trouble. There's no one in sight save me, Temra, Kellyn, and Pe—

Wait, where is Petrik? How long has he been missing? I don't actually recall seeing him after the warlord appeared.

Did he abandon us?

"I don't like repeating myself," Kymora says.

"We don't know your son," Kellyn says. "We have no idea who you're talking about."

The moment seems to grow more tense as we wait to see what Kymora will do. I need to go to her. I have to protect my sister. I have to protect Kellyn. But I still seem stuck on the fact that Petrik is nowhere in sight and my parents' murderer is right before me.

"I'm here, Mother."

Something's not right, because the voice doesn't belong to a newcomer. No, Petrik comes out of the dead smithy's forge, his hands clasped behind his back as he steps in front of us.

If it were possible for her to look more displeased, the warlord somehow manages it.

"What happened to you?" Kymora asks. Each word comes out so slowly, it feels like its own sentence.

Petrik looks over his shoulder to say, "Go wait in the smithy. I need to speak with her."

Temra's mouth unhinges, falling to the floor. "No. She's mistaken. You can't be—"

"Her son? I've wished it weren't true many times myself. Not the most loving person, is she?"

Kymora snorts at his words.

"Go inside. Now." Petrik's voice changes, and as I stare at him, I realize the similarities between the two of them. They hold themselves the same way. Petrik's skin may be dark while hers is fair, but they have some of the same features.

Kellyn recovers the quickest, grabbing Temra and me by the arms. Leading us to the smithy.

"Go round the back," Kymora says to half her men. "Make sure they don't get any ideas about leaving." She steps toward *her son* so her men can't overhear the conversation.

We get ourselves into the smithy's forge and shut the door. Temra leans against the back of it. I'd been working in here. The kiln is still raging, which means the windows are open. We can hear every word of their exchange.

"What have you been doing?" Kymora demands.

"Working on my book," Petrik says. "You know why I followed you to Lirasu. I had my own agenda with the bladesmith."

"You came because you knew I would get her to Orena's Territory. You were permitted to question her once she was in my employ."

"Well, Ziva didn't want to go with you, so I had to change my plans."

I can practically hear the warlord grit her teeth from here. "So instead of telling me of her intention to flee, you decided you would just jaunt around Ghadra with her?"

"You always manage to sound in such a way as to suggest that I owe you something. I was raised in a *library*. I saw you maybe once a year while I was growing up. I thought this journey would be a nice time for us to finally spend some quality time together. But the whole trip you were consulting with your men. Making plans for world domination, I later learn. So, yes, I didn't tell you where the smithy was going. It would have upset *my* plans."

"Your little book is of no consequence compared to what I've been working on for *decades*."

"Can you believe him?" Kellyn asks to no one in particular, interrupting my eavesdropping.

"He lied to us," Temra says, so quietly it hurts my heart.

He may have lied, but he's doing something to help us now. I'm sure of it. Why else would he drag out the conversation with his mother?

"He's stalling," I say as the realization hits me. He saved Temra before. He's trying to save us now.

"What?" they echo.

"He's giving us time. He means for us to do something. We need to figure out what it is."

"He's arguing with his *mother*," Temra says, "or did you not catch that part?" She rubs her upper chest, right above her heart, as though it aches. I don't think she's conscious of the action.

Kellyn's gaze shifts to me. "What should we do?"

"Look around. Maybe there's . . . another exit? Something underground or—I don't know."

Kellyn humors me, starts scouting the area, moving around workbenches and tables, stepping on slats on the ground. Temra is stricken, unable to do anything but stand there, her thoughts turning inward.

I do a sweep of the forge.

I have to be right. Petrik has to be stalling her. He can't have betrayed us like this only to send us into a nice little cage for his mother to collect after they're done speaking.

And why in the twin hells didn't he tell us who he is?

Would you have let him join you on the journey if you had known who his mother is?

Absolutely not.

My eyes trail everywhere. The tables, the floor, even the ceiling. Come on, Petrik. What am I looking for?

"So many things make sense now," Temra says without any emotion. "The way he barely hesitated when he joined us on the road and we warned him dangerous people were following us. He knew exactly who was following us and that she was no danger to him.

"And the time that guard hesitated before trying to kill him. Right before Kellyn saved us? Petrik must have been telling that soldier who he was. Telling him Kymora wouldn't want him dead.

"He's been with us because he never really cared if we succeeded or not. He knew he would be safe, and he wanted to pick Ziva's brain for information for as long as he had her."

She growls then, sends her fist slamming into the door behind her. "How dare he?"

"Temra, focus," I say. "We have to—"

And then I see it.

The kiln. The handles hanging out. I didn't put anything in there aside from the iron I was melting, and neither did the smithy. He wasn't working on anything. He was too curious to see what I was up to.

And now he's dead.

I swallow that thought and reach for the first metal handle.

It's attached to a cart axle, one end bright red, ready to be magicked.

The next one is a pitchfork, the tines simmering with heat.

And the final piece is a pair of tongs holding a forging hammer.

Petrik did this. He put them in the kiln, heating them for me.

He believes in me.

Enough to go against his mother.

He's chosen us as his family. Not her.

And though he may never get Temra to understand, I do.

I grab the axle and set to doing what I do best.

But first, "Kellyn, give me your sword."

He hands it over, and I shove the tip into the flames.

CHAPTER TWENTY-THREE

I 've always forged my own weapons. I enjoy the process of creating something out of nothing. The magic is wonderful, too, but I love shaping steel into what I need.

Maybe that's why it never occurred to me to magic something that was already made.

Or I guess it was never a necessity to magic something that was already made. But after what happened in the prison cell, I know that I can do this.

"The fact that you're my son is the only reason I haven't skinned you alive yet." Kymora's voice floats through the open windows.

"I love you, too," Petrik says sarcastically.

"Enough. You do as you wish, but if you come between me and the smithy again, I will not be so lenient."

"Leave her be."

"Excuse me?"

"I've never asked you for anything. Not once. But I'm asking now. Leave my friends alone. Let them go. Give up this mission you have. The economy is finally settling after the rift that splitting the kingdom wrought on Ghadra. Don't stir it up again by trying to control everything. There's peace. Leave it that way."

"You were too young to remember what things were like before Arund split the realm. You have no idea how that ruined everything."

"I don't care. I'm still asking. Let them go. Let this go. You have enough men and power to take everything even without the bladesmith. Let her live her life."

"We're done talking now."

There's a silence. I don't know if Petrik is staring his mother down or something else. I can't hear anything more that may be happening outside.

Until, "Ziva, come out. You've had a chance to say your goodbyes. I've been more than patient with you. It's time to go."

Temra, Kellyn, and I hold our newly magicked weapons. My sister and my—and Kellyn both nod their readiness.

And we exit, weapons held at the ready.

Kymora's eyes narrow at the metal in our hands. Temra wields the pitchfork, using it like a staff while she walks. Kellyn has his longsword unsheathed, both hands wrapped around the hilt. And I have my hammers, one magicked in my left, and a regular forging hammer in my right.

Petrik steps into line with us. Temra wordlessly hands him

the axle, her jaw clenched tightly. She didn't think he would side with us. I told her he would.

But she's still pissed.

Kymora looks at our line, says nothing, and backs up to her horse. She saddles herself once more. Thankfully, no one else appears to have a spear or other throwables.

"Bring me the girls. Kill the boys."

She looks at Petrik as she says it.

Her private army all drop down from their horses one by one, unsheathing their bastard swords. And then they advance.

We keep the forge at our backs so no one can get behind us. But we spread out, give ourselves plenty of room to swing.

And then we swing hard.

Petrik doesn't need to ask what the long stick of metal does before using it. He throws, watches as the tool turns end over end, striking soldiers as it goes. The axle is entirely made of metal, not so breakable as the staff was, and it spins impossibly fast. Once he catches it, he casts again. And again. And again.

The first soldier reaches me, where I stand wielding my twin hammers. He swings at my right hand, hoping to dislodge the weapon there, all the more easily to capture me. But I raise my left hand, point the hammer there right at him. His sword bounces off the invisible shield my magicked hammer creates, rebounding with the same amount of force with which it struck. He staggers backward, and I use the distraction to swing my dominant arm at him.

I may not be a fighter, but I know how to swing a hammer hard, and I do. The soldier is shorter than I am, so it's no hardship to bring the tool down on his head.

The sound my hammer makes as it connects with the skull is something I'll never forget. But I swallow the bile in my throat and prepare to do it again.

Temra is right beside me, holding out the pitchfork in both her hands. I worry for her. The tool is heavy, too heavy for her to use for an extended amount of time, but she doesn't show any fatigue yet.

She catches the sword swinging straight down at her between two of the tines. With a simple twist, the sword breaks in two, the magic of the pitchfork keeping the prongs strong and giving them the ability to break anything that comes between them. The soldier doesn't have time to stare at his broken weapon for long before Temra sticks him with the spikes.

Kellyn fights as he usually does, unable to use his sword's magic just yet.

But the opportunity presents itself soon.

Eventually, the bodies pile up, and we have to maneuver around them in order to use our weapons. Kellyn steps away from the forge, which allows a few men to get behind him.

While I was staring at Kellyn's fire-heated sword back in the forge, begging my own brain for inspiration on what to do with it, I remembered the soldiers surrounding us on all sides of the forge.

Kellyn is already a good fighter. What he needs is something to assist if he's overrun with enemies. It's the only time I've seen him thwarted.

When he's surrounded, the sword will shift in the direction he's meant to turn to catch the next advancing attack. He uses that prompting to take out as many enemies as possible. The sword knows when an opponent is about to swing. It jerks in the right direction, and Kellyn only has to shift his feet with the motion. He takes out five soldiers even when he's completely surrounded. Dodges exactly when he needs to. Swings when he needs to.

He's incredible without this ability, but with it—

He's unbeatable.

In just a few minutes, we've taken down half of Kymora's forces. She watches from atop her horse, seemingly uninterested. She doesn't flinch as soldier after soldier, man after man, woman after woman, falls to my makeshift weapons.

A dangerous feeling wells within my chest.

Hope.

Maybe, just maybe, once again I can pull my friends out of another tight spot. Maybe we'll survive this. Maybe we'll all be happy. Temra and I together. She with Petrik and I with Kellyn. Maybe everything will be as it's supposed to be.

But after a time, I realize that we're separating. Petrik is far to my right. Kellyn, far to my left. And Temra—Temra is behind me, far out of range, but handling things well enough on her own.

"Charge the smithy."

The order comes from Kymora, and I don't know how any of her soldiers can rally together in all the bedlam, but a group of them run at me straight on, smashing into my raised magicked hammer.

I go down from the force of so many, but so do my attackers. The magic of the shield sends them crashing to the ground, but I'm the first one to catch my feet. I swing my hammer at the first guard, catch his shoulder, feel the crunch as the reverberation shoots up my own arm.

But there are so many of them. They fan out, and some get behind me. My shield doesn't reach there, and someone slams into me from behind. I stumble, and several more guards charge my right side, the one holding the plain hammer. They wrest it from me before I can raise my shield.

With naught but my left hammer, I charge into the men ahead of me. They fall from the power of the shield, hitting the ground one after another.

A sharp jab hits my back—the pommel of a sword, I think. I try to catch my feet, but I land painfully on the ground. This time, someone else helps me back up.

By my hair.

More men grab on to me, and then my magicked hammer is gone, too.

Someone slings a fist into my stomach, taking the breath from me, forcing all my limbs limp. A rope materializes, binds my wrists behind my back.

And then that voice is right next to me. "Take her. I'll be along once I deal with the sister."

My breath slams back into me in time to watch Kymora drift toward Temra at a leisurely pace. My sister is too focused on the soldier in front of her to notice.

And then I lose my feet as I'm lifted into the air, being carried away.

"Kellyn!" I scream at the top of my lungs.

He turns at my voice, having just killed the last of the soldiers surrounding him.

"Save Temra!" I shout, even as the men pull me toward the nearest horse. "Get her out of here!"

An elbow connects with my cheekbone, knocking my head to the side. It throbs painfully. I don't stop the words, but they come out quietly now, almost like a prayer. "Save Temra. Save Temra. Save Temra."

I'm raised higher into the air, angled toward the saddle, kicking anything my legs come into contact with. I catch a glimpse of the sky, the clouds gray and full, almost ready to let down rain.

And then I'm falling.

I hit the dirt, the air expelling from my lungs once more. I hear a scuffle, but most of my attention is on breathing.

Come on, lungs. Remember how to work.

When air finally rushes back in, it hurts so much to breathe. I can barely think. Barely make sense of what's happening.

Kellyn is there, bent down, helping me to my feet, cutting my binds. All the guards around us lie like rag dolls on the ground.

But if Kellyn is here, then that means—

I shove him aside and run for my sister. She's just broken another soldier's weapon. The man leaps away, trying to grab one of his fallen friend's still intact weapons, but she stabs the pitchfork straight into the ground. One of the tines runs through his wrist.

But she still twists, and the bone snaps, the magic compelled to break whatever catches between the tines.

Then Kymora is there, and while Temra's distracted by the soldier she's just rendered useless, the warlord swings.

"No!"

Temra notices her just in time, dodging the strike, but Kymora doesn't let up. She sends out slashes in rapid succession, careful not to let her broadsword catch in between the prongs of Temra's pitchfork.

Kymora steps out of reach, turns her head to me, sees that I'm watching. And then she attacks in earnest.

I'm halfway there.

Kymora feints, swings for my sister's feet, but Temra jumps.

She thrusts the pitchfork forward, trying to get in her own strike. Kymora dodges and brings down her blade, and though I can't see where the weapon lands, I know it strikes true.

Temra's screams fill my ears as I bend down to retrieve my hammers from where they fell. My eyes blinded by tears, I watch Kymora strike Temra with her free hand, knuckles colliding with her skull to silence her cries. She hits the ground.

Blood spills everywhere, but Kymora doesn't finish the job. She turns to me. "You should have come when I said. I warned you what would happen. You're going to watch as I hack her apart piece by piece."

She points her sword toward the ground, resting it against Temra's side, and jerks the weapon upward, opening another wound.

And then I'm finally there.

I scream and rage and fly at Kymora with my hammers. The warlord smirks as she dodges my swing, raises her own sword.

I catch it on my shield, and the warlord's arm flies backward from the force of the magic.

And then Kellyn is there, taking up position on her other side.

Kymora crouches to retrieve a fallen bastard sword with her left hand. She doesn't blink as she takes us both on at once.

The most skilled swordswoman in all of Ghadra.

She swings her swords at impossible speeds, and I'm barely able to bring up my magicked hammer in time to catch them. Kellyn's weapon's magical ability is of no use to him now. He has only one opponent, and the sword can't help him with what's right in front of him.

Kymora is better than he is. I knew that already, but to see him pitted against her, it's so painfully obvious.

We're both blocking for our lives, neither getting an opportunity to throw our own strikes. I try once, ducking below my shield after catching her broadsword on it to swing out with my hammer.

She kicks it. Her boots must have metal at the tips, because the hammer makes a *clank* when the two strike and I nearly fall over.

"You can't beat me," Kymora says. "You're only prolonging the inevitable. Your sister will be dead in minutes from those wounds, and I can keep this up for hours."

Though sweat dots Kymora's forehead, I believe her.

She spins away and gets a sword around the edges of my shield, but she doesn't press forward; she hooks on to the invisible boundary of my shield and flings it away from me.

The hammer goes flying to the ground, and I race for it, daring to put my back to Kymora because I know she doesn't want me dead, trusting in it.

When I have my hammer back and spin around, it's to see Kymora flying at Kellyn with both swords. Only with the superior length of his longsword does he keep her at bay for one slash, two slashes.

She means to kill him before taking me.

I run. I throw myself between the two fighters, raising my hammer-shield, my grip like iron.

Kymora slams into it, but she's already used to the way the magic works. She plants her feet to catch herself from the force of her strikes rebounding. Again and again she batters at the shield, while Kellyn tries to strike her from above it.

It's not going to work.

My strength was once impressive with a hammer. I could beat at metal all day, but I've grown soft on the road with nothing to do but exercise my legs.

My strength is failing.

Only the knowledge that Kellyn will die, just like my sister did or will do soon—a whimper escapes my lips at the thought—keeps me standing. Keeps me fighting.

Because even if I lose, I can't stop if I don't give it my all.

And then a fourth figure joins the fight. I nearly sob at the thought of one of her men helping her, until I realize who it is.

Petrik.

He's finished dispatching the rest of Kymora's men, and now he's joined us.

He has not an inch of skill in fighting, but he still swings the axle. Kymora is forced to turn half her attention on him, raising one sword to block the axle, while another fends off Kellyn's strike.

With every ounce of my strength, I swing around my shield, allowing myself the vulnerability, and this time when I strike out with my unmagicked hammer—

I connect with the bone at her knee.

A crunch. A scream. I fall toward the warlord as Kellyn advances, throwing me into her, but I don't care.

Because we finally hit her.

With the three of us, she shrinks toward the ground, little by little, until Petrik finally strikes her on the head.

And she collapses, limp.

Just like Temra.

I toss aside my weapons and run for my sister. Her chest is rising and falling, but blood is oozing out of wounds on her arm and right side.

So. Much. Blood.

I press my hands firmly against the sources of the bleeding before looking up at the two men around me for help.

CHAPTER TWENTY-FOUR

My body convulses, wishing to dispel my last meal.

But I'm not allowed to do anything until Temra is safe.

She wakes not a second after I touch her, and her cries oscillate between screams and whimpers as she tries to get ahold of the pain. When her breathing turns to wheezing, tears rain down my face anew.

"This way," Kellyn says. He takes off down the dirt road at a run.

The bleeding is more severe at Temra's arm, so I risk releasing her side to hoist her up to a standing position. She screams at the movement, and I stifle a whimper of my own.

"Don't worry about Kymora," Petrik says. "I'll watch her. You take care of—" He cuts off, unable to say my sister's name.

I slide my free arm under Temra's knees and lift her up, cradling her, so I can move more easily. I've barely heard Petrik's words. I know I should probably worry about whether he'll try to help his mother get away, despite how he took our side at the end. Familial bonds are strong, as I well know.

But nothing will keep me from running as fast as I can until I know Temra is safe.

Kellyn knocks on some door and lets himself inside before anyone answers. He says very little before an older woman with long hair in gray braids instructs us to lower Temra onto a bed.

The healer urges us to boil some water. Before I turn, I watch her elevate my sister's arm carefully on a pillow, applying her own fingers to the wound.

I run out of the room, try to find the kitchen in the modest home. Kellyn is right beside me.

"I'm sure she'll be all right. Here, let me." He tries to take the kettle from me.

"Go make sure Petrik doesn't let Kymora go. I can do this on my own."

"He's no more safe with her running free than we are. He won't do anything stupid."

That may be, but I don't want him around right now. I can't bear the attention when I'm doing everything I can to keep myself together.

I strike up a fire as I talk. The wait for the water to boil might just kill me. "Please, go to Petrik. I've got this."

Kellyn stands there for a few seconds longer before leaving.

I thought I'd already experienced the worst thing that would ever happen to me. Seeing Temra injured so severely was horrible, but having to hold down my baby sister while the healer cauterizes the wound is much worse.

Feeling her fight against me, hearing her screams, knowing I'm helping to cause it.

It breaks me.

Temra loses consciousness after it's done, the medicine the healer administered finally kicking in, and I hold her to me, wrapping her in my arms while the wound at her side is stitched up.

The first thing I note when I'm fully awake is that I don't feel sticky with blood anymore.

I'm in a fresh shirt and pants. My body has been wiped clean of all blood and sweat. But I still feel dirty in a way I can't place at first.

Then I remember.

I killed people yesterday. Kymora hurt my sister. I hurt inside. Every part of me that feels aches.

When I twist my head to the side, I see Kellyn kneeling on the floor, his head slumped on the bed beside me, propped up in his arms.

His eyes rise sleepily when I prod him.

"Temra?" I ask.

"She's all right. She's sleeping next door."

"Kymora?"

"Bound and kept in my parents' garden shed. They know everything now."

I rise slowly, my muscles straining just with that simple task. "Take me to my sister."

I follow him down the little hallway to the room next door. Inside, the healer is in a rocking chair, dozing. Petrik is out on the floor. My sister looks clean and fresh on the bed, her arm and side bound heavily.

Ignoring the hand Kellyn tries to touch me with, I go to Temra, slide into the bed next to her. I let my hand brush over her hair, kiss the back of her head, push myself against her until I can feel her heat. Feel that she's alive and all right.

Both Petrik and the healer rouse when they hear my crying.

"She's alive," I say. The healer had said something about surviving the first night being crucial.

"I'm keeping her unconscious," the healer says, "because the pain will be unbearable right now, and if she fidgets about, she could start bleeding again."

"That's good," Petrik says before I can. He stands up to the bed, looking down into Temra's face.

"You should prepare yourselves."

We turn to the healer at the same time a horrible cough shakes Temra's entire body. Blood slides out the side of her mouth. I dab it away with the sleeve of my shirt.

"Wh-what do you mean?" I ask. "She survived the night."

"I didn't expect her to," the healer admits. "She lost a lot of blood, and her wounds were more severe than I originally thought. While I've stitched up her side, the sword nicked the lung. Blood is trickling in. She will continue to cough it up." A pause. "It's not a wound that will heal, and there is nothing more

I can do for her, except to make her comfortable. She doesn't have longer than a week."

"What?"

"I can wake her when you're ready to say your goodbyes."

"N-no! You're wrong. She's fine. She'll live. She's stronger than anyone I know."

"I'll leave you all alone to talk."

The older woman exits, shutting the four of us inside the bedroom.

I think I might be shaking. I think I might lose control of my limbs and collapse or rage or do something else. But I know that everything is wrong, and Temra is here and alive but it doesn't feel like she is.

Petrik stares at the door where the healer left before turning back around. He takes Temra's free hand and rubs a thumb over her knuckles.

"We need to talk about what to do with Kymora," Kellyn says.

"You can hang her for all I care," I say. "I don't want to talk about Kymora. Temra is hurt, and we need to do something."

"Ziva, there's nothing to be done."

"What do you know? You're no expert in medicine, and that old woman is a hack. We need to find someone else. Take her to someone better."

"Ziva, she'd never survive a journey."

"Then we'll bring someone to her."

"Ziva—"

"Stop saying my name like that!"

I'm being unfair. I know this. But I hurt, and I want everyone else to hurt, too.

"I've misled you all," Petrik says quietly.

"We know you did," Kellyn says. "Hard to miss what with the warlord—"

"No," Petrik corrects. "I mean yes. I obviously didn't tell you who I really was. But I was referring to something else."

"There's more!" Kellyn says. "You've got some nerve."

Petrik ignores him. "When you asked me about other magic users, Ziva, I was careful with my words. I let you believe that I only knew of two, but that's not true. I know someone who can save Temra."

I blink away my tears to try to see Petrik's face.

"Back in Skiro," he continues, "there's a magically gifted healer. I promised her I wouldn't reveal her identity to anyone. But this is Temra. We need to take her to the capital immediately."

"She'd never survive the journey," Kellyn says. "It's too far, and the road is rough."

For just once can he be helpful and positive? Just this one time when it's concerning my Temra?

"Let's go," I say. "Why are we still talking about it? If there's a chance to save her, then we're taking it."

"We're not leaving Kymora alone with my family," Kellyn says, and though he doesn't raise his voice, his tone is firm.

"You'll stay with her," I say, "while Petrik and I take Temra."

"No, he should come with us," Petrik says. "He can bring Kymora. We'll turn her over to Prince Skiro. The royal family has been wanting to pull her from power since the realm was split."

I don't hide the distaste from my face.

"Kellyn will protect us on the road as well," Petrik says in his defense, "now that—"

Now that Temra can't do it.

"Fine, he can come. We leave within the hour."

Petrik tries to offer up apologies while we get ready, but I silence him. "You came through when it mattered. That's good enough for me. Quick thinking to put the tools in the smithy's kiln for me."

"I never betrayed you," he says. "I hope you know that. I wasn't in contact with my mother. We're not close at all. I never gave her any information about you or your sister. I would never do that."

"I know."

While he collects food and supplies, the healer offers up the use of her cart. Though I know she believes we can't save my sister, she takes pity on me.

The cart itself is wood, but the wheels and axle are metal. I magic both to help Temra have a smooth journey on the road. Let the wheels absorb any bumps.

We help ourselves to the smithy's horses. He doesn't need them anymore, and we attach two to the head of the cart, lie Temra bundled in blankets in the back.

Then the healer hands me a vial. "This will keep her under while you're on the road. You have to administer it every day. Give her too much, and you will kill her; not enough and she will wake and be in agony and maybe become injured further."

She gives me the dosage, and I accept the vial wordlessly.

Kellyn ties Kymora to the other side of the uncovered cart. She's bound with what looks like no less than a hundred ropes, from her neck to her ankles. A gag keeps her from talking.

When he has her situated, I look away from the woman while we make our way to the edge of town. The three of us sit on the driver's bench in silence.

Kellyn offers his hand to me, and I don't accept it.

Kymora may be directly responsible for injuring my sister, but Kellyn could have stopped it.

If he'd just listened. My sister is more important to me than my own life. He knew that. But he came after me instead.

I would feel guilty to accept his hand or any other comfort he tried to offer, knowing that Temra is hurt.

It isn't long before I can't stand not to be near my sister. I hate that Kymora is in the back with Temra. If I hadn't broken the warlord's knee, she could have walked alongside the horses.

I climb into the bed of the cart and position myself between Kymora and my unconscious sister.

It's a week to the capital, and that's exactly how long the healer expected Temra had to live.

We're cutting it too close, but this is the only option I have.

With the last of my family on one side of me and the woman who murdered my parents on the other, I close my eyes, hoping this journey will be smoother than the last one.

ACKNOWLEDGMENTS

Book number five is here, and I can barely believe it's time to write another one of these.

As always, I like to start off by thanking the two amazing ladies who make what I do possible. Rachel and Holly: You guys are the best! Thank you for championing my novels. Thank you for continuing to believe in me and support me. Thank you for taking a chance on a feisty pirate named Alosa.

Thank you to everyone on the Macmillan team who works on my books! Special thanks to Brittany, Allegra, Jordin, Jacqueline, Starr, and Liz. And thanks so much, Sasha Vinogradova, for the beautiful cover art! I'm simply blown away by it. And thanks as well to Noverantale for the gorgeous map of Ghadra!

I appreciate everyone else who gave this book a read and

offered feedback: Dillon West, Cale Dietrich, Charlie N. Holmberg, Haley Gibson, Bridget Howard, and Caitlin Lochner.

Special thank-you to Alisa for brainstorming with me when it was crunch time and I needed ideas fast for revisions. I've never come out of one of our sessions empty-handed.

Thank you to all of my family for your continued support, even those of you who won't buy my books because they're too racy.

Mom and Tara, thanks so much for answering my medical questions. I'm so glad I have you to call up when I need to brutally maim my characters.

Special shout-out to Caitlyn Hair and Mikki Helmer for taking the time to talk to me during my low points and provide encouragement and give feedback.

And last but certainly not least, thank you to all my readers. Your enthusiasm and support are what allow me to continue doing what I love. Thanks for reaching out on social media, saying hello at events, and sharing my books with your friends. It all means so much to me!

THE ADVENTURE CONTINUES IN

More from Tricia Levenseller